EXODUS

TO

EARTH

EXODUS
TO
EARTH
A NOVEL

JIM EVRY

TWO HARBORS PRESS, MINNEAPOLIS

Two Harbors Press
322 First Avenue N, 5th floor
Minneapolis, MN 55401
612.455.2293
www.TwoHarborsPress.com

Permission given by the Joseph Campbell Foundation (jcf.org) for quotation; (The Hero with a Thousand Faces, Novato, CA, New World Library, ©2008, page 18).

ISBN-13: 978-1-63413-305-0
LCCN: 2015900504

Distributed by Itasca Books

Cover Design by MK Ross
Typeset by James Arneson

Printed in the United States of America

*Dedicated to my Mom, Dad,
Brother, Sister, and Wife.*

ACKNOWLEDGMENTS

I WOULD like to honor and thank both the late Joseph Campbell and also my writer and mythic mentor Phil Cousineau.

First and foremost I must acknowledge Joseph Campbell. This book's story follows Campbell's motif of the hero's journey. It includes references to interviews from PBS's "The Power of Myth", and "The Hero's Journey", along with his landmark best seller book "The Hero with a Thousand Faces". There are several quotes closely paraphrased in this fictional story. A specific quotation for the dedication was taken from The Hero with a Thousand Faces, Novato, CA, New World Library, ©2008, page 18. Permission was given by the Joseph Campbell Foundation (jcf.org).

I highly recommend Campbell's works to any writer, artist, musician, philosopher, or anyone for that matter looking for inspiration. Campbell's non-profit foundation's website is www.jcf.org.

I must also offer my sincere thanks to Phil Cousineau who suggested I "cotton" a book out of a screenplay I had written. His endless faith and inspiration from e-mails, meetings, and consultations, along with his books such as "The Hero's Journey", "The Painted Word", "Stoking the Creative Fires", "Beyond Forgiveness", and "Once and Future Myths", were a treasure. He helped guide me through this writing adventure. Phil is living a life that was intended for him. I would highly recommend his books and lectures. Phil's website is: www.philcousineau.net.

I want offer my loving gratitude to my Mom and Dad, Ardis and Larry. Between my Moms inspirational smile and endless energy and my Dads adventurous spirit, my brother Steve, sister DeAnne and I grew up with countless marvelous adventures and memories! And speaking of family, in regard to my mom, brother, sister, brother in-law, nephew and nieces; I want to let them all know how much I admire their strength and courage they each have endured through some tough times we have all had!

I cannot leave out my lovely wife Julie who continually inspires me with her strength, optimistic smile and spirit.

I must also include all my relatives and lifelong friends of the family of whom our family spent a lot of time together growing up.

And I can't forget a great group of friends I graduated high school with. Oh . . . the many adventures that we have had!

There are several individuals who I have to thank for offering to help critique the manuscript even though it wasn't ready and was way too long. Thanks to Julie, Steve, DeAnne, Jamie, Dane, Doug and his students.

I would like to acknowledge Doug Erickson from Orono High School for his passionate inspiration I experienced as a student. Doug is a teacher who like Phil Cousineau lives a life that was intended for him; something we all should try to pursue our whole life.

I would like to thank all the staff at Hillcrest Media for helping publish this book including Alison and Kate.

Similarly, I want to offer a tremendous amount of thanks to Ryan Scheife with Mayfly Design.

Furthermore, I would like to thank the three editors who helped keep this project intact; Jen Ahlstrom and Susan Gainen who helped in the early stages. But most of all, I would like to thank Sarah Kolb-Williams who is passionate about science fiction and helped bring this to the finish line.

And one final last note of thanks from my family to David, Joan, and Dan Jenkins/family.

Furthermore, we have not even to risk the adventure alone; for the heroes of all time have gone before us, the labyrinth is thoroughly known; we have only to follow the thread of the hero-path. And where we had thought to find an abomination, we shall find a god; where we had thought to slay another, we shall slay ourselves; where we had thought to travel outward, we shall come to the center of our own existence; where we had thought to be alone, we shall be with all the world.

—Joseph Campbell, *The Hero with a Thousand Faces*

CHAPTER 1

THE MASSIVE Evion sun was dying. As it crept over the edge of the horizon spewing solar flares from solar explosions, the temperature in the last inhabited city on the planet reached a scorching 130 degrees. By midday, the temperature had nearly doubled, registering 250 degrees.

The oldest glass buildings in Alexon, the capital city, were melting. Buildings constructed with materials that didn't burn or melt were cracking and tumbling to the ground. They imploded into huge clouds of dust, further polluting the thin, toxic air. During the night, the thin atmosphere caused temperatures to drop below minus 100 degrees.

On this particularly violent morning, Starion was gliding briskly down the devastated city's glidewalks. His shroud hood over his head and his hands in his pouch, he strategically avoided newly formed sinkholes and crevasses. On his six-toed feet he wore heat- and cold-resistant bionic e-gliders, which allowed him to move along the ground effortlessly.

Suddenly, he sensed an increase in heat, and he ducked underneath part of a demolished building. Peeking through his drooping white hood, he witnessed an Evion man caught in a sudden, snakelike solar flare. The man's body was roasted as his shroud erupted in flames. It took moments for him to die of heat and suffocation while Starion heard his awful cries.

When Starion saw the solar flare pull itself back into the sun, he felt a huge quake. Buildings tumbled while new crevasses and sinkholes developed around him. He was aware that the heat shields, built two generations ago to protect the buildings, were now either melted or worthless.

He glide-rushed into a tall glass building, one of Alexon's strongest remaining. He took the antigravity e-mover and shot up to a second-floor corner room.

Starion, the elected board president, threw his hood back and stood at the front of the Elder Room. He brushed off some dirt from his white heat- and cold-resistant shroud. He noticed a slight tear in the full-length outer layer just above his right knee. Thankfully he could tell the interior lining made precisely for his body was still intact. But now he worried the exterior lining that protected him from intense heat during the day and extreme cold at night was damaged.

He observed the six other elected elders trying to keep cool using hypercoolers powered by miniature star-power cells. As the shaking of the building subsided, he wondered what he was going to tell them. The guilt of failing to save the sun eight Evion years before overwhelmed him again.

Starion turned to address Deon, the lead researcher appointed to head the search. "What are the results of this expedition? I hope you have something. We're running out of time," he said, looking at his thin, ultra-light wristwatch. Protruding out at him was a live view from the moon of an eerie, red, half-lit Evion.

"We have found four planets within our galaxy that meet our objectives of breathable air, water, and edible foods," Deon told him with limited breath.

"What about the second envoy? Have they returned yet?"

"No, Starion, we have not heard from them for some reason."

"Where are the planets located? Do any of them have the mineral element braydium?" Starion asked, digging down deep for confidence.

Thirty-six-Evion-year-old Starion felt like he had portrayed a confident, wise, leader—at least up until a few days ago, when severe stress had changed his brown hair to brownish grey. His large and twinkling blue eyes were now dull blue. He had also become much thinner. New wrinkles had appeared on his already worried, sunburned, and frostbitten face.

Starion along with the elders monitored their hypercoolers and turned to Deon, who stood in front of the room. Just above and slightly behind him was an elliptical, glowing ultrathin screen hanging from the ceiling. Deon pointed his sixth finger, or focus finger, next to his thumb at it and produced an I-spacer of a spiraling galaxy. The panoramic image revealed where each of the four planets was in relation to Evion. First it was in 2-D, but then Deon pulled the image out into 4-D with his right hand and six fingers. The planets were spread out all over the galaxy and at different distances from Evion. Each was highlighted by a different-colored small twinkling light.

The protruding 4-D holographic I-spacer was convex and so lenticular that Deon had a hard time differentiating between the image and the actual space in the room. Suddenly the image started faltering and Deon tried to fix it.

It was very quiet as they waited for Deon to resolve the issue, and Starion wished there'd been sound from this I-spacer. If there had been, it would have been generated from the sound e-molecule, a technology that allowed sound waves to originate from all inanimate objects in a room.

Starion anticipated some reaction from the others, who sat by the long, rectangular cobalt glass table with rounded corners. When there was no response from his counterparts, he glanced outside. There he could see the ever-changing sun's pale light shining through the two warped corner windows. There were occasional light prisms. He thought about Evion's ancient history books he was now reading instead of scanning, and he decided, if not for the dire circumstances, the light prisms might have been considered an *art form*—a new term for him that somehow inspired and excited him.

Attempting a deep breath, Starion glanced at his mentor, Ardia, next to him. She had recently been inspiring him with stories from books she had found in an ancient library. The room in their historic Audiseum had been exposed after a quake.

"There is an ancient Evion story of the quest that is still valid," she had been telling him. "To discover one's inward self, and then return with a life force message or clue that has been missing or forgotten from society."

She had been the one who recommended he read these old books and stories word for word, instead of memory-scanning them. But now a new feeling kept running through him. The stories were reawakening something he couldn't quite get a handle on. The problem was that along with the inspiration he was experiencing, he'd also been instilled with other emotions that weren't as pleasant. He couldn't understand why he couldn't get rid of them—or why he'd begun to experience strange images that appeared in his mind while he slept.

Starion glanced at the doctor Judion across the table, whose brother had died tragically from a powerful solar flare when Starion recruited him to help save the sun. Even though eight years had passed, the guilt still overwhelmed him.

"Let's get on with this, Deon," Judion exclaimed, obviously irritated.

"I'm done," Deon finally told them as the floating image was now back to its original clear 4-D status again.

Starion sat down at the table on a glass chair with a sensate red cushion attached to the back and seat. Its electronically charged cloth was adjustable for temperature and firmness with the touch of a finger. He positioned his upper-arm hypercooler toward his face.

There still didn't seem to be any interest in the planets so Starion felt he had to demonstrate confidence to keep the meeting moving. Focusing all of his energy, he stood up again, using both his hands to bring the image in front of him. He examined it from several angles as he twirled it and then placed it back on the e-screen. When he finished, he noticed two of the elders yawn, which he hoped was at least an improvement from their sleep-mode. A startling rumble shook the room.

"Can't you feel it, everyone?" Starion appealed. "The quakes are getting worse."

CHAPTER 2

WHEN THE rumble subsided, Starion turned to Deon. "I really hope one of these four is our final candidate—we are running out of time. I think we're down to sixty days on this planet."

Starion was aware several elders had accused him of making false hopeful dramatic statements and political proclamations over his eight year term; especially after he had failed to save the sun when he was first elected.

Starion watched as thirty year old Deon combed his black hair out of his eyes with his right six fingers and then used his whole left hand to move this first I-spacer to the left of the e-screen. Deon performed this with the precision of someone who had done this many times before. But this time he lost control of it. The image bounced of the wall and floor before he caught it.

Starion knew Deon looked up to him and often tried to gain his attention by performing scientific endeavors. Recently Deon had tried to improve his bionic gliders by making himself look taller, but instead he messed up his sync guidance component and now sometimes glided awkwardly. When he tried to hide it, his mistake was even more conspicuous, occasionally affecting his other mannerisms as well. Starion was aware only he and Ardia found it slightly but compassionately amusing.

While Starion waited for the next image, he couldn't help but wonder; *All this technology ... will it save us?*

Deon brought up the next 4-D I-spacer. It contained a solar system with three distinct, colorful planets that revolved around its bright yellow sun. He motioned with a different finger, changing the view to a large, effervescent green planet.

This planet was the farthest of the three from its yellow sun. There were two small half-lit white moons orbiting the planet on opposite sides.

"This first of the four planet candidates is larger than ours and presently does not have any life. It is possible that it could sustain life, but we are concerned about its unstable orbit around its relatively small sun. Also, its atmosphere might have too much carbon dioxide from its massive amount of plants."

"Hmm...how ironic," Starion commented. "So much potential for life, but so little time...Deon, bring these I-spacers over the table so we can—can easily see them," Starion ordered, slightly out of breath.

He looked around the room at the listless four men and two women; most of their expressions were emotionless. Starion knew over the last three generations, Evions had coined their state "sleep-mode." Starion contemplated what it must have been like one hundred E-years in the past, what each individual's expressions might have looked like under normal circumstances then. Like in the recent ancient books he had been reading page by page, line by line, word by word, he imagined that back then he might have seen a smile or heard a laugh. However, he surmised that the keen awareness in their eyes and their mental telepathy were the result of the terrible circumstances the last three generations had to endure.

Ardia was the only elder to use her hand and bring the I-spacer of the planet candidate near her.

Starion watched as sixty-year-old Ardia, with her long grey hair and tantalizing brown eyes adjusted her thin, weightless IS unit around her waist. She searched the elders' eyes, open or not, clearly aware of the tension among some of them.

Starion knew Ardia could memory-scan vast categories of Evion literature, and then create summaries within seconds. In the past, along with her teaching, she had been a world, solar and star system traveler. She was known for her vast knowledge and wisdom, and also for her compassion.

She gently brought the I-spacer over to the table in front of her with her hand while her hypercooler blew her hair around. She examined the green planet with its moons from different angles. She closed her eyes, checking her memory of vast planetary knowledge, her eyelids glowing a brilliant blue. Then she placed the lifelike floating image back on the e-screen while everyone waited for her response.

"Yes…you are right in your analysis, Deon," she confirmed, nodding.

"Did it have any braydium?" Starion asked hopefully. "We will need braydium to create new power magnifiers and cells, along with the outer shell of our v-breakers."

"What about the actual mold castings, so we can manufacture new magnifiers and cells?" Deon asked emphasizing the word *new*.

"We lost the schematics a year ago when almost all information and data was somehow deleted from our IS units and IS banks," Quarion, the oldest of the elders explained. "The engineered design for the mold-casts had so much code that no one had it stored on their personal or home units."

"We still have two old mold-casts of the magnifier and the starpower cell that might still work." Starion reminded everyone.

Starion knew the bald seventy E-years old Quarion was an expert in Evion's energy resources. He was considered a very careful and analytical thinker, but like many Evions, he had grown tired, and his eyes had recently turned from green to a dark grey.

"Yes, the mass deletion affected us all—especially our children, who now have limited stimulation. Luckily we still retained our own personal and home data," Starion exclaimed, his head shaking side to side. "I still can't figure out how it could have happened."

Judion, wiping sweat from his forehead with his shroud arm stated, "Face it, Starion, you messed up."

Deon finally answered Starion's question moving the image as if it was in the palm of his hand. He began stacking the floating images, one atop another. "No Starion, it did not have any braydium."

"We also will need braydium for medical S-rays, Starion, so we each can continue to monitor and view inside our bodies at our homes," Ardia reminded everyone.

Deon aimed his finger back at the e-screen, bringing up a new lenticular 4-D I-spacer of the second planet. Its solar system had an array of thirteen planets of various sizes and colors traveling elliptically around a large, red sun. The image glowed brilliantly with the different hues of each planet. He focused on the fifth planet. It was medium-sized, light brown, with small blue speckled water areas spread throughout the sphere. It had no moons.

"This second planet candidate might initially work, but we are concerned about its lifespan. We think its large red sun would die within a few thousand of the planet's orbital years. It is too…doomed, and it has no braydium," Deon stated, catching his breath and anticipating Starion's question.

Until now, the elders had been going through the motions. Some were getting irritated and beginning to sweat profusely. Several of them moved their hypercoolers from their wrists to their necks.

Starion noticed the uneasiness throughout the room. He immediately turned to Deon, indicating for him to continue. But just as Deon began to speak, there was a flash of light and a terrific rumble. The room darkened and shook.

Starion and the elders could tell it was a flare with a subsequent quake. Starion was aware that as Evion sped nearer to the sun on its elliptical path, the flares and quakes had increased in frequency. The only thing he could compare it to were thunderstorms he had read about from long ago. The solar flare or wave was like the lightening, and the quake was the thunder.

The elders hung onto their chairs and table while the lights and I-spacers flickered in and out. Two lights fell, shattering on top the glass table and added to the terrible sounds of the devastation outside.

Some elders stood holding on while others went into sleep-mode. Starion's fellow elder and friend, Lazarion, dived under the table.

Starion knew the recent increased danger wasn't limited to the quakes and flares. The Evion days and nights had become incredibly hot and dangerously cold, forcing Evions to limit their time outdoors to early mornings and near sunsets for fear of death from either extreme.

Starion, holding onto table as it shook, recalled a recent patrol through a distant neighborhood where he and Ardia had viewed the results of the latest round of tragic quakes. As they survey-glided along, they saw Evions inside their homes observing them. He had sensed that another flash and quake were imminent, so they took cover in the closest home they could find. While they waited out the storm, the family next door ran outside. The two watched as the mother, father, and two small children instantly burned in the flash. There hadn't been enough time to warn the poor family—and whether they would have listened was another matter.

Starion was aware the solar flares usually happened so quickly and powerfully, their brown shoe-like bionic gliders that detected impulses from their brain weren't fast enough. Also, their shrouds weren't strong enough.

If someone was caught in a flare storm, there was nothing he or she could do if they had to make a trip to the e-commissary for fresh water and nutrition formula.

"I hope no one is out there," Ardia said, catching and agreeing with Starion's thoughts.

"On my way here, I witnessed the awful sight of someone dying from a flare," Starion added sadly.

Trying to steady himself on the elder room wall, Deon also commented, "I don't know what would be worse, roasting or freezing to death. Two nights ago, I needed some more nutrition formulas from the e-commissary. Along the way, I saw a frozen Evion woman standing on the glidewalk. She apparently had been caught outside the e-com for too long in the frigid thin air, and her lungs froze, causing her to suffocate instantly. Her poor remains stood like a lifelike statue, at least until the next day when the sun burned her to cinders."

Finally, the quake subsided. The dim orange light prisms slowly began to shine through the large warped glass windows again. Now there were new cracks on one of the exterior walls. It was even harder for the elders to breathe in the smelly, dirty, dusty air.

On another of the hanging e-screens, Zealeon unexpectedly appeared in a 4-D I-spacer that protruded out in front of Starion. Starion liked the twenty-five-year-old ambitious researcher and scientist. But he like everyone else questioned why Zealeon wore his natural brown hair in a tonsure cut.

As the elders returned to their original places, Zealeon's voice filled the room. "Starion, as per your request, I am relaying the best results we can gather after every major quake from one of our last s-rover satellites," Zealeon sadly announced and continued, "It looks like this last flare storm and quake destroyed the far north side of the city. I'm afraid we have lost another large part of Alexon...and an estimated three thousand people."

Zealeon replayed what he had seen inside the spatial image behind him. They saw a solar wave hit the north side of Alexon. Some homes burned instantly, while others melted. Much of that part of the city fell into huge crevasses and sinkholes. Tragically, there was no sign of life at all.

"Send out our v-ambulances to see if anyone has survived," Starion sadly ordered, gasping for air.

"That Zealeon is a strange one, everyone—I don't trust him. He always carries that ancient scroll," Judion sarcastically commented.

Ardia answered with her wise mannerisms, "Yes, it is possible the scroll contains the oldest story ever told of the master. The master in these ancient times was not only successful in

EXODUS TO EARTH ⟩ 11

following the hero's journey and lived to tell about it, but had gained enough wisdom to master the two worlds: the real world and the spiritual one."

"Ha—nonsense," Judion bickered.

Starion admired Ardia. He considered her a great mentor. He was aware that when she was young, she had locked herself in her home with thousands of ancient books and IS banks loaded with I-spacers. Even though she could have scanned them instantly, she read every page, paragraph, line, and word by manually flipping through the pages. She also had watched all of the I-spacers minute by minute, second by second. Afterward she had meditated about the meaning of each, sometimes spending months on a single book or I-spacer.

Starion was grateful that she had introduced him to the ancient method of reading word by word. Even though, like all Evions, he had the ability to hyper-scan written material into his memory instantly and then interpret the meaning later, Starion and Ardia were the only ones able to interpret texts, such as philosophical, mythological, fictional, or fairy tale stories, when scanning. The rest could only interpret math functions, science theories, and chemical tables when scanning.

Because scanning happened so fast, Starion realized his people missed out on the emotional and philosophical meaning of what they were scanning. Compared to the ancient Evion way of reading, in which readers felt emotions while flipping slowly through the pages, modern memory-scanning was so fast and effortless that the emotional impact or metaphorical message was lost in the data transfer. Except for Ardia, his wife, and his two children, he didn't know anyone else who bothered to learn the ancient method.

Starion, along with Ardia, had even mastered a higher level of touch-and-point scanning that allowed information to move instantly into their memories. It was the same regarding recorded I-spacers. Strangely, Starion and Ardia's data streams were always blue while the others were red.

They all turned their attention back to Deon, who used his weather-beaten hand again, using all six fingers to move the last I-spacer to his stack of rejects. He revealed a third planetary candidate and its relation to Evion. It had four planets with a very yellow sun.

At that moment, they heard—and, shortly thereafter, saw—a blue clear v-ambulance race by the window through the outside fly-way, its siren blaring. But, similar to their noninterest in the presentation, three of them didn't show much concern.

Deon zoomed in on the planet he had brought up. The elders observed a large purple sphere with one small moon that was half-lit yellow.

Starion asked, "Does it have any braydium?"

Judion glared at Deon as his hypercooler around his neck stopped working. Sweating, he demanded, "Tell us if you have something or not, Deon. I want to get home to my hyper-airflow system. It is working there," he gasped, "and it is getting hard to breathe in here. And these damn cushions are worthless in this heat."

Starion could see Judion's receding short grey hair and dark, cold eyes. He knew Judion was about the same age as himself and he always had wondered why Judion wore a black shroud while everyone else wore white.

Judion swiped the I-spacer away from the e-screen with his hand, viewed it briefly in front of him. Then he pushed it back again to a flat 2-D. Turning to Starion, he continued, "You won't find any braydium on any of these planets. It was an element native only to Evion." He yanked off his hypercooler, shaking it in frustration before throwing the cushion on the floor.

"Calm down, Judion," Starion said. "Let Deon finish … and anyway, you can't go home … you'll need to go the hospital. Zealeon and his crew might find survivors that need help."

Then Starion cocked his head, glaring at the doctor. "By the way—how do you know we are the only planet with braydium?"

CHAPTER 3

IGNORING STARION'S question regarding braydium, Judion tapped on his hypercooler in an attempt to start it. "We have two doctors on staff who can handle any emergencies."

Ardia spoke up. "*If* Zealeon has any v-ambulances left. They have been disappearing or losing their star-power cells."

Judion answered bitterly, "Well, of course, Ardia—they are being sent into dangerous areas. What do you expect?"

Starion nodded to Deon to continue but caught Deon's thinking: *You can fly off into the galaxy next time if you think this is so easy.*

Starion stared deeply into Deon's eyes, hoping to stop the telepathy so Judion wouldn't be able to access the thoughts. Thankfully, he did, and Deon didn't send anything more.

Starion was aware that Deon was losing hope during these meetings. Deon had arrived late the night before and was tired. Starion sensed he had become increasingly discouraged, heading research missions only to be rejected and ridiculed. However, he was cognizant that Deon respected him. After all, it was Starion who had recommended him. Proudly, Starion saw Deon keep his composure as he took a deep breath from the thin, dirty air before revealing his results.

Continuing while still upset, Deon fumbled, bringing up another planetary system of seven planets spread in their orbits around a white sun. He focused in on the fourth dark blue planet. "This third planet is promising, but strangely, its inhabitants are still coarse and often starving; they have hundreds of wars going on at all times. They don't have enough energy to power their planet, either."

"Does it have any braydium?" Starion asked again.

Judion rolled his eyes as he finally got this hypercooler to work. He wrapped the thin band around his left upper shoulder and aimed the blower at this face.

Deon shook his head no again as he moved the I-spacer over to the stack while he brought up a new lenticular image. Inside this new I-spacer was a strange being, nasty to the eye. It was hairy, dirty, and short, likely a male of the species, with three eyes. The image was so close to the elders that in a four-dimensional view, the alien appeared even nastier.

"This is the being I was talking about." Deon clarified.

This image pushed Judion to the edge. He stood up, glaring at Deon. "If you are trying to sell us on the idea of migrating to another planet, you aren't doing a very good job."

Judion grabbed the I-spacer and hurled it at one of the glass walls. It splattered into multicolored specks and sparks of light that appeared to cling to the wall, then slowly faded. It looked like the alien had burst into a million pieces.

"Look, Starion, this is an impossible dream. And anyway, we will safely swing around the sun as we always have…then Evion will have a full year to rejuvenate itself. Our forefathers should have taken care of things earlier! They should have noticed the sun was dying three generations ago. The generations after that should have found a solution to the dying sun, or a planet to migrate to. It's too late now."

Another of the elders agreed with Judion, nodding her disapproval. "Yes. They should have taken care of these things then," repeated Valkia, a tired elder, stroking her medium-length black hair with a deep sigh.

Starion noticed that recently the fifty year old Valkia was losing much of her energy—even more than everyone else, who he knew were much weaker than previous generations; especially their lung capacity.

Lazarion, the seventh of the other elders, spoke while trying to cross his normal arm with his bionic one. "I think we should give Starion a fair chance to provide evidence."

Judion blasted back, "You of all people, Lazarion, should be the angriest. After all, it was Starion who created the solar flare that destroyed your continent while killing my brother at the same time."

Starion noticed Judion was glaring at Lazarion, and he caught part of Judion's thoughts. Starion remembered the awful surgery Judion had to perform on Lazarion. There had been ten operations to replace damaged and missing body parts. Lazarion now had a bionic arm, a bionic leg, a bionic eye, an artificial heart, and a scarred face, among other changes.

Starion looked at the fifty-five-year-old Lazarion who had one clear blue eye with a normal pupil along with the other bionic pupil that could act as a camera. He admired Lazarion's strength and optimistic attitude after all the tragedy he had endured. The two had become fast friends.

Judion's eyes turned colder, blinking profusely.

The old Quarion chimed in. "I agree with Judion and Valkia; we probably don't have enough star-power cells to leave our planet anyway. When you failed eight years ago Starion, you used up a lot of energy."

Starion fired back while adjusting his own hypercooler, "My effort was well thought out. It should have worked—both Judion's brother and I pointed our v-breakers at the sun at a forty-five-degree angle, creating a hole to infuse more hydrogen…the massive flare that spewed out at us and our planet was just a coincidence."

"Well, it didn't work!" Judion yelled. "And now you think you can redeem yourself by forcing us to migrate to another planet."

"We have to try," Lazarion countered. "And by the way, Judion, I don't blame Starion."

"That's right, Lazarion, forgiveness is a most important virtue," Ardia stated wisely.

Starion saw Judion stare straight ahead with a psychotic stare.
Starion could see that Ardia, like Starion had just tried, was attempting to use telepathy to read Judion, but she was unable to connect. She turned to Starion. *Judion and his wife, also a doctor, have been through horrific and terrible circumstances down at the remaining hospital. Maybe this is finally taking its toll on them . . .*

Judion abruptly swiped all of the images away, and then threw them at the wall. "Let's get out of here—this is a waste of time. It's impossible . . . and anyway, we will safely sling around the Sun."

Starion was deeply disappointed. *How can I convince all the elders now—and the rest of my people, for that matter? Judion is a well-respected doctor.*

Bringing up the previous floating I-spacers again, he glared at Judion. "Just hold on for a moment—there is only one more planet candidate. Deon, go ahead."

Deon again moved the protruding colorful I-spacer to the floating stack. He brought up the final planet, while Judion shook his head from side to side.

The planet was part of an alluring brilliant solar system that included nine planets of various sizes and colors. In terms of distance, it was the farthest planet of the four in the first image of the spiraling galaxy. The planet was the third from its yellow sun.

Still standing, Judion whispered something to Valkia and Quarion while Deon used his hand to pull the I-spacer out into its large elliptical 4-D shape. He zoomed in on a space view of the planet, half lit up, from the point of view of its moon.

"This is the fourth candidate, this blue planet. It is about half the size of Evion. It has a sun very similar to what our sun was like about two million years ago."

Deon reversed the view so the sun was shining into the elders' eyes. Squinting, they put up their arms to block the light.

"Look at that starshine," Starion shouted.

Deon reversed the view back again to the half-lit blue planet. Suddenly, Starion had a vision. He closed his eyes and a blue glow emanated from behind his eyelids. He pulled out a book, *Anciente Mystical~ Blue Planet*, from his shroud pouch.

"This is a book from the room Ardia found in the ancient collection of books and artifacts in the Audiseum. It is about a mythical small blue planet far away that was surrounded by what our philosophers called the mythosphere. The stories were about its people who had fantastic and mystical adventures, including gods, goddesses, demons, dragons, and heroes."

"Ha…those old myth stories don't mean anything," Judion yelled. "And anyway, I heard a rumor that you decided to save the sun after reading one of those so-called ancient legends about an Evion sun god trying to save his son."

Ardia, Deon, and Lazarion witnessed Starion's tired blue eyes suddenly glisten and twinkle. The downward-pointed wrinkles surrounding his eyes turned upward, along with his thin but handsome eyebrows and eyelashes.

Judion continued, "Starion…as a doctor, I must tell you something. You and your old stories are drumming up emotions that are creating havoc on Evions' nervous systems. For example, Valkia and Quarion were perfectly content in sleep-mode at the beginning of this meeting, until you stirred them up."

Ardia stood up and slowly moved over to the window where she gazed up into the sky. The orange light lit up her face. With her wise tone, she said, "Judion, these old passed-down stories served a vital purpose in moving our culture forward. The hero in many of these ancient stories enters into either an intended or an unintended journey. He or she is in search of something that has been missing from their lives or their society. Along the way, the hero enters the labyrinth and must battle evil forces, in many cases—but not always—with the help of a magical aid, a mentor, a teacher, a ferryman, or a guide of souls. Once the hero succeeds, he or she must somehow find their way back to their people to provide the life force message. Sometimes, however, the task of the hero is for other reasons, such as redemption."

"Ha," Judion said, crossing his arms.

"And sometimes there is a mysterious, eccentric scientist who helps the hero too." Starion said, glancing at Deon and ignoring Judion's comment. Then he grabbed the I-spacer of the small blue planet and pulled it over near him. He examined it from different angles and moved it over above the cobalt table, increasing the view so the 4-D image was the size of the whole table. Then he created, on the spot, a 4-D I-spacer video of the planet's bright yellow sun from different distances in its solar system.

The elders were in shock and had to let their eyes adjust when the sun appeared in the image.

Some elders had to squint again. Starion displayed the sun at different times in the day from the planet's surface perspective. There was a view at sunrise, in the afternoon, and at sunset. The view of the sunset also revealed a small orange moon rising in the background.

Starion confidently held the I-spacer above the table with his hand. "This planet looks very promising. What else can you tell us, Deon? Does it have any braydium?"

"It is called Earth, and it is the third planet of nine from its sun. It rotates on its axis faster and opposite of Evion. Depending on where you are on the planet, there are a variety of climates throughout its orbit. Earths years are approximately twice as long as Evion because its elliptical orbit is longer. Its surface is seventy percent water and its seasons are similar to those we used to have on Evion long ago."

"What about braydium?"

"We found a reference to it twenty years ago in Earth's past, but we had to leave abruptly to avoid discovery from a primitive form of radar. We didn't have time to work out a way to stay hidden."

Quarion asked. "Do you mean twenty Earth years or Evion years?"

"Earth years."

Lazarion spoke up. "Since their days are shorter but the years are longer, I wonder what our lifespan would be on this planet."

Judion snickered. "Don't be too hasty, Starion, we still have time. Evion will sling around the sun in its normal elliptical path as it always has. Then the flares and quakes will end as we move farther away…and anyway, we would need to study the situation much more carefully before we could settle on this planet. Also, we need to see what Neilion has found when he returns from his galactic mission."

Starion was confused. Short of breath, he responded, "Evion will not sling around the sun. It will be pulled in as the sun increases in mass. We don't have any more time. If we can connect with Neilion, we will tell him to meet us at Earth. He has been searching a galaxy arm closer to Earth than we are."

"I demand we wait for them to return," Judion thundered, and then tossed the image against the wall.

"I don't understand. If this Earth planet has braydium, a few of us could travel there, bring the old braydium mold-casts for the magnifier and star-power cell, create a new magnifier and star-power cells, and charge them using Earth's sun. Then we would return and arrange for all of us to exodus back to Earth," Starion said recreating the I-spacer of Earth while speaking.

"This is impossible," Judion hammered, crossing his arms again.

Starion felt renewed energy. He didn't know where it came from and he didn't care, but he was confused by the negative response from three elders.

From his pocket, he pulled a small spacegazer device with an equally small e-screen on one end.

I hope this works…

CHAPTER 4

"**WHAT IS** that?" Judion asked.

"It's my orbit tester. It tests the planet's elliptical orbit speed and gravity against the sun's ever-increasing effects."

"Ha—does it work?" Judion replied, starting to move toward the door with Quarion and Valkia following.

Tapping on it, Starion blocked Judion and then grasped his arm. Starion pulled him over to the warped glass exterior and let go. He tapped the tester for a fifth time, hard, and finally it worked. A small protruding 4-D image appeared with numbers below inside the image. Starion looked closely. "Oh, no! That last solar wave and quake must have changed our orbit. According to this, we have less than thirty days!"

"Ha. That's not true!" Judion exclaimed, heading again for the door.

Ardia joined in. "You all were elected to this board. You must let Starion finish."

Judion, red-faced with sweat streaming down, defiantly stomp-glided back, clutched the chair without the cushion, and sat down hard. Deon smiled as if it pained him to do so with unused muscles.

"How can you deny the fact that the closest planet, Mercion, was pulled into the sun only ninety days ago?" Starion asked Judion.

"Because it was much closer and much smaller than Evion."

Starion, trying to think how best to continue, looked out the east-facing window, where he saw the dirty orange haze above what had been a thriving city. Where there were once corridors of tall, multicolored buildings, fly throughways or fly-ways, and glidewalks, the city of Alexon now looked like a city after an asteroid hit it before exploding into thousands of pieces. Out the south-facing window he could see a dark mountain range he knew at one time was covered with tall trees topped with white snowcaps. Next to the mountains was a deep brown crevasse that had once been a vast ocean. After the water had boiled, it had evaporated away.

Starion moved to the hanging e-screen in front. Then, with a wave of his hand, he created and pulled out a new I-spacer that demonstrated Evion's elliptical path. It showed how close the planet was and where it would go if it were to make the normal elliptical turn behind the sun. It was a solid curved 4-D line. Starion used another finger as a laser pointer to change the dotted trajectory path directly into the sun.

"In this orbital simulation, Evion will be pulled into the sun within thirty days. We must decide to migrate *now*. Scan this image into your memory. I have included the orbital motion formulas so you can each monitor it."

Starion witnessed only Ardia and Deon scan it. He understood that Lazarion couldn't because he had lost this ability after his injuries. Starion was almost envious.

Quarion and Valkia turned to see what Judion was going to do. Judion pointed at the image. "Your brainwaves are gone, Starion. How did you come to this conclusion?"

Starion continued, "As you know, gravity is related to the mass of the planet, its radius, and the universal constant g. Evion's normal speed is one hundred miles per second. Its g-force is six. So you can see from this orbit tester that we are speeding up and losing our gravity battle with the sun."

"Starion, this is just another one your crazy inventions. No one believes you—not since you failed to save the planet and killed my brother."

Deon stuck up for his mentor. "Starion is a prolific inventor. He invented the hypercooler and the e-breather for his daughter.

He also invented the toilet lifter that allows us to just point to raise or lower the seat when he was just eight years old."

"What about this star-power gaseous magnifier mixture he has been working on for eight years?" Quarion inquired, joining in with Judion.

"I'm still working on it," Starion countered. "When I do find the right gas mixture and pump it into the magnifiers upper chamber, I believe I can amplify the sun's rays enough to charge our old cells."

"Ha." Judion exclaimed as he created a duplicate image next to Starion's simulation of the elliptical trajectory path. He drew a different path while pointing his right index finger. The new elliptical line displayed Evion on its normal course, in which it would safely turn around the sun and then travel away.

"Yes, Starion, and the reason we are speeding up is that Evion is correcting itself to sling around the sun, thereby adjusting for the gravity change," Judion declared.

Without warning, there was another solar flare. It briefly lit up the room from the window walls, followed by a loud quake that violently shook the room. Inside, lights and I-spacer images flickered on and off. The blue table cracked while several empty chairs tipped over. The elders held on for their lives. Most of them started to enter sleep-mode when Starion yelled, "Everyone out."

They all listened this time and urgently headed for the door, then piled into the e-mover. They instantly dropped down to the main level, landing softly. When the door opened, they rushed out—just as the building collapsed.

"Over to the Audiseum!" Starion yelled.

Judion, who was the last one out, was caught by falling debris. Starion glide-ran back to help him while the other elders dodged newly formed holes in the glidewalks. Deon managed to make it safely while angrily trying to match up his gliders.

Starion pulled on Judion's arms, saving him from the fallen

glass, but lost his hypercooler in the effort. The two glided into the Audiseum with the rest. Judion offered no thanks.

On their way inside the large Audiseum, Starion remembered his studies as a young man about the historic building. He knew it had been built and maintained as the ultimate tribute to the Evions' history of ingenuity. The large glass dome was the oldest on the planet. Its exact age was unknown, but parts were believed to be more than nine thousand E-years old. It housed millions of artifacts, large and small. Each pie-shaped section was built with different materials, styles, and colors, depending on the time of its construction.

Starion knew the large, round, and sloped seating area in front of him was for meetings and spacegazing. It was set on a large golden plate. Similar to spacegazers in most Evion homes, the gigantic circular plate rotated slowly so the huge audience could view a particular object in space. It precisely followed the daily and seasonal planetary spin.

He observed the empty two thousand Audiseum seats individually imbedded into the sloped grey marble. Each seat had a comfortable red cushion. Spacegazers were placed next to each seat for optional viewing. He saw ten silver spacegazers that lined the top ten rows of steps to his left. Each of the steps was a different color. Each spacegazer had been pointed at a different part of the heavens for viewing at each passing age, from eleven to twenty.

Starion was aware his long-dead mentor Vincion had strategically placed these spacegazers there in order to teach young Evions about the scientific and philosophical importance of the solar system, galaxy, and universe. At the first level, the tenth step from the top, eleven-year-olds learned that their sun was just one of trillions of life-supporting stars that made up the universe. On the second to the top, nineteen-year-olds peering through their ritualistic spacegazers could see Evion from the large mirror that had been placed on the moon. The lesson was to learn an appreciation of their own living planet. The tenth spacegazer, the top golden step, was for twenty-year-olds; it pointed back in time and was supposed to teach how precious time was, encouraging him or her to make the most of it.

Starion sighed. These rituals had not been practiced for over one hundred years.

With the elders now safely inside and seated on the first row of the granite bleachers, Starion moved up to the podium, while Deon followed. They both turned to see the large e-screen behind them. Next to the podium, Starion noticed the lever that had been used to slowly start the large circular plate beneath the bleachers. Starion pointed two fingers up at the massive screen, recreating duplicate I-spacers of what he and Deon had just shown in the elder room. It was of Earth and its sun.

Judion stood with his arms crossed. "Starion, we barely made it through a quake, and it's near the end of the morning window of time in which anyone can travel."

Starion ignored him, moving these I-spacers over to the left of the e-screen, and produced a split view of two new images. One I-spacer was of present-day Evion, while the other was an image of the massive dying sun. He pulled both I-spacers out of the e-screen with both hands, moving them next to the images of Earth and its sun.

"Can't you see everyone? We are near the end. This Earth planet is our last hope."

The elder Quarion spoke up, struggling to catch his breath. "Remember, Starion, you are playing with our last twelve remaining energy cells. If we choose to migrate and go through with it, it will be final. We won't be able to come back."

"What about life species on that planet?" Valkia asked after coming out of sleep-mode.

Judion shook his head at her, using his eyes and probably telepathy to stop her from encouraging more discussion. She missed his signal.

"The planet contains a variety of life, including one species with intelligence. They call themselves Humans," Deon answered while changing the I-spacer. The leaders now viewed a massive 4-D image protruding outward, a variety of humans inside it. Several of them had small, thin screens hanging down in front of their eyes, attached to their head with a thin band. Some had a thin wire-looking device in front of their mouths. Some also had miniature round devices hanging just outside their ears.

Others, Starion realized, had a rudimentary-looking IS unit around their waists.

Valkia shook her head in disgust. "They look pretty strange to me, just like that last alien Deon showed us. Look at all those weird skin and hair colors. And look: they have five fingers along with elliptical-shaped ears. And look at their ancient form of IS units on their heads and waists … and look at those strange clothes."

"Yes, their IS units look bulky and heavy," Quarion added.

Valkia glared out the window. "Anyway, I don't want to share a planet with another species, intelligent or not. And it doesn't look like there is much land mass. Deon, were there any uninhabited continents?"

"Yes, at either pole, where it was very cold," Deon answered. "But on the rest of the land masses, the inhabitants are nowhere near as primitive as the three-eyed alien we just saw."

"Look at all the water, Valkia," Ardia added in support. "We are running low, aren't we?"

"We *were* running low, but we just found a new fresh supply deep within Evion's core that should last for a year," Valkia countered.

"We don't *have* a year!" Starion shouted.

Judion pace-glided the gold slab floor while sweat continued to drip down his face. His thin hair was blowing from his cooler. He angrily glided up to the image, motioning toward the humans with his limp hand. "How intelligent are they, Deon? It looks like they walk using their legs, just like our ancestors did."

"They are about six thousand years behind us. Their species

has been in existence for many hundreds of thousands of their years; however, for some reason, they have only made significant advances during the last two hundred or so of their orbits. They do have some space technology, but they have not invented antigravity yet."

"How do you know of this rapid change?" Valkia asked.

"While in Earth's orbit, we were able to intercept their IS planet-net. It was a similar but more primitive form of ours. It was only in 3-D."

"What about energy?" Starion asked.

Deon pulled up an I-spacer that displayed vast deserts with some type of large, tall pumps. "These humans utilized oil for about two hundred of their years, but they are nearly out. They are now desperately trying to convert to hydrogen for every form of transportation. Here is an S-ray of Earth."

Deon produced a skeleton image of Earth and the location of the oil pockets. Each pocket revealed very low levels of oil that still existed. Only one continent had a large pocket with one quarter of its supply still left.

Deon then brought up another image of an aircraft crashing into the Earth. "They tried to use nuclear power recently in place of petroleum, but apparently there was a major accident about ten of their orbits ago."

Immediately after saying this, Deon wished he hadn't.

"Show us," Quarion said.

Deon glanced sheepishly toward Starion, who nodded at him to proceed. Reluctantly, Deon brought up an image of a devastated part of Earth. "Like hydrogen power, they have not yet learned how to take full advantage of solar power either. And they have not yet discovered the benefit of their braydium."

"Ha," said Judion.

"If there is any," Quarion interjected, echoing his ally, Judion.

"Speaking of disasters," Judion said, seemingly still thinking of Evion's ancient past, "What if a hyper-asteroid should collide with the planet? If you recall our history, if we hadn't found the capability of braydium only a few years before, we wouldn't have been able to divert that asteroid—or the one two thousand years later."

"We would have no problem carefully hinting to the Earth people with metaphorical messages or clues—just like the stories in this old book," Starion countered, pulling out his favorite book, *Anciente Evion Adventura~Hero*.

"It is and would be forbidden to interfere with Earth's history, Starion," Judion shouted, glaring at Starion as if daring him to argue.

Starion shook his head and then slipped the book back into his pouch.

CHAPTER 5

STARION, SWEAT dripping down his face, changed the subject. "What about communication technology, Deon?"

Deon brought up another I-spacer of many s-rovers orbiting Earth.

"We could intercept a variety of frequencies imbedded in the signals from hundreds of s-rover satellites orbiting their planet. By the way, we left an I-cam on their moon for additional monitoring."

"Like this," Starion said confidently, pointing to an idle smaller screen to the right side of the seating area. He created an image of the I-cam. It was a large tripod with a huge cylindrical spacegazer barrel and camera at the end. "How does the signal come in, Deon?"

"Not very good from this distance," Deon told him, bringing up a live view of Earth from its moon. He adjusted the view the best he could. It was fuzzy and full of static. "But we could install our signal booster if we should visit it again. Luckily, we were able to create the views I showed you before we left the solar system. And we were able to study local solar and galactic activity in Earth's foreseeable future, too."

Judion seemed to smell a plot. "Why would you have left the I-cam there without gaining our approval?"

Valkia joined in before Judion could stop her. "Did you find anything?"

"We found a hyper-asteroid heading toward Earth in a few of their days. But it will miss by thousands of e-miles."

"Huh…do you the think the Earth people are aware of it?" Judion asked.

"No, they don't have the technology to detect asteroids at this speed. But it will safely miss."

"How can you be so sure?"

"What about air, Deon?" Starion asked ignoring Judion.

"Earth's air is full of oxygen and nitrogen."

"Oh, what it would be like to breathe in a huge breath of fresh air with lots of oxygen!" Ardia exclaimed. "Our medical staff is seeing more and more respiratory cases, isn't it, Judion?"

As the doctor tried to think of a way to combat the wise Ardia, Starion took control. "Yes, Earth's air is probably like ours was ten thousand years ago. And it would be nice to see blue skies again."

Suddenly, all the hanging I-spacers displayed wavy, moving lines while the walls produced an annoying screeching sound. A monotone voice filled the room:

"This is an emergency. This is an emergency. Please go to the nearest emergency shelter."

Starion and the elders were startled by the action in the wavy I-spacer images, along with the alarming sound resonating through every inanimate object in the Audiseum. They heard the same thing moments later from a speaker outside.

Starion, gasping, shouted, "Deon, can you turn that damn EBS off? It isn't working correctly anymore—and when it does work, we've usually already felt the effects of a quake or solar flare anyway."

"OK," Deon answered, pointing at the e-screen.

This time he brought up a 4-D dialogue box on the bottom left of the e-screen, where several options were listed. One of the options displayed on the D-box was the category "EBS," which had "On" and "Off" subcategories. He chose "Off," which caused the wavy lines and annoying sound to disappear.

"Can you delete that whole program, Deon?" Starion asked.

"I'll try, but I don't know how. Whoever developed the last update to the IS code forgot to allow for removing it. Or, if there is a way, they didn't give us proper instructions for doing so."

"Isn't there a help function?"

"Yes, but that would take a year to learn, even if I could scan it in. Some brilliant young Evion created it and no one can figure it out."

Judion didn't care. "Alright, it's time to go home, Starion. It's at the end of the morning travel window."

Starion looked at his watch. "No, we still have some time."

The eldest, Quarion, finally had enough. "Starion, what is your proposal? We need to get out of here before we roast or suffocate on our way home."

Starion pace-glided the floor with arms crossed and put his hand to his chin.

"Our search for braydium is paramount. Several of us will travel twenty years back in Earth's time. We will bring one of the last two remaining braydium magnifier and star-power cell mold-casts with us. That way we can manufacture a new magnifier and new cells on Earth. But we will also bring along an old magnifier in case Earth's sun is strong enough to charge the new cells. Who knows, maybe that's all we will need. Either way, the twelve remaining star-power cells should be enough to get us there and back with plenty to spare for our uses here on Evion."

"How many cells would you need?" Quarion asked.

Starion looked over at Deon, who answered, "Four."

"That would use up a good portion of our twelve remaining star-power cells," Quarion warned. "Besides, we would need more than eight to send the rest of our people there. We would have to use several v-breakers."

"Well...even if we should fail bringing back new energy from this Earth, I think I am close to a new gaseous mixture that will amplify the diminished sun's rays in the chamber of the magnifier and store the energy in a more compressed version. If it works, we can charge more cells that way," Starion clarified. "But I think our best bet is to travel to this Earth first."

"What about the other envoy? We need to wait for their results," Judion adamantly stated.

"And I agree," Quarion said.

"Me too." Valkia added.

Starion thought of a political move. "Deon, keep trying to contact Neilion. If he has found a better planet we will consider it."

Starion's strategy worked. Quarion, still a part of the discussion said, "By the way, you have been working on a new star-power magnifier gas mixture for eight years. If you are successful in your lobby efforts and we choose to migrate to this planet, there had better be enough power or we could end up stuck somewhere in between while starving or suffocating. This seems impossible."

"It might help if we can figure out where our cells are disappearing to," Starion added pointedly.

"Everyone in this room has the authority to disperse those cells," Judion announced.

Quarion interrupted, "Starion, how do you know there will enough braydium on Earth—or, for that matter, any of it?"

"I believe in Deon."

Judion chimed in again, pace-gliding in front of everyone. "Starion, time travel was outlawed more than two thousand years ago. The consensus was that it is universally unethical to change any form of history anywhere in this universe."

Valkia joined in with her eyes half open. "Let's say that this all works and we migrate to Earth. Will we be accepted, and will we be able to cohabitate?"

Deon answered. "According to our research, we have very similar DNA to these humans."

"But we would have to be attracted to each other. I could never be attracted to a primitive Earth man. Would you like it, Ardia, if these Earth men tried to romance you? With their five fingers and odd-looking ears?"

Ardia paused, smiling seductively. "Why yes, I would, if he was a gentleman and I was attracted to him. And especially if the survival of our people was at stake."

Valkia, obviously irritated from all the dialogue and action, finally opened her eyes all the way. "Well, no wonder you're not married."

"We could study some love and romance rituals from Earth to help ensure success. Their old stories are probably like our ancient love stories," Ardia explained.

"Eww!" Valkia replied. "What good did those old myths do?"

"They help explain in metaphorical terms the mysterious life force attraction we have with the opposite sex. Even our scientists were never able to explain it."

"Are you saying that if I should go to this Earth, I will be somehow magically infatuated with the human women and you with the men?" Judion blurted.

"I'm saying that love is the most powerful and mysterious force in the universe."

Deon changed the subject. "By the way, the Earth people have many strange but interesting customs."

Starion's eyes opened wider in anticipation.

"For example, I have brought back some of the instruments these Earth people use to create their music. They're over in that room," Deon said, pointing to an Audiseum room.

Lazarion, who had been feeling increasingly ill from the heat and thin air, choked, "I have to go—I'm not feeling well. Please, take a hard look at Earth. I believe in it."

"Wait, I'll help you," Starion offered.

"No, I will be fine. I'll hop a v-breaker down there," he whispered, pointing out the window.

Judion grumbled, "He'll be fine."

Lazarion walked out of the Audiseum.

All at once, there was a bright flash and subsequent small rumble. The elders rushed to the door and looked out just as

Lazarion, who hadn't made it to the v-breaker, was hit by a solar flare. They heard him yell in anguish as he fell to the ground.

Starion started for the door, but Ardia and Deon held his arms. It was no use. It was too late.

Everyone slowly moved back to where they had been. Some plugged their noses to avoid the stench. Ardia, Deon, and Starion put their heads down in grief. Starion felt especially devastated. Lazarion had been a major inspiration to him lately. He sat in a bleacher seat and put his hand on an idle spacegazer. As he stared up out of the heated glass dome, he sadly reminisced about his friend.

Ardia consoled him with a telepathic message of comfort. *He was a good man . . . a good man, Starion.*

"Starion, why so quiet?" Judion asked sarcastically. "All of a sudden you don't have the votes, do you?"

"Can't you see Starion is grieving?" Ardia shouted, losing her objectivity for a moment.

Deon ambled over to several purple bags of miscellaneous Earth artifacts, struggling to keep his bionic shoes in control. He distributed the bags to everyone. Judion defiantly pushed his away with his right foot glider.

Tucked in at the top of each bag was a small tank of Earth's fresh air with a mask and small hose attached to the cylinder.

"I have a bag of Earth items and an e-disk of information for each of you."

"Did you scan or bring any of Earth's books back?" Starion inquired sadly.

"Just one called their dictionary, so we can learn their language. I didn't have much time."

"I'm not touching any of that stuff," Judion proclaimed.

Struggling to breathe before each sentence as he felt it getting hotter, Starion now tried to honor his friend's death by politically suggesting, "Let's try some of Earth's air. It is getting dangerously hard to breathe."

"I wouldn't if I were you," warned Judion. "Who knows what bacteria or viruses could be attached to the air molecules? And, for that matter, what kind of diseases these people carry?"

Starion, slightly worried but still feeling the loss of Lazarion, murmured, "Deon was just there, and he is fine."

"Is he?" Judion said, looking deeply into Deon's eyes. "I must test him and whoever he was with."

"Glenion was the only other Evion with me on Earth, and we are both fine."

"Don't be so sure." Judion stood up, ready to leave. Quarion and Valkia were also poised to leave.

"Be careful on your way home," Starion reminded everyone, still grieving for his friend. "We will meet tomorrow and vote."

"You will all need to scan in this dictionary first, everyone," Deon told them.

Quarion and Valkia rolled their eyes as they left the room, reluctantly carrying their bags of Earth items.

Deon remembered one more thing. "And there is some of Earths water in small, clear containers that you can try."

"Don't anyone drink it before I can test it," Judion warned.

As Ardia walked out the door, she sent a quick telepathic message. *Good job, Starion. I'm so sorry about Lazarion. I'll be happy to help with the presentation for tomorrow.*

Starion replied telepathically, *Thanks, Ardia—and thanks for introducing the old stories to me while encouraging me to read them.*

He left right after, not caring whether Judion was still there or not.

CHAPTER 6

STARION PULLED his hood over his head and hustled out of the Audiseum. He avoided the site of his friend's death by hurry-gliding to the opposite side of the glidewalk. He could feel a surge of heat near his right knee. Then he remembered he had torn the outer layer of his shroud earlier.

He found one of the city's few v-breakers parked on a designated area below the fly-way, where v-breakers once traveled in between the tall Alexon buildings. The shuttle was about eight feet wide and twelve feet long, manufactured from a heated mixture of braydium with water. It visually looked similar to glass but was extremely strong and had a slight blue tint to it. Even though it utilized antigravity technology, it still required wings on each side in order to take advantage of air molecules for steering.

Each wing on this particular v-breaker extended outward four feet and was angled backward at forty-five degrees. There were three ways to enter. There were airtight doors on each side of the ship just in front of the wings, along with a back hatch.

Starion remembered the term *v-breaker* had been chosen after the inventor Bellion, some five thousand years before, yelled that he had broken gravity, and also the fact that it was v-shaped. Luckily, the outer shell of the remaining few v-breakers had withstood the terrific swings in temperature—so far, anyway.

Before entering, Starion looked for other Evions through the hazy, dirty air. He wished he had seen someone picking up the daily ration of nutrition formulas and water from the e-com. He wanted to see their eyes and demeanor to see if he or she had any hope. According to an old story he was reading, maybe he could connect while drawing strength.

He saw the galvanized green glass dome that was supposed to maximize the sun's diminishing rays to grow plants used for nutrition formulas.

Just then he thought he saw someone, but he soon realized it was an IS-man, one of Evion's robotic city maintenance men. These robots were black and silver and operated from chips similar to those used by IS units.

Shaped like an Evion man, Starion knew IS-men had been used in Evion's thriving times to perform tasks such as cleaning and repairing the fly-ways and glidewalks.

This particular IS-man was about six feet tall and a foot wide. It had two legs and four arms, so it would be stable enough to lift large, heavy garbage cans from the city glidewalks. The IS-man had been melted in its upright position.

Starion sensed a flash coming and heard a rumble in the distance. It wasn't very strong. There was a small flare that fell short of hitting the planet.

Once Starion was safely onboard, the IS bank scanned his eyes. Because he gave no specific instruction, the IS bank followed the default program and started ascending at an angle for Starion's home. He set his bag of Earth artifacts on the galvanized clear braydium floor behind the manual pilot seat. Starion started to sit in the front of the first row of ten chairs. Glancing below, he noticed someone waving at him through the clear bottom.

"IS unit, please land."

When Starion was back on the dangerous ground, his neighbor Ripeon rushed inside with a small bag.

"Hi, Ripeon," Starion said with surprise.

"Hello, Starion. Thanks for picking me up," he said with a nervous twitch. He tossed his hood back and took off his six-fingered white gloves.

"Going home?"

"Yes. I was just picking up my ration from the e-com."

Starion was aware Ripeon was the same age as himself but shorter, with grey hair. He was married with no children. He was an average, expressionless Evion who had a strange twitch about him. Every once in a while he would twitch his shoulder and eyes at the same time. No one understood why. Neither the doctor Judion nor Judion's wife Kircia, who was also a doctor, could diagnose it, which was a lasting frustration for the two.

As a nutrition expert, Ripeon had helped Starion's wife Aphelia make sure that there was an ample supply of nutrition for the remaining Evions.

The ship took off again; there was no sound due to the powerful star-power antigravity technology. When they flew over the large e-center—the planet's last remaining control center—Starion observed two figures below hustling into a room where the star-power cells were stored. "Hmm," he mumbled. "Who is that?"

As the ship flew higher, Starion peered out one side of the clear blue tinted shell. He gazed at the hazy orange landscape and sky. He thought about the long, successful history of his planet. Would their existence have all been in vain? He decided to view the planet briefly from a higher perspective.

"Ripeon, I'm going to take a brief look at our planet."

Ripeon went into sleep-mode.

Starion used a voice command. "V-breaker, please fly two e-miles higher."

The ship jettisoned up to where Starion could see more of the planet. In the distance, he viewed the barren brown plains, dark brown mountains, sinkholes and crevasses, and a variety of different sized faults made from ancient lakes and oceans. Very limited amounts of water remained. It was now toxic from the constant direct ultraviolet sun rays and the thin atmosphere. Starion knew that over recent years, the only fresh water left was deep inside the planet and had to be pumped out.

Starion pointed at an idle e-screen just below the clear shell-roof of the ship. He brought up a D-box that had several options to choose from. He chose "Evion's History."

Nothing appeared. This v-breaker, along with all the others, had lost most of its data.

Continuing to look outside, Starion could see where the edge of largest continent once had a vast ocean filled up next to it. Way off in the distance, he could barely see the only other small continent, now totally barren. He sadly remembered Lazarion's death, and his own responsibility for the destruction of the small continent eight years before. A rush of guilt ran through his soul again.

As they flew along, eerily quiet, Starion turned his attention outside again, viewing trees that were either burned or petrified. Much of Evion looked like large wooden poles.

"Hey, Ripeon...wake up."

Ripeon slowly opened one blank eye.

"Ripeon, can you imagine what this planet was like a hundred years ago? It must have been beautiful."

Ripeon nodded cautiously, answering, "Yes, I suppose."

"Wouldn't you like a chance at that again? Ripeon, back in the Great Era, some of those trees were enormous. They provided our people with immense pleasure and satisfaction. They were used for home building, fuel, and wood products; as well as shade."

Starion was aware Ripeon was still in sleep-mode, but he kept talking. He checked his watch by instinct, but he didn't care what time it was; he loved flying.

"I have been reading some of our ancient archives Ardia found in that uncovered old library. Some trees were so huge that when the leaves fell in autumn, there were so many that someone invented hyper-fans to blow them away. There are several ancient stories of Evions getting lost in leaf piles and suffocating. It was a sight to see when the large trees were harvested, according to the accounts," he told his neighbor.

Suddenly the v-breaker took a dive straight down. Luckily, it corrected itself. It appeared to have found a limited air pocket.

Starion heard the IS unit's monotone voice: "*Warning… Warning… Energy low… Energy low.*"

He glanced at the v-panel in front and checked the star-power energy gauge. It was very low. He opened a compartment in the bottom of the craft that stored the star-power cell. There was a faint blue glow from the convex lens. He picked up the cell, shook it, and put it back. Below it he could see the lower flap doors, where cells could be replaced from underneath the ship as well as from inside. He looked at the gauge again and saw the needle had moved slightly in his favor.

Starion continued with his one-sided discussion. "Ripeon, wake up…did you know our star-power cells and antigravity technology were the only reasons we were able to travel into Evion orbit, plus deep into the galaxy? With the cells, we can hover or travel at any speed. But going beyond the speed of light was banned generations ago, after a devastating incident that changed part of our history."

Starion stood up. Now that he was talking about one of his favorite subjects, his adrenalin had kicked in.

But then he sensed a flare. He realized that if it were a large one, he and Ripeon might be doomed. He looked up at the sun through the clear roof again. Luckily, it was a small, swirling flare that pulled itself back into the sun.

He continued his monologue with the enthusiasm of an inventor talking about his favorite subject. Deep down, Starion was aware he was rationalizing his flying by giving this lecture to his neighbor; he knew he should be heading home.

"Bellion invented the star-power cell right after braydium had been discovered. He devised different-sized cells for different functions. We use small cells in the hypercoolers we each wear, and medium ones for hyper-air blowers that heat and cool our buildings. Each of these cells can last for thirty years. The larger ones are more powerful and are used for v-breakers. Unfortunately, they don't last long. Shortly after that, Vincion invented the v-breaker."

He continued on through the thin atmosphere and again reveled that he was flying. He missed it. He hoped that if they migrated to Earth, he could fly to his heart's content there. But he remembered the warning about introducing new technology. Perhaps he might fly Earth's aircraft, no matter how far behind they were.

Starion thought about the Great Era, when star power was plentiful and almost every family had its own small v-breaker. Evion workers were able to commute to work on the opposite side of the planet on a daily basis. This had allowed many of them to live in tropical climates but work in cold or dangerous areas.

"Trips into Evion's orbit and nearby planets had become routine. Some v-breakers housed thousands of Evions and toured the solar system for weeks at a time. These required huge amounts of star power."

He decided to give his neighbor a break, mumbling quietly to himself. "Most v-breakers had what was called a v-air threshold. This vertical intersection of breathable air and dangerous vacuum of space allowed an Evion to jump back and forth between the two. It was near the back hatch and could be easily turned on or off. This made it much easier for an Evion to spacewalk or to jump out onto a planet, asteroid, or moon."

Starion continued to recall their history. Sadly, he understood that when the news of the dying sun became evident, Evion's leaders had to ration star-power cells, keeping only a limited supply for local travel. The cells were stored in the e-center inside a locked room. Only the elders had access.

Then he remembered seeing the two figures at the e-center earlier. *Who were they and what were they doing?*

Suddenly a flash passed through the ship so fast Starion had to close his eyes. He began to sweat profusely and had to blink his eyes to wipe the tears. *I can't let something happen to Ripeon.*

The v-breaker shook violently and went into a fast dive. It heated up instantly. Starion could smell the interior starting to burn. "IS unit...I want to take manual control."

"Manual control approved."

Starion took hold of the v-stick and pointed it upward to the left, leveling the ship. He sat down in the overheated pilot seat. "Ouch!"

Starion looked down as they neared Alexon's outer edge. Through the dirty air, he saw an ancient, dried-up river. He had been reading old stories about explorers traveling up and down it. Next to this was a wind farm that had taken advantage of Evion's wind for energy long ago. Adjacent was an ancient solar panel field that had been used to store the Evion sun's energy before star power was invented. Its one-piece tinted glass was miles long and wide but had since melted.

He turned back to Ripeon, whose eyes were still tightly closed. He nudged his shoulder again with his hand. "I think we have found our new home!"

Ripeon twitched while Starion manually landed the v-breaker. Even though he was out of practice, Starion brought it in perfectly. Once parked safely between his home and Ripeon's, he shook his neighbor, "Wake up! Wake up!"

"OK, OK," Ripeon muttered, awakening from sleep-mode.

Starion wrapped up his neighbor's shroud, pulled up his hood, and put on his gloves. He sent him on his way. Starion, looking on from the v-breaker, watched as Ripeon's wife greeted Ripeon and then glared back at the v-breaker, giving Starion the evil eye.

Before stepping into the scorching heat, Starion reached for the bag of items from Earth. He made sure his hood was securely wrapped around his face, and then he put on his heat-resistant gloves. He should not have taken the long way home and should have been safely inside a building before now.

When he stepped outside, he felt a blast of heat enter his hood. It was so hot he had to wrap the hood around his head even tighter. There was now just a slit of fabric through which he could just barely see. He felt a terrible burst of pain on his left wrist along with his right knee area. "Ohhh!" he shouted.

He noticed he had failed to completely secure the glove on his left hand. He set the bag down, pulled up the glove to cover his flesh, and hurried toward his house, still feeling excess heat near his knee.

Looking out of the corner of his eye, were the few homes that still stood along with the remnants of those that had been destroyed. Smoke still billowed from one that had been melted the day before. He knew his other neighbor, Hephion, had perished inside. Suddenly, Starion could smell burning flesh and became sick to his stomach. The fire must have found his neighbor in the debris.

Starion turned back toward his front door. He observed the barren brown and dead terrain. He imagined what it might have been like, a hundred years before, to stroll up to a home in glorious bright sunshine under blue skies. What was it like to smell the fresh air and fragrances from the surrounding vegetation?

He was reminded of a story his grandfather had told him when he was a boy. The old man had told young Starion about a time long ago, when Evions could tell the time of day along with the season by the smells and the shadows made by the sun. He wished he had that ability, but the sun's diminished rays no longer created shadows.

Through the slit of his hood, he could see his large galvanized half-spherical home that, like the warped window in the elder room, illuminated different hues of orange.

The autodoor scanned his eyes for security when he stepped onto the entry threshold. Just before he glided in, the recent emotions of guilt and anxiety started running through him again. *Why?* He wondered. Ever since he had started reading instead of scanning the ancient stories, he had been feeling both negative and inspiring emotions at the same time.

Did one have to experience both types of these emotions, like those in the old stories?

Even though the outside elements were extremely dangerous, Starion hesitated for a moment before entering his home.

CHAPTER 7

THE DOOR opened. Starion rushed inside, where he was greeted by his wife, Aphelia. He could tell she was worried and concerned about his late arrival. She glide-ran over and hugged him while he undid his makeshift face mask, took off his gloves, and threw back his hood.

"Starion, where were you? You are past the dangerous time of the morning…and your kids miss you."

Starion looked at his slightly younger wife with her long, gorgeous red hair. She had a twinkle in her brilliant green eyes. She had not been exposed to the outside elements as Starion had been and therefore was able to keep her exquisite looks.

He saw she was wearing her semicircular ultra-light silver IS unit around her waist. Starion knew Aphelia was vitally involved in anything related to her children. She also was instrumental in the growing and nutrition quality of Evion's food sources in the e-com greenhouse.

Starion contemplated Lazarion's question regarding their lifespan and that of the Earth's peoples. Would Aphelia be considered young or old for having children when she did?

"I took a short trip a little higher than usual to take a look at the latest damage."

His daughter Bria ran out of her room and hugged him. "Hi, Dad," she said with a slight wheeze.

Starion reciprocated the hug wrapping his arms around her skinny ten year old body while looking into her clear, curious blue eyes.

He felt his e-breather invention of a small, shiny, black

respiratory tank strapped to her back. It had a thin hose and mask attached. He knew she had recently been losing her lung capacity and therefore required help to breathe, especially when she slept.

Starion's son Dustion stayed in his room. Starion was sadly aware he shied away from himself and Aphelia. A typical sixteen-year-old, he was suspicious and rebellious.

"Hello, Dustion," his father called.

"Hi," came the despondent answer after a short pause.

Starion winced at his son's pain, trying to remember what it was like at his age with all those raging hormones. He also remembered the awkwardness of being scrawny with a large head.

Starion looked at Aphelia. She had the same stare she always had when they argued about his constant time away from home. But before she had a chance to speak, Bria noticed the bag Starion had brought with him and asked, "What's in the bag?"

"OK, my daughter. I will show you later. Now back to your schoolwork," Starion said, gently patting her rear end.

When the girl had gone, Starion turned his attention to his wife of twenty years. "I am so glad we decided to have children. They inspire me to keep going every day. Most decided not to."

"Me too."

Starion set the bag of Earth artifacts on the floor. Aphelia glanced at it but then looked away. She had noticed Starion's tear on is shroud leg. She quickly found and brought over a small device that instantly repaired it.

"How did the meeting go?"

"I have some bad news. We lost Lazarion today," he said, lowering his head.

"Oh, Starion, I am so sorry…I know you two had grown to be great friends."

"But I think we have found our new home."

Trying to relax, Starion sat on a blue chair in the center living room. It was made from soft but firm foam that molded to his body. It didn't work; he was too wound up. He stood up and started pace-gliding the floor. He remembered he had tried a new gaseous mixture in his star-power magnifier that morning before he had left for the meeting.

He hurried into the e-mover, arriving instantly above inside the skyroid. He immediately inspected the thin disk star-power cell below the magnifier. He hoped to see a bright blue glow. But, as in the past eight years, there was only a dull yellow glow shining through the top concave lens. What had always bothered him the most was the paradox, that even though the sun was much closer now, its light rays were much weaker.

He stared at the old black magnifier. Arched in shape, it was three feet long by one foot wide. Even though much smaller, the magnifier reminded him of arched entryways he had seen pic-spacers of long ago.

His hope was that someday, with the right gas mixture pumped into the convex magnifier lens, the sun's rays would be amplified enough to charge the old cell below.

Discouraged, he took both objects with him. He shot down the e-mover and over to his lab. Aphelia followed him. He lowered his head in defeat.

"I have to try to relax for a minute," he said. Aphelia watched him shuffle-glide out the room and over into the e-mover room.

He shut the door behind him, pointed at the large wall screen, and pulled out a D-box with the options "E-Mover On" and "E-Mover Off." He chose "E-Mover On" and the room lost its gravity. He aimed at another option, "Music," choosing a song that filled the room. It was a song without singing but with synthesized melodies. He began to float, finally closing his eyes to meditate.

While drifting, he remembered the many times years ago he and Aphelia, before the children were born, had used the antigravity room for romance.

Within seconds, he found himself near the inside wall by the door. Judion popped into his mind. He reached out with his leg and pushed so hard he found himself instantly at the other side of the room, near the warped arced glass outer wall. He had to reach out his arm and push again in order to not slam into the glass.

"This isn't working," he said aloud. He pointed to "E-Mover Off" and his body started slowly floating to the floor. Once safely down, he rushed back to the living room, took the Earth bag, and hustled into his lab.

Starion was inside his favorite room. It included a cobalt glass desk, a spacegazer in front of a large arched window-wall, and a small chemistry lab with glass bottles. These flasks contained different-colored gases. He saw the star-power magnifier he had just brought back from the skyroid, with a star-power cell below it. He turned toward his collection of ancient petroleum and hydrogen engines, along with his water splitter. He knew when he acquired the hydrogen water splitter it had almost cost him his marriage.

Next to this was a large bookshelf with ancient books from Ardia's discovery.

Aphelia followed and watched him take one Earth book out of the bag. "This is what the Earth people call their dictionary. It gives definitions of their words."

He touched it, closing his eyelids. "Interesting," he said with eyes glowing blue.

When totally scanned, he plopped it on a shelf and panned the other shelves. They were full of ancient Evion books and included self-reliance books, chemistry and physics texts, and old books of ancient Evion mythology.

There were several copies of his favorite book, *Ancient Evion Adventura~Hero*, one of which he kept in his shroud pocket. It was written in an ancient Evion dialect. The book had a black cover that included two faint-looking mythological figures that no Evion had ever seen before. Starion was fascinated by it. He and Ardia had tried to find out its origin, but with no success.

Starion reached into the bag and pulled out the Earth air tank. Then he pulled out several other objects. There was a bottle of some kind of light brown liquid, and a small white container with hundreds of small solid objects inside that he could hear when he shook it. There were packaged items he tried to open but couldn't. Finally he found several clear bottles of what he figured were water. Deon had mentioned them before everyone left the meeting. Then he remembered Judion's warning and put them back in the bag.

Starion turned back to Aphelia, who had been waiting patiently to hear more about the day's events. She was now curiously looking over the Earth items.

"We met today and found a planet that I believe is our answer," he told her.

"You mean that small, primitive blue planet you mentioned?"

"Yes, but it is not as primitive as I thought. Even though the people are significantly behind us in technology, I know it will work—and besides, we are running out of time. My orbit tester shows we are down to thirty days."

Bria yelled from her room, "Dad, can you help me with a chemistry problem?"

Starion yelled back, "A little later, I want to talk to your mother first."

"OK," Bria loudly answered back, wheezing and coughing.

Starion grimaced, as did Aphelia.

"I wish she wouldn't try to yell. She knows she can't do that," Aphelia worriedly whispered.

"I suppose we weren't any different until we became adults. It is called blind faith, and I admire her for it. It's funny; when we become adults we lose all hope...why?"

Aphelia saw the tank and asked, "What is that?"

"That's a sample of Earth's air."

Aphelia, concerned, asked, "Even if we should decide to migrate to this Earth, will we be accepted? You said the people are quite a bit behind us."

"I don't know, but we have something to bargain with that will be of tremendous value to the Earth people."

"What's that?"

"Alternative energy sources."

Starion sat at his desk and turned on his clear e-screen with his finger. He pulled out the small e-disk Deon had placed in the Earth bag, and then inserted it into a connector on the bottom of the screen. He brought up a 4-D image of a spectacular view of Earth. He pulled the I-spacer toward him and Aphelia. He twitched his finger, changing the image to the red surface vehicle Deon had shown at the meeting.

He pulled it out into the nearby air space with his hand. He held it from different angles. Even though the surface vehicle was sputtering while intermittently starting and stopping, he admired the ancient metal, glass windows, and rubber tires. When he zoomed in on the back, he read the words "historical antique" on the license plate. The driver stopped and opened up the hood. Starion could tell it was a prototype of a hydrogen engine. He glanced between it and an old, ancient hydrogen engine in his collection.

"They apparently can't quite finalize hydrogen technology for their surface vehicles and small aircrafts. But even if they do someday, similar to us long ago, they will face a shortage of water, too. Then they will need to change to star power like we did—that is, if there is braydium, like Deon believes there is, and if their scientists discover its uses."

Starion brought up an Earth I-spacer of hundreds of oil pumps. "According to Deon's research, they have nearly exhausted their oil supply."

Starion turned his attention to another old dusty engine in his collection. "Transportation is tremendously important to these people, like it is to us."

He watched again as a young man on Earth adjusted something underneath the hood, and then tried it again. The young man had no success, and the vehicle intermittently started and stopped again. Starion saw a side view of the young man. He looked strangely familiar.

"What's the next step?" Aphelia asked.

"Deon believes Earth has braydium, but he only found reference to it from Earth's archives twenty years in Earth's past, when they apparently started to recognize they had limited oil. Unfortunately for them, they never made the connection to its uses for solar power or its other uses. As I said, they have urgently turned to hydrogen for now but also have apparently been experimenting with atomic power for transportation."

Starion pace-glided the floor. "We need to go back to that time on Earth, find the braydium, and charge star-power cells from their healthy sun, then travel back to the future, here."

Starion scurried over to a corner of the room. He pulled a cover off two objects that were just slightly larger but had the same shape as the magnifier and cell. The coloring of these was a dull black along with speckles of grey. "I wish we could make a fresh new magnifier mold-cast and a new cell mold-cast somehow. That would allow us to pour the mixture of Earth's braydium and water inside it. Then we could create new shiny star-power magnifiers and cells; these are almost worn out. But the engineering schematics were lost in the mass data deletion."

Starion looked over at the dull black magnifier and the cell he had just hauled down from the skyroid. "But maybe these will still work fine and we won't have to try to make new ones from the old mold-casts. By the way, Aphelia, I am going to leave these here. I will take the only other two mold-casts that are down at the e-center in my office. I have been trying different mixtures there also. Same with this old magnifier—I will take the one at the e-center. So if anything happens to me, remind Deon they are here."

Noticing Aphelia's worry and wishing he hadn't said that, Starion motioned up at a clock displaying the same eerie image that was on his watch. He observed Evion, half lit up red while it protruded out in 4-D. "It must have been nice to see the healthy Evion on the clock long ago, Aphelia. Some people even put the clock on their bedroom skyroid domes so when they woke up at night they could see what part of Evion the sun was shining on."

Aphelia, concerned, asked, "Speaking of going back in Earth's time, I thought we couldn't interfere with another planet's history. It is strictly forbidden, right? As you know, Bellion, the inventor of time travel, went back and met his grandfather, who he knew was going to die in a v-breaker crash. He saved him but altered their whole family tree. Some relatives who had been alive instantly vanished, while some who were never alive on Evion strangely appeared...it was a cultural mess."

"That story happened so long ago, some think it's been mythologized," Starion said gazing into the depressing sky through the warped arced glass exterior. "We have less than thirty days to live, my wife. I will do anything to save us. I know it will work. And that reminds me: I have to notify our people."

Starion rushed over to his cobalt desk pulling up an I-spacer with a D-box. He chose the option "Evion Planet-Net."

"Can't you contact them using your DTI?" Aphelia asked, looking the small slightly indented hole on his neck.

"It would take too long. And speaking of our DTIs, we may have to hide them somehow if we should migrate there. I suppose the Earth people would think it odd to place a small ultra-miniature data transfer interconnect on their children's necks."

"Why, I grew into mine in less than year when I was five," Aphelia commented.

"Even though it is skin-magnetized and easily deciphers subtle voice patterns from one's voice box and then send sends and receives transmissions, it probably is way ahead of their technology."

Now, in front of him on the e-screen, a smaller blank I-spacer protruded out from the larger one. "I want to send a message, IS unit," Starion ordered.

"Proceed."

Starion was then visually recorded live inside the smaller image. "Fellow Evions, I believe we have just thirty days to survive. However, we have found a planet called Earth that I believe will work. The council is meeting tomorrow for more discussion and to vote. Please come down to the Audiseum tomorrow to see for yourselves."

"Are you ready to send?" the IS unit asked.

"Yes."

Starion watched as the small protruding I-spacer slowly disappeared. But then he heard the IS unit again:

"Message undeliverable."

CHAPTER 8

STARION TRIED again to send a message with the same results: "Message undeliverable."

"Hmm...I wonder what's wrong."

"I can try to contact our people one by one, Starion," Aphelia offered.

"OK, do the best you can, and I will try to keep sending this too. I will even use that annoying EBS system, if I must."

Aphelia motioned to the children's rooms, giving Starion a concerned look. "If we migrate to this Earth, will we be able to continue on with our race? Will our children have a decent life there?"

Starion also turned toward the children's rooms. He pointed his two fingers again at his e-screen and produced images of a variety of humans on Earth that had been shown at the elder room. There were images of many different skin colors of people wearing a variety of clothing while performing different tasks. Some had awkward IS units.

"They sure are an interesting-looking race. And they all look somewhat different. Are you sure we have similar DNA?"

Starion pulled up a category called "Human DNA from Deon's disk." After a moment he replied, "Yes we do, except..." Starion changed the image to a rough-looking man holding a spear and wearing animal skins.

"There is some question on Earth whether DNA from this being has survived," Deon's voice suddenly narrated.

"As long as we can all get along," Aphelia commented, look-ing away. With a worried look, she stroll-glided out of the lab down the hall and into the bathroom.

Starion was aware that when she was ner' combed her hair. He secretly followed her, wa in one side of the I-mirror combing her hair. T the other side of the I-mirror, where there was a of the back and the top of her head.

On her way out, she noticed the gold-colored toilet seat had been left up. She pointed her focus finger and lowered it using her husband's childhood invention.

She yelled, "Dustion, please put down the toilet seat when you are done."

"Why?" he yelled. "It only takes a second for you to point and lower it."

"That's the point. It would only take a second for *you* to lower it with your finger."

On her way out, she passed by the floor-length S-ray mirror. She could see her insides from a live 4-D image. Thankfully, she didn't see anything to be concerned about.

Starion moved over to the lab. From the doorway, he watched her stroll-glide along the circular hallway, passing the children's rooms.

Starion could tell that she was extremely concerned, and he mosey-glided over to the partly melted glass exterior while looking at the devastating view.

Aphelia entered and followed him. "What's next?"

"The leaders are going to review and, I hope, memory-scan the material tonight. Deon, Ardia, and I are going to put together some more information to present tomorrow."

Just as he finished, there was a terrific flash that lit and heated their home momentarily. It was followed by a small rumble. The quake shook the solid glass floor. Several books fell from the shelves. Starion and Aphelia glared outside. They hoped no damage had been done to their neighbors. To their relief, there wasn't any.

Aphelia remarked, "That was a small one."

Are you kids OK?" he yelled.

"Yes," they both answered.

Moments later, the annoying emergency broadcast sound and wavy lines appeared.

"That damn EBS system," Starion exclaimed, moving back to the desk where he tried to send the e-message again. He failed again.

"There wasn't much support for migrating or even studying this blue planet today. I don't understand it, Aphelia. Before the mass deletion, we would have had the support we needed. If Lazarion had lived, I know I would have had enough votes," he lamented, shaking his head. "Instead, I will contact our people directly via the planet-net."

He looked up into his wife's eyes for support, switching to telepathy.

Maybe they are right. Maybe this is a waste of time. Judion seems to be totally against the migration for some reason that I don't understand. Valkia is also skeptical and doesn't think there would be room for us. Quarion thinks we won't have enough energy to transport all Evions that far anyway.

Aphelia didn't use telepathy to respond. "You know I want to do anything we can to keep our family alive and help our children live a normal life."

Just then they heard Bria cough, desperately gasping for air. They both hurry-glided to her room, as did Dustion.

Starion shook the e-breather and tried to adjust the mask. It didn't work.

Bria, extremely short of breath, appeared close to death.

"Do something!" Aphelia screamed.

Starion hurried out and returned with the tank of Earth's air. "Bria, put this mask on."

Aphelia telepathically asked him, *Are you sure it's safe?*

Starion held the mask up to his daughter's face and turned the lever on the tank.

"Take a few deep breaths, Bria."

Bria followed her father's orders. Then her eyes opened wide while she smiled. When she spoke through the mask, she had noticeably more energy. "Wow. My lungs really liked that. Can I have some more?"

Aphelia's eyes filled with tears, and she moved into the hallway to hide her emotions.

Starion also felt a tear in his eye. "You can use this tank instead of your e-breather for now, but when the air in the tank is gone, you will have to return to using the other e-breather machine."

Starion saw Dustion was relieved too, from his glowing blue eyes; except he still had a look of rebellion about him. He brushed his long brown hair backward over his rectangular ears with his six fingers, then patted his sister softly on her back and headed back to his room.

Bria pointed her small finger at her w-screen and then to an old, tattered book on her desk called *Evion Medical Journal*.

"Look, Dad," Bria said, feeling well enough to take off the mask. "We are studying ancient diseases and medical practices in school. There were some really bad ones. One was called cancer."

Shutting off the tank, Starion answered, "Yes, I remember that in my studies in school, too. There were some great men and women who invented cures. A woman named Dea invented the S-ray that we use every day to see inside our bodies. Afterwards, she created a cancer vaccine that killed any cancer, and called it K-cancer. She was one of our greatest inventors. Perhaps you, too, will be a great inventor someday."

"I don't know. I'm not too good with chemistry."

"Have you memorized your periodic table of chemicals and elements?" Starion asked.

"We did that when I was three."

"Well, it wouldn't hurt to brush up."

"I'd rather study ancient Evion and the old adventure stories, like you."

"How do you like reading these books the old-fashioned way?"

"I like it, but sometimes I don't have the patience, and I scan it in anyway."

"I know, but then you might miss out on the writer's true message. Remember that in some of these stories, there is a message telling us that we are all different and that we all have to follow our own paths. Maybe your path will be chemistry, astrophysics, philosophy, or something else. You may not know what you want to do for many years, but never stop trying to find out...a vital person vitalizes everyone around them."

Starion glided back out into the hallway and past Aphelia, who was wiping away a tear, and into Dustion's room. There he put his hands on his son's shoulders while his son played an interactive IS game. "Do you need help with anything, Son?"

"No, I'm figuring out everything I need to on my own, Starion."

Aphelia spoke sharply from the hallway, "Dustion, you call your father 'Dad.'"

Starion ignored his son's patronizing tone. "Good job. Sometimes we ask for help too soon and miss out on the reward of figuring something out for ourselves. A wise person knows when to ask for help and when not to. How is school? Is the signal coming in OK on your w-screen?"

"Yes—it seems to be working, now that you adjusted the s-rover dish."

"How many students are connecting to your teacher's I-spacer?"

"Today there were only nine of us."

"What are they teaching you?"

"We are learning about ancient arts, including old music," Dustion answered, becoming agitated while playing the IS game.

"Does that interest you, Son?" Starion inquired, trying to ignore Dustion's cold response.

"Yes."

"Remember what I have always told you, Son: If you follow your passions, life will be more fun, more interesting, and easier. Opportunities will open up for you where they wouldn't for anyone else. But that doesn't mean you give up responsibilities. What's the old saying? You have to eat? So you may need to keep your passion alive part time at first."

"Do you really think I have a chance to live out my life and be passionate about something?" He asked jerking his head backward to get his hair out his eyes.

Starion didn't know what to say. He wished he had the experience of listening to his own father's advice when he was a child. The sad emotions hit him hard as he remembered his father disappearing when he was only five E-years old. But again he was happy for the inspirational ancient stories he had been reading, and he tried to concentrate on those.

"You know, Son, I believe Deon brought back some of the Earth's musical instruments. Earth is a planet we are looking at for possible migration. Maybe we can take a look at these instruments together sometime."

Dustion shrugged his shoulders in his teenage way. "You mean like this stupid old IS game? It is ancient. It is in 3-D."

"I know, but it was the best I could find. We lost all the others during the mass deletion."

"It's not the same. In 4-D I am encompassed by the 4-D image so realistically I feel like I am part of the game," Dustion explained.

"Yes…I know, Son," Starion conceded.

Starion sighed, peeked at his watch, and left for his lab.

Starion was drawn to the spacegazer standing idle on its small circular rotating slab. He hopped up on the slab and turned its silver barrel into the sky, where he could peer into Evion's dying solar system.

Adjusting the lens, he was able to see the farthest planet, Sagion, over eight hundred million miles away. The thin air had settled enough for him to see right down to a square inch of the pale red surface. Viewing large holes, he could see where the planet had been mined thousands of years before. Then he aimed at the next planet between Evion and Sagion called Galion. He knew this planet had been the favorite among Evions in the past due to its brilliant orange, white, and yellow rings. But now, most of the rings' particles had been pulled away by the massive sun. There were now only straggly-looking groups of particles that were reddish in color.

He turned away in despair and noticed his favorite pic-spacer of his mentor Vincion hanging on a wall. It was a static 4-D image of him looking up into the sky. Starion remembered his one-way discussion with Ripeon earlier that day, when he told him how successful their civilization had been. Starion was proud to be an Evion.

He pulled out his favorite book, *Anciente Evion Adventura~ Hero*, and turned to the chapter "*Adventura~ Pathos.*" He had read it so many times he knew it by heart. It was about the quest Ardia had been discussing with him. "Each individual must follow his or her intended and unintended adventures if their soul calls for it," he stated to himself.

He was also aware of the next chapter called "*Adventura~ Denial.*" He was familiar with this chapter as well; it explained, metaphorically, the negative implications of hopelessness that one could experience if the internal call was denied.

Starion was inspired. He hopped off the round metal plate and glide-ran to his desk. He decided he would turn his attention full force to this blue planet Earth and to the presentation at tomorrow's meeting. He wasn't going to quit. The old stories told him to keep "digging down into the well." He had to keep fighting as the heroes did. No matter what the obstacles were, he would overcome them, somehow, some way.

He pointed his finger at the e-screen and brought up the image of Earth for inspiration.

Then he tried to send a message to his people again. "Send e-message again, IS unit."

"Message undeliverable," it pronounced.

After that, he tried the Evion planet-net, but it had no link.

Finally, as a last resort, he tried to pull up the EBS system, and found that there was no link to it either.

"What is going on?"

CHAPTER 9

LATER THAT same day, Starion was studying Earth while strategizing on what would be best to discuss at the meeting. He noticed the massive spewing sun sinking lower on the horizon. It grew eerily darker orange by the moment as dusk set in. He knew the temperature would swing from 250 degrees to minus 100 degrees within an hour.

He had tried all day to connect with his fellow Evions via the e-message system, the planet-net, and the EBS with no success. Frustrated, he glanced at his watch and decided it was a good time to perform his daily patrol of the city.

"I'm heading out on my evening patrol," he told Aphelia, stopping to hug her.

"That's the first time you have touched me in over a year," Aphelia told him affectionately.

"Any luck connecting to anyone with your DTI?" he asked on his way out.

"No, Starion. So far everyone I have tried to contact has it turned off…they must all be in sleep-mode."

He hurried outside, entered the v-breaker, and traveled downtown.

Along the way, he surveyed the sights below utilizing a massive white spotlight on the bottom of the v-breaker. He looked up through the top of the clear shell, where he could see the daily turbulence had settled for now. He saw the full red moon against the thin twilight sky.

Starion searched for signs of Evions in distress, but thankfully, he didn't see anybody. He landed near the center of the city. He quickly checked on the hospital, the e-com, and the Audiseum. On his way to the e-center, he passed what was left of the Sporteon Center. This was where Evions had come together to watch e-ball, their favorite sport long ago.

Starion felt fortunate that he had been able to experience e-ball as a boy. He remembered excelling in the antigravity technology that allowed him, his teammates, and the opponents to move readily around the game floor and air space. He was quite the athlete and was good at anticipating the gravity changes forced upon them at random throughout the game. If the gravity was lowered just as he pushed off the floor, he would careen past the basket and occasionally hit the ceiling. When the gravity was increased, he would only jump a few feet as the crowd cheered and laughed.

When nearing his last destination of the e-center, his main task was to check the remaining star-power cells inventory. Suddenly he was struck with horror as he came across the burned bodies of two Evions, their shrouds still smoldering. There was nothing he could do. *Were these the two I saw earlier from above?*

He entered the star-power storage room, but instead of the twelve star-power cells that were mentioned at the meeting, there were only nine.

"Where are they disappearing to?" he yelled.

Discouraged, he headed back outside. As hard as the task was, he turned over the smoldering bodies with his legs and gliders. There weren't any cells underneath them. Just then, out of the corner of his eye, he caught a faint blue light across the street inside the one and only remaining I-mover. It had not been used for over one hundred years.

Starion curiously headed over to the door, but it was frozen and he had to push hard to open it. After much exertion, he succeeded. Once inside the lobby, he marveled at the ancient design and blue dimly lit ambiance. As a boy, he had snuck in there with some friends, and he remembered the magical smells, sloped seating, and curious large white screen. But why was the light on?

"Hello? Hello!" he shouted.

No one answered.

He wandered the eerily quiet building and into the main seating area. He noticed the magnificent downward sloping red cushioned seats, along with the large I-mover screen at the front. At the bottom of the screen was a small stage, with long embroidered red curtains on each side. Above the large I-mover screen, fantastic and mysterious monumental creatures were forged into the top part of the wall.

He was aware the stage long ago had been used for live action stories. When 4-D was invented, sometimes an I-spacer and a live performance were shown simultaneously.

While exploring, Starion remembered reading about a writer's encounter with the I-mover fifty years before. The writer had explained that he could feel the mustiness of memories that permeated the air. Starion felt the same, and he reveled in his imagination.

He sat down in one of the weathered, dust-covered chairs and gazed up at the enormous, elliptical, smudged white I-screen. He felt at home, and a warming peace came over him.

He couldn't believe how comfortable the chair was. The foam upholstery molded to his body so uniformly he didn't even know he was in a chair. Next to his chair was a small, artfully crafted wooden table for storing items during long I-movers.

He played with a lever next to him, moving from sitting upright to a forty-five-degree angle to lying down flat. He remembered stories of I-mover ushers who often had a hard time emptying the I-mover when it closed for the evening, because these particular Evions had been there all day and had fallen asleep. While looking up, he could see the enormous domed roof that had been opened during warm, clear nights.

Then he turned the lever the other way and was now standing

upright. Afterward he adjusted it so he was back to the sitting position.

Starion sat in silence. He tried to imagine what his ancestors watched on these large screens during the Great Era. During these times, Evions were able to use their four-dimensional technologies to create intense, magical experiences for the moviegoer. He remembered that I-mover buildings long ago had been built with huge hydraulic cylinders below the floor. From what he understood, there had been a special IS I-mover unit somewhere in the building, which the director could use to manipulate the building's movement.

This IS unit could anticipate and sense what was happening on the large 4-D I-screen. Then, simultaneously, it would move the whole seated or standing audience along with what was happening. When a scene of something falling approached, the I-mover IS bank would gradually lift the entire building structure up into the air so I-movergoers were not aware of it. And when the cylinders brought down the I-mover structure, the audience would also drop, feeling the experience.

He also remembered reading what it was like when antigravity technology was introduced inside the I-mover. With this new innovation, when there was a scene in space, the audience members were lifted out of their seats. They followed along with the characters in the scene. But unfortunately, when that happened, I-movergoers always bumped into each other as they floated. And when the gravity was slowly brought back to normal, most were not above their own seats anymore; it was a mess. Some even suggested providing seatbelts to keep the I-movergoers in place. But most Evions told the production companies, "Who wants to watch an I-mover with a seatbelt!"

Just then Starion thought he heard a noise. He turned to look behind him, where he saw seven back v-rooms. He knew these rooms had been used for Evion students, teachers, researchers, and scientists for film study. He remembered that during an Evion film or documentary, Evions could stop the large 4-D I-mover image and study it from one of these back v-rooms. And before that, long ago, the rooms had been reserved for the Evion elite.

On the far end of these back rooms, he saw one room that included a small skyroid with a spacegazer. The room had a two-sided mirror. One side was tinted in order to keep the light from shining into the dark I-mover. He understood that this room had been used to view space while the film was being shown simultaneously on the holographic screen.

It was getting colder. Starion realized he had to get home or face another scolding from his wife. Just as he stepped out of the I-mover lobby, there was a bright flash and an explosion off in the distance. *That's odd,* Starion thought. It was rare to have a flare and quake at dusk.

Then, Starion witnessed a huge ball of fire and smoke billowing from the area where he lived. He thought for a moment about taking the v-breaker but decided to run-glide the mile to his house.

Fast-gliding home, avoiding sinkholes and crevasses, he hoped with every part of his newly reawakened soul that his wife and children were okay. One crevasse was so large he glide-ran down into it and up the other side, fighting off the loose dirt as he climbed. He finally reached the top and kept gliding. He stopped several times to catch his breath from the thin and dirty air.

When he ultimately managed to reach his neighborhood, his worst fears were realized: his house had been demolished.

There was just enough light for him to see Ripeon helping Bria out of the debris. He ran over to her and held her small, frail body in his arms. "Are you OK?"

She nodded but was obviously dazed.

Starion asked, "Where's your brother and mother?"

"I don't know," she responded.

Starion heard a faint cry out for help. He followed the sound and finally found Aphelia underneath pieces of glass. Tossing the debris aside, he saw she had been very badly injured and was unconscious. Ignoring the harsh weather elements, he took off his shroud to protect her. He threw her over his shoulder, looking for his son. Just then Dustion arrived from the same direction Starion had.

Starion greeted him with a smirk; he didn't have time to ask where his son had been. Then he took off, shouting, "Take care of Bria while I bring your mother to the hospital."

Starion started back toward the city, but slowed momentarily and yelled back to his neighbor Ripeon. "Will you watch my children?"

"Yes Starion, I will."

He immediately glided toward the city, past the e-com, the e-center, the Audiseum, and finally to the hospital.

Inside, Starion was surprised to see Judion as the doctor on staff. Despite their differences, Judion was still a doctor. He put Aphelia on a floating gurney while motioning to Starion to wait there.

Starion pace-glided the floor with no one else in the hospital. Judion finally came out into the waiting room with his cold eyes. "I'm sorry, Starion."

Starion was aware that Aphelia was either dying or had already died. He hurried into the hospital room to find her lying on a white bed next to a warped glass window. Outside he could see a touch of orange light shining through. Aphelia was in and out of consciousness, softly moaning. Starion sat down and held his wife's hand. She was wearing a silver medical monitor on her wrist that displayed her vital signs, including her heartbeat.

When he reached for her hand, she clutched Starion's arm with her six fingers in pain.

"How are the children?" she asked, closing her anguished green eyes.

"They're fine. They are staying at Ripeon's." Starion spoke to her softly, starting to weep. "Aphelia, please don't go—please."

Aphelia painstakingly placed her hand on Starion's head. "It's OK, my husband…everything is going to be OK."

Starion wept while searching for water to give his dying wife. He found a cup and brought it over to her, lifting her head gently from the white pillow.

As she tried to take a sip, he told her, "I am so sorry I haven't been spending much time at home, Aphelia. Please forgive me."

He gently laid her head down on the pillow again. He lowered his eyes before continuing.

"I have something I need to tell you that I've never told anyone, Aphelia."

"What?" she asked in agony while both felt a small rumble. Starion put his hands on her body to keep it from shaking. Thankfully, the rumbling stopped.

"As you know, my mother died when I was very young, and my father disappeared shortly after…I was raised by my aunt and uncle, who were very loving. But when I was eighteen I felt hopeless."

He shook his head slowly from side to side. "Anyway, while I was flying my v-breaker near the mountains on the other side of the planet, where I was planning to crash, there was a sudden bright light that forced me into a more level landing. I still crashed, but I didn't die. I only injured my leg and was knocked unconscious. When I awoke, there were seven old Evion men and women with orange shrouds standing over me."

"You mean those old philosophers everybody talks about?"

"Yes. They helped me, and we talked for two days about many different subjects. While my wounds healed, at one point they asked what I was doing over in this part of the planet. I told them I'd gotten lost. I know they knew I was lying."

Starion stood up and pace-glided the floor. "They asked me where I was on my journey. When I told them my journey had ended, they explained that one's journey never ends, and they gave me this book." Starion pulled out his very old, tattered copy of *Anciente Evion Adventura~Hero*.

"They also told me that each person must live the life that was intended for them and never refuse the call or give up their dreams. Also, be open to fate. They all forced me to stand up and continue. There was one with a long beard who seemed to be the leader. He asked if he could count on me while writing something down in a small empty book with a wooden stick."

Aphelia groaned. "Yes…before the quake, I was reading from an old book in your study. It was about wishes and dreams our people had long ago. My dream is for you, our children, and all Evions to go to this Earth, and for you to find love with a good Earth woman."

"I don't care about any other woman—here, on Earth, or anywhere. Besides, most think traveling to Earth is impossible."

"Nothing is impossible…and you will find love again," she whispered.

"Please don't go, Aphelia. Please."

She writhed in pain again and dug into Starion's body with her fingers harder than ever.

"I want you to go to this Earth and save our children and our people. That is my dream. It is not impossible…and find a good Earth woman. Please, fulfill my dream."

With her last dying words, the small oscillating line on her wrist medical monitor went flat.

Starion laid his head on Aphelia's bosom and wept.

CHAPTER 10

AFTER A few moments, Judion came into the room and put his hand on Starion's shoulder.

"I'm sorry, Starion."

Starion glared up at Judion's cold eyes with his own sad wet eyes. "I want her ashes."

"Nobody asks for the ashes anymore, Starion. That practice has been gone for many thousands of years. What are you going to do with them?"

"Never mind," Starion fumed, standing up and giving him an angry look.

Moments later, Judion came back into the waiting room and handed him a small pouch with Aphelia's ashes.

"Starion...it's getting very cold out there. You'd better go home," he warned while leaving himself.

Starion stayed in the room for several hours staring at his lost love's ashes, even though it was dangerously cold outside. He wished he could have cleared his conscience of one last thing.

He wanted to tell her of his second encounter with hopelessness; when he'd failed at rejuvenating the dying sun and killed Judion's brother during the attempt, not to mention killing millions who lived on the only other smaller continent while badly injuring his friend Lazarion.

All these thoughts and emotions swirled around in his mind and newly found soul. Starion placed the small bag of his wife's ashes inside his shroud pouch. When he did, he felt his book, *Anciente Evion Adventura~Hero*, again. He pulled it out and read the handwritten words again on the first page: "I have faith in you, my son."

He gazed out the window and up toward the sky. Surprisingly, he observed several stars he hadn't seen in years. "Aphelia…I vow to you that I will go to Earth and fulfill your dream. No matter what, I will save our children and people," he pronounced out loud.

He wrapped his hood across his face and headed outside. There he felt the frigid slap of cold air through the slit of his hood. He could see his breath. He hurried over to the e-center, but just before entering, he was startled again by the two bodies he had seen smoldering earlier. But now they were frozen cinders.

He hurried inside while the automatic light slowly came on. He was devastated. There were no star-power cells in sight. He searched everywhere. His heart sank. Someone had taken the rest of them—but who?

Starion sadly glided back to his neighbor's home in the dark, frozen air, where he knew the children would be waiting for him.

When he slow-glided into his neighbor Ripeon's home, Ripeon telepathically caught what happened to Aphelia. "I'm sorry, Starion…the kids are asleep."

Starion nodded but had to see for himself. After seeing them safely sleeping, he took a seat in his neighbor's living room, staring out into the dark, warped window.

"Starion, please rest," Ripeon told him, nervously twitching.

"I will…thank you. In the morning, I will take my children over to a nearby home I know is vacant."

Starion suffered the rest of the night, overwhelmed by all the events and emotions. Not only had he lost the love of his life, but now he couldn't fulfill his wife's dream. These inspiring old stories he was reading hadn't helped after all. Like Quarion had said in the meeting, maybe he was offering false hope.

After what Starion felt was forever, a touch of morning light showed through the window. He realized he had to face the daunting task of trying to console his children. He slowly moved into the children's temporary room, where they were both sleeping on the floor.

What was he going to tell them? He started to leave, but Bria had just awakened.

"Where's Mom?"

"She has gone to sleep."

Bria cried. Dustion screamed in pain after hearing the news and glide-ran into another of his neighbor's rooms.

Starion allowed them to grieve in their own way for a while. When it was nearing the safe time to travel, he told them, "I have found a great new home just two houses down...OK?"

Neither of them said anything. They were clearly in shock at the tragedy of losing their mother and home.

Starion thanked Ripeon and the three of them left the house, grieving while gliding slowly to their new home. On their way, they had to avoid new sinkholes and fight for air.

Starion was aware of a family who had recently been killed by a sudden solar flare when traveling to the e-com—and he knew their house was basically ready for them to live in. He felt awful about this scenario, but he had no choice.

Once inside, he felt very strange about it. This was not his home where he, his wife, and his children had life's memories in abundance. He set up the children in their own rooms.

He left for about an hour to rummage through the debris of his demolished home. He found several items in the rubble to make their new dwellings as homey as possible. He was able to find many personal items from Bria and Dustion's rooms. He also retrieved some of his own items, including most of the books from his bookshelf. Luckily, he also found the old star-power magnifier and cell braydium mold-casts, along with the old magnifier and cell he had been trying to charge. He also found his orbit tester and several of his hydrogen engines, as well as his coveted ancient hydrogen splitter. But everything else was either burned or covered in melted glass.

Starion hauled everything back to the new home. The three of them made the best of the situation, but it was very quiet that whole day. Starion could tell both Bria and Dustion were having a very difficult time adjusting. For the first time, he witnessed something in his daughter he thought he would never see. He saw a hopeless expression, along with a melancholy demeanor.

Dustion was also despondent. But at one point he confronted his father in his new lab without his gliders: "Do we need to stay here from now on?"

"I'm afraid so, Son."

"Why weren't you there, Father—why weren't you at home? You could have saved Mom!" Dustion cried, running into his new and uncomfortable bedroom. Starion heard the sound of his son punching a wall.

After losing his wife and seeing his children in this state, Starion felt hopeless, too. He tried to act normal while organizing his lab the best he could. He sat gazing out the window into the dim orange horizon, so depressed he drifted in and out of sleep-mode, something he had told himself he would never do.

On the table next to him, he had set down the book *Anciente Evion Adventura~Hero*. He kept noticing it out of the corner of his eye.

For some reason, he couldn't stop hearing his wife's request at the hospital when she told him to fulfill her dream and go to Earth. Her wish kept running through his mind over and over again. He also had vowed to save everyone. But now he realized he couldn't.

Starion had enough. All of these thoughts finally took their toll. He was tired of the book on the table; he had had enough of those old stories. They obviously weren't helping. This was impossible. He couldn't save his people. The evil forces had won. He was now in the labyrinth and couldn't get out.

He grabbed the book and threw it at the wall. It broke into different sections and scattered all over the floor.

Bria and Dustion heard the commotion and hurried into

the room. "What's wrong, Dad?" Bria asked.

"Nothing, Bria," he replied.

Bria could see the new hopeless look her father's face and worriedly asked, "Are you giving up?"

Starion, afraid to look at them, put his head down.

Dustion, tears in his eyes, reminded his father, "You have always told us never to give up. You told us to keep our hopes and dreams alive…you told me that just yesterday."

"I know I did, Son, but there is just too much to overcome. There isn't enough energy to get to Earth…and someone or something is sabotaging my every move. I don't have any more energy. I'm tired. I am truly sorry."

Dustion slowly walked back into his room without his gliders again.

Bria started to cough. Starion reached over and put the Earth's air mask on her, which instantly helped. He watched her draw in Earth's fresh air. She immediately looked better.

Bria hurried over to where he had just thrown the book. She carefully picked it up and put it back together in the proper order. She brought it back to Starion, handed it to him, and smiled. She glanced back and saw she had missed some pages, so she hurried and brought them back. He looked down. He read the words of the chapter heading aloud: "*Adventura~Denial.*"

He took the book and the pages, placing them in the right order. He hugged her as never before. "You never give up, do you, my daughter? You never give up."

Just then, out of the corner of his eye, he saw a small blue glow illuminating from the star-power cell he had been able to salvage in the rubble. He gazed up and out the arced view. He had an idea.

He grabbed the star-power cell, took his daughter's hand, and led her down the hallway to where Dustion sat staring at his blank wall screen. Starion sat Bria next to his son while he held the book in his other hand. Dustion's eyes made it clear he had not forgiven him.

Starion turned to his children and said with the best smile he could muster, "Don't worry, I have an idea. Are you two with me? Can I count on you?"

Bria nodded yes right away, and after a long pause, Dustion gave a small nod as well.

"Let me read you a short story, and then I am leaving for a while."

He opened his tattered book. The three sat in the dim orange light while he flipped to a story called *"The Anciente Hero's Adventura~Pathos."*

"Long ago and far away," he began to read, "there was a young Evion boy and girl who had been lured out into a dark forest and had gotten lost. Suddenly, they were confronted with an enormous evil dragon, but soon an old woman with a cane appeared. She guided them into a dark, mysterious cave and through a secret passageway to a wide and dangerous river. There, an old man with a wooden staff ferried them across the river in an old wooden boat. He wisely pointed them on the right path, which had never been taken before..."

When Starion finished, Bria had fallen asleep on his lap. Dustion was listening but didn't acknowledge it.

"OK, I will be gone for a while. If you need anything, Ripeon's is only two houses away."

Starion brushed Bria's blonde and Dustion's red hair with his hand. He headed into his new lab, shut the door and glide-paced the floor. Finally, he pointed at the e-screen on the desk.

He brought up an image with a D-box labeled "Time Travel."

CHAPTER 11

STARION MOTIONED for the category of time travel to appear with instructions, but nothing came up. *It must have been deleted during the mass deletion,* he thought. He shuffled through some of the old books he had in his new bookcase. He found an old and outdated book called *Time Travel: Fact or Fiction.* He instantly scanned through it and gathered up some extra clothes. He took his orbit tester and put it in his pouch. When doing so, he sadly felt the small bag of Aphelia's ashes. He became more determined.

He almost forgot his favorite book. When he rushed back to the shelf for it, he took two more copies, just in case. He put everything into a large white bag.

He started to grab the mold-casts, but he remembered he had decided to take the only others in his office at the e-center instead. But he did take the dimly lit cell he had been trying to charge. He tossed it in the bag and threw it his shoulder.

"I'll see you in a few hours?" he tentatively told his children, hoping his time travel plans worked properly.

"Okay, Dad...good-bye," Bria replied, hugging her father. Dustion just nodded. Starion searched for any kind of support from him. Just as the door shut, he thought he noticed a touch of regret in his son's face.

Once outside, Starion struggled to breathe. He pulled out his orbit tester and aimed it at the sun. This time, he wanted to be one hundred percent sure his tester was pointing directly at the spewing sun without any glass in between.

As suspected, Evion's orbit was losing its battle with the sun.

His heart sank. He, his children, his people, and the entire planet were now down to three days. He tapped on the orbit tester and pointed at the sun again to confirm his reading.

"Oh, no!"

Starion hustled into the v-breaker, the dark orange ever-changing light of dawn shining through the clear-looking shell. He flew toward the e-center through the thin, dirty air, careful not to be seen in case anyone was out.

Once landed at the center, he took the star-power cell out of the floor compartment of the v-breaker and put it in the bag along with the one from home. He hurried inside. He took the e-mover to the top fifth floor, where he knew Deon would be working.

He looked at the panoramic view through the circle-shaped room. He could see his devastated planet and city out the partly melted and warped glass exterior.

Deon gave him a puzzled look when seeing Starion holding the large white bag.

Next to Deon was Curion, a curious young blond man twenty-five e-years old with large, ambitious green eyes. He looked up to Deon as Deon did Starion.

"Hi, Starion," Deon said. "I was explaining the possible next step with Earth regarding mining the braydium. Depending on where the braydium is on Earth, we will be using our laser ray from our v-breaker to poke a hole in Earth's surface to locate it—unless we are lucky and find braydium on the surface."

"Will we be introducing our technology to them?" Curion asked.

"We can't, Curion...you know there is an Evion law in our charter that says we can't interfere with another planet's history," Deon told him.

"I wish we could use old the I-spacer DNA molecule technology so we could watch the team of Evions who travel to Earth from right here on Evion."

Deon, looking at an impatient Starion, continued. "We still

have to win the vote tomorrow at the meeting. Plus, I don't think there are any old IS towers that still have that program installed. And anyway, it wouldn't work, Curion. Whoever should travel to Earth will be in the past time continuum…furthermore, they will be trillions of miles away. It is ironic, however; the technology only works beyond our solar system. So, in other words, the signal must be far enough away but not too far."

"If it did work and the Earth people have similar DNA, wouldn't their signals show up too?" Curion asked.

"Their DNA is similar, but it wouldn't work. It would have to be an Evion."

On his way to his private office, Starion saw Deon create a protruding I-spacer of an Evion man within an invisible sphere surrounding him. He continued showing Curion the sphere changing while the man glided along. "This is how it works in theory. And by the way, this same inventor was also close to inventing the fifth dimension, whereby an Evion could interact with the I-spacer in live time and space."

Starion motioned Deon over and shut the door with a point. Starion could still see a bewildered look on Deon's face as he scurried across the room underneath the skyroid. There Starion picked up his second pair of old magnifier and cells mold-casts and brought them over to the door entrance, setting them down. Next to these were three half-charged cells, the second of his actual old magnifiers, and his bag of clothes and books.

"What are you doing?"

"I am going to Earth on my own. Will you help me?"

"I don't know, Starion. What about the vote tomorrow?"

"I don't care about the vote. I just lost my wife." Beginning to weep, Starion continued, "I care about my children and our remaining people. I was elected to save our race. This is our only chance…unless you connected with Neilion and Shepion?"

"No, Starion. It is very strange. We have never had that problem before." Deon watched Starion glide-pace the floor. "I'm sorry about Aphelia. She was a good person."

Starion stopped pacing and, with a worried look, told him, "I just checked my orbit tester, and we are down to three days. Deon, listen to me: what if you had never had the chance to be a scientist? What if you were never able to feel the joy of flying into space and seeing the other planets in our solar system? What if you were never able to dream about the future? Like me, you're old enough to know what it was like to have at least a little hope. Please help me, Deon. Please."

Deon locked his eyes onto Starion's. "What do you want me to do?"

Starion pulled out the book he had brought from home, *Time Travel: Fact or Fiction.* "Deon, I need you to help me chart a course to Earth and travel back in time twenty of its years—and hurry. We don't have much time. I scanned this old book. Here are the equations you need to plug in."

"OK, but as you know, it will require at least four of our remaining star-power cells, as I told you before."

"Actually, Deon, our cells are all gone—I checked on them last night. Someone has taken them all."

"How are you going to make it to Earth then?"

"I brought one from home, one from the v-beaker I used to get here, and if I use the one here in my lab room, I have three half-charged cells. I think I would have just enough power and speed to make it to Earth's past."

"I just traveled to Earth, Starion, and that's not enough power...especially if you are going to attempt time travel. And how about the trip back?"

"Deon, I have to try to make it to Earth and find braydium, then charge new cells—either from this old magnifier and these old cells, if their sun is strong enough, or maybe I can even manufacture a new magnifier with the last of our two remaining mold-casts I will bring along."

"This is impossible!"

"Deon, I have to try—I made a vow to my wife."

"There's something else, Starion. I was about to contact you about it. Look, this is a live view from Earth."

Deon produced an I-spacer from a hanging e-screen in Starion's office. It was fuzzy. It showed a newscaster speaking, the words "Special Bulletin" scrolling below him. They heard him say, "Take cover, everyone; an attack on the United States is imminent. Apparently they are after Earth's last remaining oil." The signal faded.

Starion caught Deon's worried look and said, "I will be going back in time, Deon, so whatever this is, it won't affect me."

"What if you don't make it back?"

"My other magnifier mold-casts are at my new home, along with the only other magnifier two houses down from Ripeon's. If something should happen to me, keep trying new gas mixtures. Also, I suppose it's possible the envoy might find braydium too, if they come back."

Starion picked up the three partially charged star-power cells he had placed on the floor. Deon saw the dismal, slightly glowing cells. He shook his head. "I think you will need at least one more fully charged cell...but anyway, I'll say it again: this is impossible. Remember, Starion, the IS bank on the ship won't allow you to fly past the speed of light."

"I think I have a fix for that."

Deon awkwardly glide-paced the floor in doubt, then stopped. "I think there might be one more cell left in one of the old blimp v-breakers...let me check. I will get a v-breaker ready for you," Deon said, still shaking his head.

"Please hurry," Starion told him, looking at his watch. "And store enough nutrition formula and water for one way. Once there, I need to try to survive on their food and water in order to ensure we can survive there."

"You'd better take that watch off when you get to Earth, Starion...it probably won't work anyway."

While Starion pulled up a live I-spacer of Earth, Deon took the three other half-charged cells. He accidentally dropped one but picked it back up.

"Don't tell Curion—or anyone else for that matter about my trip." Starion demanded.

Deon left the room, avoiding Curion, and shot down the e-mover to the v-breaker hangar area. He rummaged through one of the old gigantic v-breakers.

Moments later, Deon was back. "I have a v-breaker ready for you. And I found one more partially charged cell. It is very old. So now you have four partially charged cells. I still don't think it's enough.

"Good job, Deon. Please haul my things down there. Were you able to input the time travel trajectory path?"

"I think so, but this is uncharted territory. I hope it is correct…otherwise, who knows where and when you will show up—if at all."

CHAPTER 12

"**I WILL** leave Evion, and hopefully, no one will see me," Starion announced. "I'll also need your space log from your last visit to Earth, along with all research materials…and give me all your information on the reference to braydium."

"This is what I have," Deon answered, pointing to an e-screen. He pulled out an I-spacer. The image included a blue link. Deon clicked on it. A recorded news broadcast began to play: "On the science front, researchers have just discovered a new element called braydium. However, its origins and potential uses are still up for debate. If you would like to see it, it is being displayed at the Museum of London."

"How did you get this?"

"Like I told you at the meeting, the humans have invented a global planet-net. I think they called it 'Internet.' I was able to search it. The link to this broadcast stated it was created in June 26, 2060. This date of 2060 is almost exactly twenty of Earth's previous orbits around its sun before when I was there; according to what were called their digital newspaper stands, it was June 26, 2080."

"Where is this London on Earth?" Starion asked.

Just then, Ardia surprised the both of them, arriving from shooting up the e-mover. She was carrying a bag of clothes over her shoulder.

"I told you not to tell anyone, Deon," he said as Ardia approached. "I don't want anyone else to get in trouble if I should fail."

"Starion, you don't have to do this alone. There are some of us who, like you, have hope," she told him. "And I am sorry about Aphelia. She has joined with the universal life force."

Starion put his head down in despair.

"You will join with her when it's your time, Starion, but it's not your time."

Ardia set down her bag and glided over to Starion, wearing her waist IS unit. "I have been studying Earth and have created a global map that you can transfer into the v-breaker navigator. And I understand you will need to find what is called 'London' first to find braydium. Here is the location."

Ardia pulled out a 4-D I-spacer of Earth from an e-screen with her hand. It contained latitude, longitude, names of continents, countries, oceans, rivers, lakes, mountain ranges, and even city names. She twirled it around like a globe then stopped it. She used another finger to highlight a specific area.

"Starion, this is called 'England.' From my brief research, the people here are known to be very 'proper' or 'stiff.' I'm not completely sure what that means, so be careful."

Starion gave her a curious look.

"It looks like you can possibly land in the water near that area to hide and camouflage the v-breaker. Do you have enough nutrition formula and water?" Ardia asked.

"I have enough to get to Earth, but once I'm there, I'll have to sustain myself on the Earth people's diet. I have to make sure we can survive there."

"I hope Judion is wrong about diseases," Deon said worriedly, taking a few deep breaths. "I feel fine after being there…so far, anyway."

Starion glanced at his watch.

Ardia asked, "Do you know how far back in time you need to go?"

"Yes—from the information Deon found in reference to braydium, I need to travel back twenty of Earth's previous elliptical orbits around its sun to this particular time."

"It's amazing the Earth people started marking time only about two thousand revolutions ago," Deon observed.

Starion was nervous. Ardia caught it and telepathically connected with him. *Starion, do you feel like you are living the life that was intended for you?*

I thought I was.

If you are, the path will open for you where they wouldn't for anyone else.

Starion wasn't so sure.

Ardia continued. *Learn from this, Starion ... not just their customs, but learn ... find out if the people are living our ancient stories of the quest. And we must learn about their psychology and philosophies. I think it will be extremely important.*

Starion nodded.

And one more thing, Starion—you are doing something that has never been done. You must boldly go where no Evion man has gone before. But if you feel something is wrong while going back in time, you have to stop—you may be affecting the time continuum.

"Yes. This sounds like something I have heard before somewhere."

Deon caught the telepathy and asked Ardia, "What could happen?"

"There are some forces in this universe we don't understand. If we start believing we are more powerful than the life force, that's when these heroes in the old stories get into trouble."

Ardia handed him the bag of clothes. "I went into one of the old Audiseum rooms and found these clothes the ancient actors used. Hopefully some of these will help you fit into Earth's population more easily, especially this hat," she said, handing him a light blue flat hat. "Make sure you cover your ears with it ... and I also put another pair of gliders in there, just in case, along with some nutrition formula. Plus I put in a few of Earth's water bottles Deon brought back. And one more thing, I found some skin-colored gloves with only five fingers. I don't know why our ancient actors would have created these."

"Thanks, Ardia," Starion said, stuffing the items into his bag.

"Starion, if something should happen and you are stranded there, you must try to survive at all costs."

"I don't want to get involved with their culture yet, Ardia. My mission—I mean, my adventure—is to find braydium, charge more cells with my magnifier, and head back."

"Starion, you must survive. That is the way of the hero. And if you are open to the adventure, there will appear a magical aid, a guide, a ferryman, an old man with a cane, a teacher, or a mentor of some other kind who will point you in the right direction. It's a mysterious fact, Starion—just like the life force of love."

Starion shook his head doubtfully. "I can never forgive myself for failing at saving the sun and not being able to save Aphelia."

"Starion, you must forgive yourself in order to move forward with the adventures in your life."

It was nearing the dangerous part of late morning. They all glanced outside at the devastation.

Deon spoke up. "Starion, I loaded up everything along with the signal booster so you can deploy it on their moon…I wish you would try to find more energy to make it to Earth and back in time. After putting the cells in the v-breaker, I checked the energy gauge and it only shows half-full. If that's not enough, you will be stuck in space."

"We don't have any more time. If that happens…please look after my children, you two."

We will—and be safe, Ardia telepathically said. *I have faith in you… always be open to fate.*

Starion nodded, remembering the same statement the old man in the mountain cave had said to him long ago.

"Oh…one last thing, Starion. I put some lead in the ship. I forgot to tell you, but you will need what the humans call 'money.' I believe you can use that lead and exchange it for this money at what they call a 'gold exchange,'" Deon informed him, telepathically sending him an image of one.

"Remember Deon, if your two envoy recruits should find braydium...whether I make it back or not, the last two braydium mold-casts are at my home."

Starion turned to Ardia, who smiled in her peaceful way. He felt better as she telepathically reminded him again, *Learn...learn...and find out if the humans are following the ancient stories of the quest, like our ancestors did. I believe the ancient story is universal.*

CHAPTER 13

STARION FOLLOWED Deon down the e-mover to the e-centers enormous hanger. There he observed several v-breakers. They were all different sizes. Most were old and worn out.

Deon guided him over to the v-breaker he had prepared. Starion hesitated for a moment and then entered the ship with his things. Just before he closed the door hatch, he told Deon. "I'll be back."

When the door shut automatically behind him, Starion took a deep, worried breath. He sat in the red pilot's chair in front while he watched Deon stumble over to a wall full of IS banks and levers.

Deon flipped one of the levers, and the dome roof opened. Starion felt the scorching thin air fill the hangar room along with the interior of the ship. Deon pulled his hood over his head.

Starion flew the v-breaker up into the thin, dirty Evion sky.

"IS unit, I want to take manual control," Starion told the onboard IS unit.

When Starion cleared Evion's atmosphere, he shot out into the solar system. He was aware he had a long journey ahead of him. He watched the devastated planet of Evion grow smaller as he passed by its red-lit moon. He wished he could have taken his son and daughter with him, but he would never forgive himself if he should run out of energy on the way. He had to save all the Evions or die trying.

He also wished that after his mission to Earth, he could arrive back home just a little earlier to save Aphelia—but he understood the universal physics of that was impossible. It had been tried before, but time travel only allowed a one-way time lapse. The return trip had to bring the traveler back to the launch time at the earliest. Usually the traveler actually lost some time.

Starion now questioned if he was seeking the impossible, like Deon had told him. He had to go back twenty Earth years in the past, then he had to create enough energy to travel back to Evion while at the same time bring along enough power to migrate his people to Earth.

As these thoughts filled him with worry, he felt a sudden urge to turn back. He put his hands in his pouch to rest his weary arms. He felt *Anciente Evion Adventura~Hero*, the book his daughter had put back together. He pulled it out and opened it up to the chapter, *"Adventura~Denial."*

He became inspired again. He wasn't going to refuse the adventure. With a wave of his hand, he turned on all the necessary IS banks and guidance systems on the ship's v-panel. He glanced at several gauges, including gravity level, inside air, velocity, and energy level. Starion inspected the v-breaker Deon had chosen for him. In front were two comfortable slanted pilot chairs that conformed to the Evion body with v-sticks for steering in front of them. Behind these chairs was a three-foot-high, two-foot-wide, flat horizontal Navigator IS bank. This device allowed the pilot to create I-spacers of the desired trip path or destination in 4-D.

Behind this navigator were twenty-three other red seats. Behind them was the large cargo bay, where Deon had placed the signal booster.

Starion turned forward. Out the front window was the eerie, reddish light reflecting off the other planets along with space ahead of him. Beyond that, he saw the rest of the galaxy and vast universe.

He turned to the main IS e-screen just to the left of the front windshield and brought up the same 4-D I-spacer of the Milky Way Galaxy Deon had revealed at the meeting—but instead of the four planet candidates, it now displayed only Earth and Evion.

"IS bank, proceed to the coordinates Deon just input. I want to time travel to this planet," he ordered, pointing to Earth. "I want to land on that planet twenty of its past elliptical revolutions around its sun."

The IS unit took control of the image, performing hundreds of calculations. It replied, "This velocity is not allowed."

"IS unit, you are correct…we are not allowed to travel at this speed. But just for analysis purposes, what would be the speed required to travel back in time to this planet twenty of its years ago?"

There was short pause while a text D-box on the screen filled with numbers of 0s and 1s, then the IS unit answered back with a monotone voice: "Three billion e-miles per second."

Starion knew the text D-box would override any voice command, so he pointed his finger at the number on the screen. He held it. "OK, IS bank: what is the maximum speed allowed?"

"186,000 space units per second," it responded.

"OK, take me to the Earth destination with that speed."

After a short pause, the IS bank announced, "Destination planet Earth in Optim part of Milky Way Galaxy at the speed of 186,000 space units per second confirmed."

Starion still held his finger on the number in the image.

"That is correct. Proceed."

His plan worked. He was instantly hurling past the last planet of Sagion.

Starion turned his head back at the diminishing view of his small Evion planet along with the other planets. Like in the old stories, he hoped he could fulfill his destiny and save his family and people.

Suddenly, he saw the massive sun spew its violent energy in all directions, including the planets and his ship. This was not a flare or a wave but a huge fume that engulfed the whole solar system. And even though he realized sound didn't travel in pure space, he heard an awful heart-wrenching sound. He felt the heat as the craft accelerated faster and faster. It went into a tailspin. His items were hurled everywhere. He was thrown against the side of the ship, and then hung onto a chair. The braydium magnifier and the cell mold-casts slammed into the side along with him, both smashing into pieces. He also lost the magnifier. Looking behind, it looked like the signal booster was intact.

Starion yelled, "Stop! Stop, IS unit!"

Starion's earlier tinkering with the IS unit had messed up its processing ability. It was locked up, but had at least corrected from the spin. He was still accelerating away from home. Looking backward, he had to put his hand up to block the deadly solar rays. For an instant, there was a short break in the light. Disturbingly, he witnessed the last planet, Sagion, explode.

He tried to see if he could spot any sign of Evion, but the ship had now sped up to an astronomical level. It was difficult to see anything.

Starion shouted, "Can you detect if the planet Evion is still there?"

"According to my analysis, Evion has vanished," the monotone voice stated after a few moments, stuttering slightly.

Starion felt sick to his stomach. He ached with more guilt.

He sat in pure psychological torture. Everyone was gone: Dustion, Bria, Ardia, Deon, and the rest of his people. Did they suffer? Were they burned, or did the planet explode instantly? His whole civilization had vanished. Could he have done something else? Should he have taken as many of them as he could have instead of going alone? *I wish I had died with them.*

Finally, the pain was too much for him. He blocked out everything. He laid down on one of the back seats behind the navigator. He felt his ship accelerate further while streaks of light became thinner and thinner.

Starion had always tried to block sleep-mode because he didn't believe in it, but now he welcomed it.

CHAPTER 14

STARION WAS jolted awake without warning. The ship was slowing down just as fast as it had taken off. His eyes opened slightly. He observed the streaks of light become thicker outside as he lay depressed.

Suddenly he heard the IS unit blurt out, "*Warning... Warning... Energy low.*"

Still lying in a prone position, he saw a star ahead becoming larger and larger. Traveling closer, he could see the array of colored and different-sized planets in their elliptical paths. He had to put up his arm to partly block the sun's bright shining light. But he didn't care about anything.

First he passed by a small light brown planet. Then he flew by a large, dark blue planet, and then by another that was greenish-blue. Next was a pale yellow one that reminded him of one of his own solar system's planets, Galion. Next, he traveled by an enormous orange planet with white bands. Finally, he passed by a red, barren planet, while feeling the ship slow even further.

As the craft approached the blue and white swirling planet Earth, Starion saw its white orbiting moon along with it. Then he saw two more planets between Earth and the sun: a gaseous yellow planet and a small grey planet that reminded him of his own destroyed Mercion.

As the v-breaker approached Earth and its moon, he couldn't help but think to himself how closely this blue planet resembled ancient Evion.

He remembered the book he had shown everyone at the elder room meeting about a mystical blue planet. The planet had a magical mythosphere, a place whose people had fantastic and mystical stories about gods, goddesses, demons, dragons, and heroes. There were outlandish and exciting adventures.

"Ahhh..." he said to himself. "Everyone...we were right...she is beautiful...but it's too late."

The sight was too much for him. It brought back the sick, aching feeling he had felt when he left Evion. He closed his eyes, listening to the ships IS unit again: *"Danger. Danger. Planet's gravity pulling ship into its atmosphere. Turn on emergency guidance system. Turn on EGS."*

As he lay there, he felt the ship hit Earth's healthy atmosphere. He could feel the hot resistance on the shell heat the interior as Earth's gravity pulled the ship in.

"Warning... Warning... Low on energy... Low on en—"

He understood that he was supposed to point and turn on the EGS located on the front v-panel in order to save himself, but he didn't care enough to make the effort. And besides, he apparently was out of power.

While the v-breaker streaked toward a vast mountain range with flames surrounding him, the terrible time when he had tried to kill himself, when he was younger on Evion, entered his mind. He hoped this time the ship would disintegrate on impact in a remote part Earth. He closed his eyes tightly, ready to die.

Unexpectedly, he felt the v-breaker start to level off and slow down.

"Emergency guidance system on," The IS unit stated intermittently with low power.

The ship slowed, and then safely landed in a mountain pass. Starion opened his eyes.

What happened? I didn't turn on the EGS.

In a daze, he step-glided out the right side door, down the stairs, and out onto the rocky terrain. And even though he was engulfed with Earth's fresh air and abundant sunshine, he was despondent.

After a short while, he lost his balance due to the faster opposite rotation of Earth. He started to stagger. He felt like something was pulling him from his left side. When he over-corrected he fell, hitting his head on a rock.

When he awoke, there were seven human faces looking down at him with the flickering light of a fire. They were wearing orange shrouds and had different types of skin colors. Four appeared to be men and three women. He opened and closed his eyes several times to try to focus. *Am I in sleep-mode?*

Panning the room, he realized he was in a cave. He could see the bright sunshine and blue sky out of the cave entrance.

"Where are you on your journey?" one of the men asked.

Starion understood him from his scanning of Earth's dictionary, but he did not answer. He was still in a dazed state of mind and didn't know what to say.

"Where are you on your journey?" a woman repeated.

"Do you have a question?" another man said.

Starion answered carefully, sifting through the vast memory of new words. "Where am I?"

Starion, still trying to gain focus, saw them look at each other.

"You are here with us in this cave within the Himalaya mountains. We are the Earth Life Guides."

Starion looked around the cave again, smelling the cozy and flickering fire that filled the room with a smoky haze. The fire lit up a bookshelf with old, tattered books. Next to this were two free-standing racks with clothes hanging from them.

"We are a group of religious leaders who put our individual faiths aside once a year to study new ways to guide our fellow humans through their life's adventures," a second woman spoke up.

"So, where are you on your journey?" a third man asked.

"My journey has ended," Starion coldly stated.

"Your journey never ends," a fourth man told him in a strong, wise tone.

Starion had to squint at this man. He couldn't quite see his face with the angle of the light from the fire, but he appeared vaguely familiar.

"All my people, my wife, and my children are all gone," Starion sadly told them.

"We have all had losses…all of us," the second woman explained, holding up a tattered black book. Starion noticed the cover had figures of creatures strangely familiar to him. Before he could look closer, she opened it and handed it to the first woman, who proclaimed, "The hero in all these stories never denies the adventure path they have been called to do."

"Yes, I have heard that before…but I don't have any strength left," Starion told them, seeing them look at each other again. He closed his eyes.

A voice spoke: "The biggest battle you will face will always be the battle with yourself…we are here to help guide you through the labyrinth and get you back on course."

The first man's voice continued: "Throughout history, people have ventured out, exploring and searching—but actually, the journey is inward. The adventurer always encounters danger-ous and mysterious obstacles, and usually he or she falls into the labyrinth. Then, somehow, usually but not always, with the help of a magical aid who points the way, the person succeeds and returns to his people with a revelation of the life force."

"Yes, I have heard that before, too—but my people have all perished."

"Your people have not perished. We are all part of the uni-versal life force."

He opened his eyes. "But I don't think I will fit in here…I am not from here."

The third woman answered him. "Look around you. We are all different. That's what makes life and your adventure interest-ing. It would be very boring if we were all the same, wouldn't it?"

Now, all seven of them forced Starion to stand up while they all spoke at once in chorus.

"Continue on with your journey, and always be open to fate and the magical aid for guidance. Look for inspiration in everything you see and experience: people, nature, literature, religions, philosophies, and all the arts, which include music, paintings, sculptures, and motion pictures. Follow the story of the quest...discover the inner person that you are."

He remembered Ardia telling him the same thing about his own ancient people's metaphorical messages. He felt better.

They all gave him a nod and a smile, then pushed him out of the cave.

Still dazed, he slowly and awkwardly glided down a path toward his v-breaker. He could feel his gliders battle the Earth's opposite rotation.

CHAPTER 15

ONCE INSIDE his v-breaker, Starion sat looking at the dimly lit instrument v-panel, then outside to the new, fresh environment of the mountains, green vegetation, and blue skies. He shook his head, trying to regain his composure and equilibrium. He opened a window and took deep breaths of Earth's air. Finally he was able to get his focus back.

He didn't know what he should do next; he was still in a state of disbelief at what had just happened to him. He decided he needed some time to think.

He took manual control and instantly escaped Earth's stratosphere, a word he found in the section of his memory where he had stored the Earth dictionary.

On his way, he observed a few distant Earth aircraft. Once in space, he headed slowly toward the moon, avoiding any s-rovers or anything else the humans might have in Earth's orbit. He hoped no one had seen him enter Earth's solar neighborhood or land on Earth.

He gazed down through the ship's clear bottom at the astonishing view of Earth. He put his hands in his pouch. He felt his orbit tester, his old book, and Aphelia's ashes. He pulled the book out and opened it up at random. He was on the chapter with the title "*Magica~ Aid.*"

Then, out of the corner of his eye, he noticed a green light flicker on the inside of the shell. It was coming from the back area. Hurrying there, he discovered it was illuminating from the signal booster Deon had loaded. He examined it closer and noticed that the flickers had a pattern.

"What's going on?" he shouted out loud.

Again the flickers continued with the same pattern.

He smacked his hand on his head. "That's the old Evion e-code...but what's it saying?"

Starion closed his eyes, recalling his old studies. His eyes rolled around. He opened them again and followed the intermittent signals.

"Starion, this is Deon. We are with you. We are looking forward to your safe return. You can be assured we are all OK...you may have seen Sagion destroyed, but most of us are alive, including your children and Ardia, and the planet is still intact."

Starion was so happy he jumped and hit his head on the ceiling of the ship. He stood with renewed energy, looking at planet Earth as a tear rolled down his face. For the first time, he could really appreciate the view outside his v-breaker of Earth, its sun, its moon, and neighboring planets.

Suddenly, he realized he was hungry and thirsty. He found some of the nutrition formula in the bag and a bottle of Earth's water and consumed them both. But then the terrible circumstances back home urged him on.

He moved up to the pilot seat. He flew over to the white sunlit moon, squinting in the brightness. "IS unit, please locate optimum location on this orbital moon for a signal to reach Evion."

The IS unit instantly performed its analysis on an I-spacer image shown on the front e-screen. The v-breaker landed on the moon then sent out a solid laser ray that pointed toward Evion.

"*Low on energy...Low on energy,*" the IS unit pronounced.

Starion was aware that the light didn't point exactly at Evion, because it had to adjust for the relative gravitational pull of the galaxy's spiraling arms, suns, and all matter in between. He realized the signal would intertwine with them all by the time it reached Evion.

He put on his clear, lightweight spacesuit. "IS unit, deploy v-air threshold," he shouted.

Starion knew this would allow him to easily step out into the vacuum of space or a different atmosphere without losing the required air in the v-breaker.

Within moments, he could see a thin outline that separated the air in the ship with the now vacuum of space near the back hatch. He stepped through into the vacuum and opened the hatch, then hauled out the signal booster.

He pointed his finger at a switch. A bright laser ray shot out toward space. Starion adjusted this ray so it was parallel with the one from the v-breaker.

He wished he could send back a message to Deon. He would have to thank his friend when he arrived back.

Just before he climbed back into the ship, he noticed a round enclosure in the distance that appeared to be made of glass. It reminded him of a small version of an Evion home. He couldn't resist, and he hop-glided there and circled it. It contained one s-rover dish pointing out into space.

Why don't they have an s-rover dish pointing back at Earth?

Once back inside the ship, he shut off the v-air threshold and took off his suit. He noticed a strange image coming from his watch. Looking closer, he saw half of the bright blue Earth lit up in the small I-spacer. He remembered what Deon had told him: that the watch probably wouldn't work. He happily experienced what his ancestors had seen on their watches long ago.

Now, with all the recent occurrences of the mysterious intervention when he was supposed to crash on Earth's surface, meeting the Earth philosophers, the signal Deon had sent back in time—at that instant, his conviction of Ardia and the Earth philosophers regarding the magical aid in the old stories became stronger. He felt confident he would succeed. He didn't know how or why, but somehow he felt a renewed sense of purpose and strength to save his children and people.

He transferred Ardia's telepathic stream of Earth's global map into the navigator unit. Suddenly, a 4-D image of Earth appeared, containing all the necessary information he would need: longitude and latitude lines, land mass names, names of bodies of water, and city names. He found London in the image and flew directly above it but still safely beyond Earth's atmosphere. He could see blue, vibrant water below next to the land mass.

He realized the location he had to travel to would soon be lit up with the sun. He stopped for a moment to let the starshine hit London. He treasured the vibrant, slowly rotating blue planet below, with its swirling clouds and blue oceans, along with its brown and green terrain.

"She is beautiful," Starion said aloud.

He felt his heart racing. His curiosity overwhelmed him. He took off downward. This time he was aware of the difference between Evion's thin air and Earth's healthy breathable air. He could feel the resistance on his ship's outer shell.

"What's the altitude?" he yelled to the IS bank.

"One e-mile."

"OK, stop here," he instructed. "Please check air and atmospheric pressure."

Even though he knew the air was safe, he wanted to log all the information he could to show his fellow Evions.

A small flap opened on the side of the ship while the IS unit performed analysis. "Atmosphere and air pressure safe."

He opened the sliding windows on each side of the craft. A surge of fresh sea air permeated the craft. He took a deep breath, remembering when his daughter had inhaled Earth's air. This time he could really enjoy it. But moments later, sadness overwhelmed him. He missed everyone back home already.

Remember the task at hand ... remember the task at hand.

Suddenly, he heard a strange noise outside. When he looked through the clear v-breaker shell, he could see a huge silver aircraft fly above him. He saw faint images of humans looking out small windows. He was amazed at this ancient aircraft technology. It was similar to ones back at home in the Audiseum. Puzzled, he wished he knew what kind of fuel it used.

Then he remembered something he'd forgotten. He yelled, "IS unit, allow any radar and sonar tracking waves to pass through the ship." He hoped they hadn't seen him or his clear v-breaker.

"All radar and sonar waves will now pass through the ship."

Starion remembered Deon had trouble with Earth aircraft detecting him when he was here. Just in case, he decided it would be best to fly just above the water until he reached land.

When he was a few feet above the roaring dark blue waves, he was pleasantly surprised when he witnessed a large blue creature on the surface spewing water, her offspring swimming next to her.

He was mesmerized. He remembered the old stories about Evion's oceans and the life that had once lived there. This also jogged his memory-scan of an ancient Evion story in a book Ardia had uncovered in the Audiseum. He wondered, now that he was in this blue planet's mythosphere, if there were any other similar stories.

While pondering this, he heard the IS unit again. *"Warning... Warning... Energy low."*

The gauge was nearly empty. He hoped he had enough energy to find the braydium.

On the floor were smashed pieces from the mold-casts and magnifier that had been made from braydium long ago. He wished he had the schematics to build new ones. The virus that had deleted almost all the planet's data a year before still bothered him. *How could that have happened?* He still contemplated.

Now, even if he should find braydium, he would have to find a different energy source to bring it home.

Flying east toward England in the same direction as the Earth's rotation, he pulled out a handheld spacegazer. He located an isolated place just outside of London. It seemed like a good spot to land and hide his spaceship.

CHAPTER 16

STARION SCRUTINIZED the area intently, making sure no humans were near. He landed hard on the beach next to the water, using the early morning light instead of the bright landing lights. He peered through the clear shell, hoping again that no one had seen or heard him.

Starion's heart was pumping adrenalin like never before. Nervous, he pulled out some of the clothes Ardia had found from the ancient room in the Audiseum. He took a guess on what would be the best for him to wear based on Deon's information.

While taking off his shroud, he felt the orbit tester, his favorite book along with Aphelia's ashes in his pouch again. He left them while draping his shroud over a chair. He put on a pair of brown pants and a blue long-sleeved shirt with a high collar that covered his small DTI. Next, he put on skin-colored gloves, which allowed two of his six fingers to fit comfortably together, giving the appearance of five standard Earth fingers. Finally, he put on the hat Ardia had given him, pulling the sides down over his ears.

He was aware of the extra pair of gliders Ardia had given him but decided he wouldn't need them. He put some of rest of the clothes back in the bag, tossing it over his shoulder. Then, without warning, several aircraft streaked by above him. He decided he had better move fast.

He nervously opened up the hatch and hopped out, but then remembered that according to Deon, he would need the element lead. He hurried back in and put a chunk in a pocket.

He glided out onto the light brown sandy beach, where he could smell the green grass, the ocean, and Earth's vibrant air. The brightness hurt his eyes, but he didn't care. He squinted, small drips of tears running down his face.

Starion immediately felt lighter. Then it dawned on him: Earth was much smaller than Evion and therefore had less of a gravitational effect compared to home. He hadn't come to that conclusion when he had landed in the mountains because he hadn't cared enough to notice. And as far as the opposite rotation of Earth, his equilibrium along with his gliders had now adjusted.

He pointed his two fingers at the v-breaker, maneuvering it into the water until it was covered. He was now all alone standing on a beach on this new alien planet. He felt a flush of embarrassment, as if in front of an audience, and his knees went weak.

Just then, three low aircraft with strange propellers on top surprised him with their powerful roar. He hurried over to a large tree, hiding below the branches. Had they seen him? He peeked through the bustling green leaves to see if they returned again. Luckily, they didn't.

"I wonder what type of fuel they use. It has to be either petroleum-based or hydrogen," he contemplated again.

Standing underneath this tree reminded him of his discussion with Ripeon about Evion's trees long ago. He pulled off a leaf and smelled it, then tasted it. Reading about it didn't come anywhere near the actual experience. He was ecstatic.

He started his journey in the dawn hours toward what Deon and Ardia had called London. He could see the tall buildings way off in the distance. He traversed down a long, winding country road, breathing in as much as he could of the fresh morning air and fragrances. His twinkling blue eyes were moving constantly, viewing the vital life-producing rolling hills of abundant green foliage. He could see a multitude of trees with the blue sky above as Earth's sun crept over the eastern horizon. He squinted happily.

Gliding effortlessly along the twisting and hilly road in the low-gravity environment, he noticed farmland, and the scattered homes along the surface-way made from stones imbedded in the ground.

Just then he stumbled and fell on a stone that was a little higher than the rest. Picking himself up, a fresh new batch of emotions hit him hard. He looked around, hoping no one had seen him. Surprisingly, he could feel his face turn red. He couldn't recall the last time his gliders had made that mistake and he had fallen back on Evion. He thought he had adjusted for the different planet's spin and gravity. Finally he decided the stones were of elements the gliders had never experienced.

Moments later he was startled by two graceful brown four-legged animals with long, skinny legs. He ran this through his memory-scanning of Earths dictionary and deduced that they were deer. He had awakened them from a matted bed near the road. He watched in awe as they bounded away across the rolling fields.

Searching the fields more closely, he observed a variety of green grasses and plants. At some point he would have to eat these to make sure his people could survive there, but he decided to wait a while.

Still gliding along, Starion smiled as a gentle breeze blew the morning fragrances into his face and nose. He wished he could have glided, breathed, smelled, and enjoyed the experience forever.

Then, something startled him again. Several small creatures sped by above him, flapping their wings and chirping.

Continuing on his way, off in the distance he witnessed an Earth man feeding several different four-legged animals with fuzzy short white hair and long dark noses. Searching his memory, he decided they were sheep.

He could see the hazy morning dew glistening from the morning sun's rays on the green grass pasture. Then he viewed five large animals with four legs and long necks, in a variety of majestic colors, looking over his way near several large trees. He believed they were called horses. He could see lively shadows from them displayed on the opposite side of the sunshine. He had never seen such a sight in his life.

As he edged closer to town, he started seeing other Earth people bustling about. He started to worry someone might notice him. He was having a hard time syncing his glide again. Then he recalled two words that had caught his eye in his favorite book. They were *risk taking*. He had to take this risk. He had to.

Checking his memory bank again, he discovered the glide-walks he was seeing were called sidewalks, and the surface-ways were called streets or roads. It felt surreal. Unlike on Evion, here he was surrounded by life. These experiences unexpectedly and very keenly affected his nervous system. He remembered the doctor Judion's warning about this at the elder meeting. Flashes of ancient Evion stories popped into his mind.

He saw someone riding a red two-wheeled type of vehicle, his legs and feet powering some kind of sprocket mechanism. The human rode past him so closely the sudden brush of air startled Starion. He was fascinated by this ancient form of transportation as he watched the human ride down the road behind him.

Continuing on his way, he glided by an elderly man and a woman walking toward him. The man was wearing tan pants along with a red patterned shirt, and had white-grey hair and a pipe sticking out of his mouth. He was using a cane. The woman had gorgeous grey hair tied back in a ponytail and wore yellow pants with an orange shirt and a scarf around her neck.

When he had met the old philosophers in the cave, he didn't have all his faculties, and the encounter was just a blur. Aside from that, this was the closest Starion had ever been to an extraterrestrial. It was so new and strange the hair on the back of his neck stood up. He was so close now to an Earth human he could see for the first time their real live facial features and mannerisms.

When the elder man glanced at him with his mysterious blue eyes and bushy eyebrows, Starion reeled from the conflicting emotions he suddenly felt. These new emotions were mysteriously exciting. He was in such a euphoric state of mind he could barely keep his composure. He wished he could say something to the elderly couple, but he thought better of it for now. He instinctively tried to connect using telepathy, but he found he couldn't. This made the encounter even more exhilarating.

As this elderly couple passed behind him, he slowly turned around so he could keep watching their ancient form of walking—but he noticed they had been staring at him as well. It dawned on him he'd better be careful, so he turned back toward his city destination. After a moment, he glanced back to see if the elderly couple was still watching him. To his relief, they had continued on with their morning walk.

His heart and emotions were racing so hard his bionic shoes sensed he wanted to hurry. He glide-ran without his brain's approval. He passed a young man who was manually running for some reason. The young man noticed Starion effortlessly move by him. Starion saw him stop while holding his head down.

Starion finally forced himself to slow down by meditating.

Moments later, several surface vehicles constructed from some type of clear material drove by him. He could tell it wasn't braydium. Starion could see the passengers staring at him while driving by wearing small eye protective devices. After that, he saw another kind of two-wheeled vehicle zip past him. He could hear and smell the used-up petroleum coming from the exhaust. It smelled similar to his historic ancient engine back home.

Still observing, but wishing he could explore instead, Starion saw another surface vehicle constructed with the same type of clear substance race by him. It had two humans in front with nothing between them and the airspace. Similar to the person on the two-wheeled vehicle, he could see they were wearing strange-looking tinted devices in front of their eyes. Their hair was blowing backward. *That must feel wonderful,* he thought, *to feel the Earth weather on their face and bodies while traveling, smelling the life-fulfilling air.* He would have to try this if and when his people migrated here. *Maybe this open-air traveling could be applied to v-breakers.*

Alarmed, he heard a strange noise above him. There was a flock of geese flying over him, honking to each other. At that moment, something splatted on the ground near him.

The sun was now high enough on the horizon where he started to see the local inhabitants moving about from their houses.

Soon after, thirty of Earth's aircraft soared above him. To avoid being seen, Starion carefully hustled into town, joining the other people.

It was the strangest feeling in his life. Here he was, gliding along with an alien race. What was going on in these people's minds? And what were these devices some were wearing around their heads and waists? What type of information were they storing?

He had all he could do to not stare at the beautiful Earth women. But, like he had told Ardia, he wasn't there for love.

He took in the cobblestone streets, trying to be more alert that his gliders were breaking new ground. He observed the old wooden and brick buildings. He marveled at their different colors, imagining this was what the view might have been like on ancient Evion. He experienced several flower gardens that lined the street between the sidewalks and homes. He viewed their walkways leading up to the door, where he could see a whole array of more flowers and shrubbery. The colors and smells were indescribable. There were yellow flowers, red, green, purple, white, and orange. Behind them the sun's glow created shadows that danced in the slight breeze.

He remembered just the day before, when he'd entered his home, wondering what it must have looked like back on Evion long ago, when his grandfather could see the shadows and know what time of the day it was. This sight was unexplainably pleasing and peaceful. He would have to show this to his people.

He stopped to smell the fragrances but was suddenly

frightened by a small, orange, hairy animal with long whiskers that had been hiding in the flower patch.

Then a tiny yellow creature flew up near his face, buzzing, then scurried up and away. All these new sights, experiences, fresh air, and animals overwhelmed him, and a tear fell from his eye.

"Oh…if they could only see this back home!" Starion remembered Curion asking Deon about the I-spacer DNA technology before he left. He wished he could have shown his fellow Evions this view live back home.

Continuing, he glided by three roughly teenage Earth boys, who stared at him and laughed.

"What a weirdo," one said.

"Yeah, what a creep," another yelled while positioning his wrist at his mouth and talking into a small device.

Starion wondered what these words were, but he didn't have time to run through his memory of the dictionary. The first task on his list was to make sure he had arrived at the proper time in Earth's history.

He searched for anything that might give him the date.

Finally, he glided by a digital newspaper stand he recognized from what Deon had instilled in him. On top were the words "Download" and "Paper Copy." Below this was a headline scrolling across the screen: "Breaking News: Strange Object Detected Hitting Earth's Atmosphere near Himalaya Mountains." Below this, he read, "Congress Still Battling Universal Healthcare 70 Years Later," and finally "Cancer Still Number-One Killer, I-Jet Flyer Collisions a Close Second."

He kept looking for a date and finally caught one: "*The England Digital Times*, July 29, 2060."

He sighed in relief. Deon had said the date when he was there was "June 26, 2080." Starion apparently had not quite made the twenty years, but he thought it should be close enough.

Lower on the digital screen, he read the scrolling words, "The Renowned Scientist Leonard Vincy strongly suggests that new energy sources must be invented…Hydrogen to be the best alternative."

Further down, he noticed "Top Grossing Box Office Hits":

1) *Star Wars XXXIII*
2) *Spiderman XXIV*
3) *Hunger Games XXVIII*
4) *Dumb and Dumber XXXI*
5) *Iron Man XXVI*
6) *Lord of the Rings XXXV*
7) *A Population Explosion*
8) *The Deadly Virus*
9) *World War IV*
10) *A Cosmic Life*

Now that he thought he had been successful with the right time on Earth, he had a destination in mind. Deon had telepathically instilled a building in his memory. He had to get money.

He searched along the streets for a while, watching the interesting humans interact. He couldn't get enough of the curious-looking Earth people and their different clothes, looks, walks, and discussions. And what were these face panels and miniature devices hanging next to their ears?

There was a young man ahead of him wearing the ear device. He sped up so he was next to the man but slightly behind him. Starion put his ear up close the man's head. He heard music. *Oh—those little devices are e-speakers.*

Then he saw a young woman walking ahead of him wearing something strapped to her head. She also had a bag containing several books strapped to her shoulders. In front of her face was a thin, clear panel. Starion hustled up to her but stayed just behind to the left. He could see two images in the panel. On the left part of the screen was a live image of where she was walking. On the right side was a 3-D I-spacer of a teacher in front of a class. He felt a strong urge to touch this gorgeous woman but fought it off.

Then, to his right, a young boy was kneeling while holding a small item that looked like the lens on the star-power magnifier. The boy was holding it at an angle so as to make the sun's rays as small as possible on a piece of paper. Soon after, Starion witnessed a small hole being burned in the paper while a tiny puff of smoke rose up. He wished he still had the magnifier; it would have worked for sure.

Suddenly, from behind, a young human man scooted by him riding on a small thin wooden board. It had a set of four tiny wheels underneath. Occasionally he would push on the ground with one of his legs and feet.

Then another sped past him. The woman riding on this one was wearing one of the face panels he had seen. Starion noticed she didn't have to manually push off to propel herself. The inventor in him wanted to find one of these and take it apart. He also would have liked to study their surface vehicles, aircraft, and strange IS units.

Gliding on, gazing at the humans but realizing he had a mission; Starion remembered Ardia's telepathic message to him: *Learn . . . learn . . . see if they are living the ancient stories of the quest.*

CHAPTER 17

TRYING NOT to be conspicuous, Starion intently viewed the bustling businesses lining the sides of the streets. One building had two large yellow arches including a digital flashing sign: "Big Mac & Veggie Burger only $29.99." Above this he read, "Over 100 Trillion Served."

While Starion admired the sign, a surface vehicle turned right in front of him into some sort of pumping station. Starion viewed another sign: "Gas $175.59/gallon." Below this he read "I-jet Air Tanks $1,299/Tank. The man in the vehicle hopped out and pumped a liquid into his vehicle. Then he flashed his wrist at a scanning device and drove off.

Startled, Starion heard a thrusting sound and felt the air swirl directly above him. He looked up and saw a woman wearing a tank on her back with an exhaust-looking hole on the bottom. The woman was holding onto two handle-looking devices that wrapped over her shoulders while her long red hair blew upward. She softly landed, blowing Starion's hair and clothes around. She subsequently exchanged her tank with a man behind a window and then aimed her watch at some type of scanner. Smiling at Starion, she shot straight up and away. He would have to try it if and when they migrated to Earth.

Finally, Starion found what he was seeking: a sign with the words "Gold Exchange." He saw light illuminated inside the building. Then a human five-fingered hand changed a small sign hanging in the window on the door from "Closed" to "Open." Then an old man with a long grey beard opened the door carrying a broom. He was wearing a white uniform with a brown cap similar to his own.

The old man proceeded to sweep away any dirt that lay in front of the door. As he swept, he noticed Starion. "Good morning, sir."

Starion nodded back, but he was nervous. After all, here he was on a new planet where he wasn't supposed to be. He was suddenly interacting at random with a strange human being, an alien race he didn't know anything about. He didn't even know whether he would be susceptible to their diseases, as Judion had warned him about.

He took a deep breath, entered, and waited for the right moment to make his move. He observed the magnificent paintings on the wall that were in 2-D. He could even see the brush strokes. *Hmm . . . an art form.*

He turned his attention back to the task at hand. He studied how a transaction worked as another man came into the shop to sell his gold watch. Then he witnessed another transaction.

Finally, Starion was comfortable enough to walk-glide over to the display case counter. He inspected the watches, jewelry, and miscellaneous gold and silver items for sale.

The old man behind the counter asked, "What can I do for you?"

With his camouflage gloves, Starion pulled out the small chunk of lead Deon had given him. It was about the same size of a small copper-looking coin Starion observed on the counter next to him. When he set the lead down on the counter, he wished he had practiced speaking their language first—but he was pleasantly surprised at how well his brain matched his language to the Earth dictionary he had scanned.

"Is this worth any money? I need money for an exchange of goods and services."

The old man laughed. "Is this a joke? And what kind of accent is that?"

"Why?"

"This isn't worth anything. You need to have gold or silver, like this," the old man informed him, pointing to the items in the display case.

When the old man turned away for a moment, Starion analyzed a gold coin in the case with a laser stare of his eyes. Afterward, he pointed his smallest outside finger at the piece of lead, which instantly created a slight gold-colored glow. The chemical composition of the lump changed to gold on the spot.

Starion pointed to the gold piece he had just created. "What about this?"

The old man wiped his eyes several times. "Holy cow! What a nice trick. Where did you get that?"

Starion replied, not thinking, "It is from my planet, Evion."

The old man laughed again. "That's a good one. Let me weigh it." Starion watched while he weighed the gold. "That's worth exactly three hundred dollars."

"What will that get me? Is that a lot of money?" Starion asked.

"Well, it's nothing to sneeze at."

"What?"

Just then a cute young Earth woman walked in and smiled at Starion. He could see she was wearing some type of substance on her face, along a vast amount extra coloring around her eyes. She wore a short red dress. Trying not to stare, he observed a small image painted on the top of her right breast that was partially exposed. In Starion's eyes, this was new and very seductive.

Moved toward the counter, she spoke to Starion, "Good morning."

Starion was flabbergasted. He couldn't say anything. He fought hard to remember his task at hand. He wanted to leave, but he felt a rush of passion. He felt compelled to stay. He felt powerless.

The gold shopkeeper gave Starion his cash. He turned to do

business with the young woman, and then glanced back toward Starion. "It's not polite to stare."

Starion got the message and headed out the door. Once outside, he stood in a daze with the cash he had just been given in one of his hands. After a few moments, the young woman came out the door. She called over to him, "I didn't think you were staring. Were you?"

"No, I wasn't…well, maybe a little," he responded sheepishly.

The young woman laughed and then noticed the bag over his shoulder. "Are you just back from a deployment?"

"What?"

"It looks like you just hopped off a ship, right?"

Starion answered, "Right."

"Well, I am always interested in helping out our sailors. Let me cook you something to eat."

Starion, realizing he had been getting a little hungry and thirsty, eagerly nodded yes.

"You sure have a weird accent. Where are you from?"

Starion didn't answer but instead tried to fight the powerful compulsion he was feeling. "Do you know where the Museum of London is?"

CHAPTER 18

STARION WAS awakened by the sound of a large surface vehicle that drove by with a loud whisking sound. Then he heard the hum of aircraft and surface vehicles. As he struggled to pull himself up to sit, he felt like his head had been slammed into the ground. His stomach felt like it had been filled up with a disagreeable chemical of some kind.

He noticed he was in a bed. It had white sheets, two pillows, and a yellow blanket, all in disarray. Next to the bed on the floor was an empty glass bottle, along with his gliders, clothes, and hat.

Outside, he could see the light from the sun shining from a different direction than when he had arrived.

He reached for the bottle and smelled the few drops left in the bottom. Then he felt his stomach gurgle and he violently threw up a tremendous amount of green vomit all over the floor next to the bed. Luckily, he missed his clothes. After the first unexpected projectile, he had enough sense to run to the bathroom, where he quickly pointed his finger at the white porcelain toilet seat. But, unlike back home, it didn't automatically rise. He disgustedly lifted the seat with his hand, heaving another large amount of what he thought were all of his insides.

After several more sessions of this torture, he stood up from the toilet. He looked at himself in the left side of two mirrors above a sink. *What happened?* His coloring was very pale; his eyes were red with some yellowish streaks. He turned his eyes to the right-side mirror, expecting to see a live shot of the back of his head. Then, on his way out, he found a full-length mirror. Expecting an S-ray, he tried to view his insides and brain. He wanted to see if either was damaged. But, like the toilet seat, this didn't work either.

When he felt it was safe enough to leave the bathroom, he sat on the bed staring out the window. There was a red neon sign flashing the word "Motel." He attempted to assemble what had happened.

He remembered he had been invited into the room, where the young woman had offered him liquid refreshment. He recalled he had felt the liquid burn as it ran down his throat. But he couldn't remember anything after that.

He panned the room for any sign of the young woman, but she and her belongings were nowhere to be seen. "I wonder where she went. I don't even know her name," he mumbled to himself. He noticed his bag of clothes was still there.

He closed his eyes and performed a rewind of his recorded visit in his memory. His eyes rolled in a circle. He began with the rebroadcast of his visit, from when he had started to fly past the speed of light witnessing the awful solar flare from space. He fast-forwarded, feeling sick to his stomach when seeing the tragic occurrence again.

He stopped at the point where he met the young lady at the gold exchange. From there, he forwarded slowly to where he entered the room. He saw the young woman grab a bottle and hand it to him. It was the same empty bottle next to his bed.

He observed himself take a drink of the liquid, subsequently hearing himself cough uncontrollably. Right after, the rebroadcast went dead. He kept fast-forwarding, seeing himself wake up on the bed, sit up, and throw up all the vomit.

Starion put on his clothes, hat, and gloves. When he stepped outside, there was a uniformed woman outside the lobby. He noticed that she was wearing a name badge that read "Manager."

"Have you seen the young woman who was with me in this room?" he asked.

"Why, yes. She left a little while ago."

"Did she say if she was coming back?"

The manager started laughing uncontrollably. Starion had never seen this before in his life.

"Are you kidding? You will never see her again—I hope she didn't take all your money."

Starion reached into his pockets, feeling for his money. It was all gone. He stared into the manager's eyes for support and was puzzled why she had laughed.

"That's all the money I had."

The manager's eyes changed instantly and were now similar to the compassionate Ardia's back home. "You look like you have had a hard life. Here are a few bucks to get you on your way."

Starion remembered the old stories. *If you are open, there will always be a magical aid to help you on your way.*

Starion gladly took the money, but he was already perplexed by these stressful interactions with the humans. The Earth people were more complex than he'd imagined. This was going to be harder than he could ever have anticipated.

"Do you know where the Museum of London is?" he asked her, stuffing the money in his pocket.

She pointed down the street. "About seven blocks that way; you sure have a weird accent."

He didn't know the words "thank you" yet, so he nodded to her gratefully.

When he started on his way, there was a digital newspaper stand outside the hotel. It scrolled, "UFO Sighting Over England."

"Oh, no," he whispered to himself. "I wonder how they saw me..." He would have to be extra careful with his presence from now on.

Even though his stomach was still turning, he liked gliding down the street with the warm sunshine beating down on his face and body. *Oh... if they could only see what I am seeing,* he told himself again. He forced himself to concentrate so as to not bring attention to himself by allowing his e-gliders to take over.

He was astounded at the variety of surface vehicles and

aircraft that filled the streets and airspace. He noticed more of these interesting single-person flying contraptions also, but there were not very many, for some reason. He figured maybe they had only recently been invented. Why hadn't Deon showed these at the elder meeting? He noticed they were flying much lower than the other aircraft. He presumed it was for safety reasons.

Continuing on his way, Starion began to feel the stares and glances. He tried to remain inconspicuous while viewing the wide variety of shops, stores, and buildings. He made sure he didn't stare too long at the different clothed and uniformed humans performing their daily professions or leisurely activities. He wondered if his own ancestors had been so industrious and adventurous.

Just then he noticed a man in a black suit-uniform with a black hat staring at him. When Starion his eyes met his, the man looked away.

Starion hurried along, passing by a store with thousands of books inside. He turned and ducked inside.

He was ecstatic looking at all the books. Over on another side of the store, he read: "3-D DVDs." He thought about his own meager collection of books and I-spacers back home. He realized he didn't have time to read each book, but could point-scan everything for now. He scanned any and all categories of Earth books he could find. He had made a mental note to highlight the word "braydium" or any type of mineral similar if he should come across it, especially in the science, energy, and physics categories.

When he was done, he closed his eyes, running through trillions of words. He found no reference to braydium, and he shook his head in puzzlement. He concentrated on any information regarding energy. He created a category of Earth's energy in his memory and set aside the words "nuclear," "hydrogen," "atomic," "electric," "rocket fuel," and "solar energy."

Next to this was another bookshelf: "Classic Science Fiction." He saw author's names: Isaac Asimov, H. G. Wells, Jules Verne, Ray Bradbury, Suzanne Collins, J.R.R. Tolkien, and Frank

Herbert. He was deeply drawn into these while scanning. On several occasions, his scanning suddenly skipped over the book as if he had already scanned it. He shrugged his shoulders.

Finally, he saw one more bookshelf. He couldn't resist; it was labeled "Mythology." Among others, he scanned categories referenced "Greek Mythology" and "Arthurian Romances." In the same section a book with the title, "The Hero with a Thousand Faces" caught his attention. He noticed the authors name was Joseph Campbell. He closed his eyes for a moment, connecting the metaphorical message to many of his own Evion stories he had been reading.

He accidently glanced down at the floor. There was a strange, small object made of hard paper. He curiously picked it up, examined it while admiring the ancient ingenuity. Inside were thin strips, each with a red tip. From his newly expanded memory, he concluded they were matches for creating fire. He put them in his pocket while at the same time scanning a story called "Prometheus." When he realized the connection, he wondered if it was a coincidence.

On his way out, he was drawn to one more bookshelf. He scanned the books: *Speed-Reading for Dummies, Radar for Dummies, Hydrogen Power for Dummies*, and *Will Solar Power Work for Dummies*, and every other Dummies book on the shelf.

Finally he saw one last book that caught his attention. It had the title, *Which Country Will Be the Last to Own Oil?*

Just before heading out the door, he remembered the opposite side of the store, where he had thought there were Earth I-spacers. He scurried over to scan one of the thin disks. He realized right away that they were I-spacers. Remembering Ardia's statement to learn, he point-scanned everything in sight. When he hit the science fiction section, he wanted to continue scanning, but he felt an overload in the temporary storage area of his memory. He knew he was in trouble: his eyes were starting to give off a more visible red glow instead of their normal blue glow.

Sure enough, Starion noticed the woman in charge whispering

something to another human man. He decided he'd better leave right away. "I can't keep delaying my mission," he said, smacking his forehead with his palm.

Outside hurrying down the sidewalk, he was compelled to stop for some reason. Gazing into a window, there was a sign: "Now Available: Microsoft 3-D Windows Version 24." And then another sign: "Xbox Newest Edition 81 Available Soon—escape inside the Xbox pod in your own home and lock the door!"

Moving along, a middle-aged couple walked by Starion arm in arm, suddenly taking an interest in the image of Earth protruding up from his wrist. "Hey, is that a new Timex or I-watch?" the man asked.

Starion didn't know what to say. He hustled on his way, putting his watch in his pocket. He heard the man say, "What a creep."

This time Starion had to find out what the word creep meant. He instantly found the meaning and felt sad.

Just then, he noticed he same man in the suit-uniform and hat across the street leaning against a tall wooden pole. The pole looked like the dead petrified trees he had seen with Ripeon back home. The man was casually looking over at him, talking to himself. This time the man had the panel attached to his hat down in front of his eyes.

The man started toward Starion.

Starion hurried down the block, passing by a building that reminded him of the I-mover back home. There were words displayed on the marquee: "Star Wars XXXIII."

He turned the corner and found a door to his left. He tried the handle but couldn't open it. He pointed his index finger between the door and the door jamb, melting the lock, then opened it and hustled inside.

Starion breathed a sigh of relief, feeling safe in the dark ambience. He marveled at the sloped seating in front of him, along with the large screen illuminating flickering images to his left. After a few moments, his eyes adjusted to the darkness, and he felt like he had when he landed: as if he was in front of an audience. This time, he was. He noticed most people wore a similar ultra-clear face panel while watching the film. Most of them turned to look at him.

Starion hurried up the steps toward the back. It was eerily familiar to his visit to the I-mover just before his wife had died. Once in the back row, he sat down in a chair. Luckily, no one paid attention to him anymore. He noticed there was no lever or table near any chairs. Looking back, he saw no back rooms. Looking up, he saw there wasn't a retractable domed roof.

He took a deep breath, smelling something very enticing. Staring at the large 2-D screen, he was amazed at the mythic story unfolding in front of him. He witnessed the spectacular scenery and the characters coming to life in a space adventure.

Starion contemplated who the hero was in this particular story. Who was the magical aid or guide, and who were the evil forces? And what life force message would the hero bring back to his or her people?

CHAPTER 19

STARION DIDN'T have time to watch this. He headed out-side—through the lobby this time—and carefully searched the area to see if the man with the hat was still lurking. He didn't see him, so he headed on his way.

Moments later, four young men asked him for his money while one pulled out a knife. Starion was frightened right down to his soul. What was this all about?

Starion melted the knife while instinctively lifting a phrase from a movie he'd just scanned in at the bookstore: "That's not a knife."

The men ran away, terrified. One yelled out, "Creep!" Again Starion was sad and confused by the human actions. Maybe they were more primitive than he had thought.

Finally, he was relieved to see a sign: "Museum of London." When he crossed the street, he was shocked as two surface vehicles collided right in front of him. It was all he could do to keep from wetting his pants. Immediately, several humans rushed to help. Moments later, a surface vehicle arrived that reminded him of v-ambulances back home. He couldn't believe the humans that had hurried to help. These people could not have all known the victims, he surmised. He shook his head in disbelief.

He hurried over to the entryway, ready to open the door, when he heard a voice to his right. "Hey buddy, over here. That will be fifty dollars," the man demanded.

Starion reached in his pocket and pulled out the money the hotel manager had given him. The man took it all and gave him a ticket. Station headed inside, where he found himself in wonderment at all the Earth's artifacts. Some items were similar to what was in the oldest part of his own Audiseum.

This was someplace he could explore while looking for the braydium. He toured the history of Earth's surface vehicles and aircraft. When he read signs labeled "The Bronze Age" and "The Stone Age," his curiosity skyrocketed. He scanned everything. Then he saw two other signs: "The Industrial Age" and "The Computer Age." He entered and scanned everything again.

He kept searching for any sign of braydium. Moments later, an elderly lady with long grey hair similar to Ardia's, utilizing an old wooden cane, shuffled up to him. With her wrinkles and a twinkle in her eye, she asked, "Can I help you?"

"I want to see the display of braydium, please, and I would like to know where it is found naturally on Earth."

"Never heard of it, sir," she told him.

"I was told it was here in this museum twenty of your years ago."

"What do you mean, *our* years? Besides, that doesn't make sense. Twenty years ago is a long time."

"I'm sorry, I mean now."

"I don't believe there is anything like that here…but I will check our records, if you like."

Starion nodded in disappointment while continuing touring.

Momentarily, the old woman returned as Starion was admiring an old ship. "There was a traveling exhibit with that mineral about a month ago here, but it didn't generate any interest. I think it moved on to the University of Berkeley in San Francisco."

"Where is that?"

"Across the pond."

"What?"

"I mean ocean," the woman explained with a wise tone, pointing west. Then she shuffled away with her cane.

When gliding out the door, Starion looked for the man with the hat. Thankfully, he didn't see him.

He decided he would go to this San Francisco. Hopefully he would have enough energy both for his ship and himself.

After leaving, he glided by a man with one leg, who acknowledged him. "Good day, sir."

Starion nodded back, not knowing what to think. But then he was reminded of his friend Lazarion, who had also lost a leg back on Evion. Starion smiled slightly, but the muscles for doing so weren't used to the effort, so he had to stop.

Soon after, he passed by a boy shooting a ball at a basket above him. The ball rolled over to him. It reminded him of e-ball back home.

The young boy offered, "Take a shot."

Starion's emotions were racing after thinking about Lazarion. He jumped up way beyond the height of the basket then dropped the ball through effortlessly on the way down.

"Wow!" the boy exclaimed.

Starion shook his head in disgust and continued on his way. *I really shouldn't have done that.*

When he headed down the same winding and hilly country road he had glided into town on, he unexpectedly found himself caught in a small rain shower. The light rain fell softly onto his face as well as into his opened mouth while he gazed into the sky, feeling suddenly invigorated.

When he finally arrived at the v-breaker, he searched the area and sky to make sure no one had been watching. Off to his right above the landscape, there was the most unbelievable sight he had ever seen. There was a full rainbow. He had read and scanned about it from Evions history, but nothing could compare to witnessing it.

Suddenly, he felt a sting on his neck. He instinctively slapped himself. The miniature creature fell to the ground. Starion felt a little disturbed.

What was that? Then another one attacked him, buzzing near his face. *Maybe this little creature knows who I am;* he contemplated with his new memory of creative Earth literature.

He maneuvered the large ship out of the water onto the beach and happily used a wave of his hand to open the door hatch. He hurried in.

It feels good to be back in familiar surroundings again, he thought, flying immediately up high enough to where he felt he was safe. He hovered there for a while to regroup.

"IS unit, please monitor any radar and inform me."

"What frequency range?" the unit asked.

"All of them...from 0 to 1,000,000,000 waves per second."

"Monitoring activated."

Starion thought about his encounters with the Earth people. They were more complex than he had thought. Even if he were to find braydium and also find enough power to get home, would his people feel comfortable cohabitating with humans? From what he had witnessed so far, he wasn't so sure.

All these new emotions were affecting the scientist in him. He started wondering if he really was back in time and if Evion was still safe. He had been learning, like Ardia had suggested, but he figured he'd better get on with his main mission: to find braydium.

He pointed at all seven of the v-breaker's hanging e-screens, pulling out any and all I-spacers he could think of relating to his family and Evion. He stared at all the 4-D images that protruded out as far as possible to his body and face. He sat in one of the first-row seats and changed one of the I-spacers to images of his Aphelia, Bria, and Dustion.

I must succeed!

CHAPTER 20

STARION WAS startled by the onboard main IS unit notification: *"Frequency wave of nine hundred thousand cycles detected."* Then he heard an aircraft fly near him.

This particular craft was closer to Starion than any of the others he had seen. He thought he'd better move higher, so he flew up another five e-miles.

He was perplexed for a moment why the IS unit hadn't caught the aircraft sooner. But then he understood what had happened: Evion hadn't used this frequency for thousands of years. Then he remembered Deon had to leave because he couldn't figure it out when he was on Earth.

He closed his eyes. He found the book *Radar for Dummies.* He instantly studied it but couldn't figure it out. He felt ashamed.

"IS unit, can you block out this range?"

"Negative."

"What altitude above Earth would this signal be undetected?"

"There are safe altitudes above nine e-miles and below one e-mile."

He would have to be very careful from now on while flying above Earth.

He brought up the floating globe above the horizontal navigator. "IS unit, travel to San Francisco."

He took off immediately over the Atlantic Ocean westbound at the nine e-mile altitude. Within moments, he flew over the edge of the east coast of what he now knew was the United States.

He couldn't resist and descended to the one e-mile mark.

There he observed a large statue of a lady holding a tablet of some kind, remarkably standing in the water.

He pulled out his floor spacegazer and zoomed in on a tablet she was holding. Just after he scanned it, three very fast aircraft headed toward him. He shot up through the clouds and out into Earth's orbit. He waited for the Earth to turn enough so the area called San Francisco was in the shade. Even though his ship was clear, he knew his v-breaker would be less conspicuous traveling in the dark.

He waited impatiently in Earth's orbit, but finally he couldn't wait any longer. Taking a risk, knowing it was dangerous and would draw more energy, he decided to fly down to where he was earlier where he had seen the statue. Then he would slowly and silently follow the Earth's moving shade until he reached this San Francisco.

When he entered Earth's atmosphere, he found himself in clouds again while descending. Finally below them, he was fascinated with the brilliantly illuminated city lights twinkling up at him. He decided it was now safe to fly slowly across this continent, opposite the rotation of the Earth. He lowered to just under the one e-mile altitude the IS unit had recommended. He silently traveled over the growing shadowy part of Earth, happy there was only limited company flying around him.

Ahead of him, he could see the evening sunset-lit sky and occasionally a piece of the large orange setting sun. It was almost like he was following the sun. The IS unit startled him: "*Warning...Warning...Low on energy.*"

"I know, I know," Starion said angrily.

He couldn't see below very well, so he dropped lower. Just like in the old stories, the heroes always seemed to do something they weren't supposed to do—or so he rationalized. He put his hand out the window to feel the cool air push against it. He opened up the v-breaker skylight above him so he could see the starlit sky.

Soon he flew over three large interconnected lakes. There was a large city on the south end of one. He adored all the city lights glistening off the large lake. But then he saw twenty scattered aircraft circling the city. He could have looked at the navigator to see the name of the city, but why? It didn't really matter for now. If he were to come back, then he would want more details.

He veered out over the lake and headed west again. He loved flying over the edge of the land and sparkling water. Almost right away, he had reached the farthest edge of this lake, so he headed north, flying above another city.

Keeping an eye on the shade, he still traveled north along the shoreline. He continued until he observed another large lake off in the distance, all the while ignoring his low gauge.

He followed this shoreline west until it ended over another city that appeared very hilly. Then he veered southwest, where there were minimal lights below. Feeling safer, he descended down above the vast variety of trees, fields, and numerous lakes. He could smell the night's mysterious fragrances. With his silent v-breaker, he could hear the enticing night's sounds of what he figured were insects and animals. He put his hand outside again so he could feel the soft spring air. After a while, he even put his head out the window to catch all the fresh air and smells he could.

But his enjoyment was short-lived. The IS unit announced, *"Danger. Danger. UFO approaching."*

Starion saw a small aircraft just above him to his left. He couldn't fly up, so he dropped down, into a small lake. He splashed into the middle of it. The ship slowly sunk down to the bottom, where he landed softly. He could faintly see weeds and sand out the exterior. He turned off all instrument lights so as not to let the light reach the surface above him.

When his eyes adjusted, he was startled. There were two large fish looking at him. From his memory-scanning of both the dictionary and the bookstore, he decided one was a northern pike while the other was a walleye.

Out the other side, he saw a strange object. He briefly turned on his landing lights. "That's a surface vehicle," he curiously blurted out, as if talking to the IS unit. "I wonder how it got there."

When he felt it was safe again, he pointed the ship upward, propelling it up to the surface. Feeling comfortable no one was near, he jettisoned straight up and continued his flight.

His memory-scanning kicked in again. He was reminded of an Earth book. *Is this Lake Wobegon?* If so, this might be a good place to live—or at least visit—if and when he came back. He definitely would have to check out this Sidetrack Tap place. As he recalled more of the book, he wondered if he would like this "lefse" and "hot dish."

He continued southwest at the one e-mile mark, where below he saw a long, winding river below. Again, his new memory library synapses fired up. He could picture a boy traveling down a river in a raft. *Is this the same river?* He also could envision the dried-up riverbed he had seen when flying with Ripeon back on Evion.

He traveled south above the river, still waiting for the sun's rays to disappear to the right of him. He saw the remarkable twinkling lights emanating up at him from homes, buildings, and streetlights below. At one point there were two cities, each across the river from one another. They looked amazingly alike, he thought, like twin cities. He also saw surface vehicle lights below. He conjectured what everyone was doing and where they were going. He hoped his people would fit in.

Continuing on, ahead of him were several large aircraft circling to land. He decided he'd better fly up higher.

He closed his windows and flew west-southwest toward his destination. With his delay heading west, Earth's shadow was now considerably ahead of him. He was pleasantly surprised by the moon that suddenly appeared behind him. The moonlit view below was magnificent.

Moments later, he could see mountains with a large city in front of the foothills. It reminded him of Evion one hundred

E-years before. He wanted to fly over the city, but he saw more aircraft approaching. He headed slightly north, and then back west again.

He couldn't resist the call to fly close to several of the mountain peaks, as he had done on Evion when he was younger. He experienced the mountain terrain and pristine sparking lakes lit up by the moon. He also could see a white substance on one of the peaks. He found the word "snow." He wished he could have flown around these mountains forever, but knew he couldn't.

Finally, San Francisco was in his sights. He had to confirm it by looking at the floating Earth globe. The sun's rays had just passed by the city. He was fascinated by the bright city lights and moonshine that lit up the surrounding area. He was amazed at the vibrant and sparkling city lights reflecting off the Pacific Ocean. He opened the windows experiencing the fresh night sea air. He circled above the San Francisco coast for a while, but the vast amount of large aircraft nearby deterred him again.

He suddenly thought of something. This was nighttime. He should have flown the opposite direction from England, directly to San Francisco. He decided there wasn't much he could do while the humans slept. Also, he had to ration his low star-power energy the best he could. He decided to head up into space again until the San Francisco area was starting to light up again.

He traveled behind the moon, admiring the local solar neighborhood along with universe view of stars, galaxies, and nebula. He shut everything down.

He closed his eyes trying to sleep. The day's experiences were swirling through him while his eyes grew heavy. He opened and closed them several times.

He had a revelation—a new word he had learned from the humans. He now comprehended the difference between sleep-mode and actual sleep. Sleep-mode was a way to ignore life's struggles, while sleeping was a natural way for the body to rest.

He fell fast asleep.

CHAPTER 21

_____

STARION WAS awakened by bright sunlight shining in his face. The moon had continued its orbital path around Earth. He had been in a deep sleep. Strange images had been permeating his mind. One was of Aphelia, running through a green meadow of grass. There were large puffy clouds floating above her in a perfect blue sky.

Wiping the sleep out of his eyes, he recalled the words Ardia had once spoken to him: "There seems to be a connection to the old stories that were apparently necessary to move our ancestors' culture forward...and if these clues or metaphorical messages were not supplied from these old stories or creative art forms, I believe these images had to be somehow supplied from within, such as through dreams."

Gazing at Earth, the sun's rays were now almost hitting the eastern part of San Francisco. He stood up, shot over to Earth and then descended to the nine e-mile mark. From his floor spacegazer, with the sun shining on him, he was able to scope out a good place to land between a large golden bridge and downtown San Francisco.

He beat the sunlight, flying downward. When he landed on the sandy beach, he looked for his bag of clothes. "Oh, no," he said aloud. He had left it at the hotel in England. Oh well, he thought, he wouldn't need it anymore. He would find where this braydium was in this San Francisco, and then find a way to get home anyway.

This time he changed the lead to gold inside the ship.

He wanted to bring along the copy of his favorite book he

had taken along to England. Then it dawned on him that he had placed it in the bag. "Oh, no!"

He put another copy of his favorite book in his back pocket.

Just before leaving, he noticed the spare pair of gliders Ardia had given him. He thought it might be a good idea to bring them along.

He guided the ship into about thirty feet of water, like he had done in England.

At that moment, four aircraft streaked by above him again.

Starion scurry-glided over to a rocky, then grassy surface toward the early-morning San Franciscan lights. Soon he could see a touch of morning sunlight creep up over the east horizon.

He instantly fell in love with the cool breeze from the ocean and the smell of the salty air. He breathed in as much as he could while watching the birds flying above him looking for their morning breakfast.

He heard something behind him. He turned back and discovered an object flying next to a long golden bridge. It looked like a human holding onto something in front of him with his hands. Then it disappeared behind the bridge. It reminded him of the woman who had landed near him in England and the others he had seen. He respected the humans for their ingenuity of the bridge.

When he entered the outskirts of the city, he witnessed the local shop owners getting ready for the busy day, while surface and aircraft traffic gradually started to appear everywhere, including several of these single-person flyers. He smelled enticing aromas and wondered where they were coming from.

He had to find the gold exchange again, so he effortlessly glided up and down the hilly streets to downtown San Francisco. He lauded the variety of homes and the creative buildings.

Just then, a young man cruised by him up a hill, riding on one of the small wooden boards Starion had seen in England. The man was gliding along effortlessly. Starion now realized the device had to be powered by some kind of battery. He was impressed.

Then he observed something he had to look twice at. He saw a large, long surface vehicle gliding along with a thin piece of metal attached on top to a long wire. It was apparently running on electricity.

Hmm . . .

Continuing on, he viewed many homes that had large flat solar panels on roofs. He admired the fact that the humans were trying. But he only saw two homes that had a skyroid on top, similar to the ones back home. He felt pity that more humans did not have skyroids for spacegazing.

He stopped by a large red home with distinct rooms and protruding windows on the roof to examine its construction. There was a young man above him standing on a ladder with a brush changing the color of the building. The young man had a book tucked away in his back pocket like he had done with his own book. Starion felt some kinship with him.

Moving on, he was awestricken with the stores that lined the sidewalks and streets. One in particular caught his eye. In the window was a fake human with some type of contraption on his back, along with two handles that wrapped around the shoulders. The sign read: "I-jet flyer." This is what Starion had seen while in England and on the way here above the bridge.

Once finally downtown, Starion found a gold exchange building and came out with a roll of bills. He hurried on his way down the sidewalk, where he came across a scruffy, sunburned young man with long hair. The man was playing a guitar on the sidewalk with a hat in front of him. He was singing a song, *"For the times they are a-changin . . ."*

Starion interrupted the young man, "Where is this Berkeley?"

The scraggly-looking man pointed over across the bay to the bridge, "You can either take the sky escalator or the ferry across the bay to the college, because you can't walk across the bridge."

"Why not?" he asked the young man while multitasking and searching his memory for the word "college."

"I don't know."

"Thank you," Starion offered, happy to be getting used to the language customs.

Next to the man was a hat on the sidewalk with some coins in it. Starion didn't understand. He felt his eyebrows turn downward.

He traveled down to the water, where he found a long tunnel-looking escalator arching over the bay. Nearby was an old wooden boat floating next to a large wooden pier.

He couldn't forget the story he had read to his children before he left, about the young Evion boy and girl who were lured out into a dark forest and then had gotten lost. They were confronted with an enormous evil dragon ... but an old woman with a cane appeared, guiding them into a cave, then out a secret passage to a wide and dangerous river. There, an old man with a staff ferried them to safety in a wooden boat, wisely pointing them on a path that had never been taken before.

He decided he would take the old wooden boat. If there was magic in these old stories, he needed all he could get.

As he boarded, an old man wearing a dark worn out shroud with a hood covering most of his face held out his frail hand for money. The old man steadied himself using a waist high wooden cane with his other hand. Starion noticed his long thin hand looked almost like a skeleton. The old man took the money and then nodded Starion to come aboard.

Floating along in the old boat, again synapses in his memory were firing. Hundreds of stories he had scanned in, about a magical aid that helped the hero succeed, engulfed the inspiration portion of his brain.

When he landed on shore, the old man nodded at him on his way off the boat.

As he headed down a street, Starion confronted five smiling disabled humans. Three were running with one real limb and one prosthetic leg, while two were pushing themselves in a two-wheeled chair. Starion remembered the smiling young man back in England with one leg. Starion couldn't understand why these disabled people were so vibrant, vital, and happy. Certainly they must have some sort of prosthetic devices. *Surely the humans aren't that far behind us…*

Starion noticed one of the men getting tired pushing his two-wheeled chair with his arms, his legs hanging limp. Starion remembered the spare pair of gliders Ardia had given him. He reached in his pocket, took them out, and said, "Here, try these."

The young man examined them, and then looked at the strange-looking Starion. "These are just shoes…even though they are very light, they can't help me."

Starion still held out the shoes. The young man finally took the gliders from his outstretched hand. "Thank you…but are you sure? You look like you need these more than me."

Starion nodded. "Where is this Berkeley?"

The young man pointed down the road.

Starion headed on his way. He turned back to see the young man putting the gliders in his pocket. He suddenly remembered the warning Judion and Quarion had given him back home about not interfering with Earth's history. He reminded himself not to interfere anymore.

When he arrived at the college, he adored the architecture of the buildings and campus surroundings. He didn't know which building he should enter to find out about the braydium exhibit, but he felt invigorated by the young, energetic young humans hustling and bustling about with their books in hand. They were talking and laughing against the background of green trees, bushes, and grass.

Just then, two young men landed next to him with their I-jet flyers. They were talking about something with raised voices all the way down. One asked the other, "Are you going to enter the contest to be the first person to fly nonstop around the world with your I-jet flyer?"

Once landed, they lifted the flyers off their shoulders then locked them onto some sort of metal stand, which also held several of the two-wheeled contraptions he had seen traveling on the surface.

Continuing, Starion came across the library with all its windows. He wanted to hustle in and scan all the books, but he saw a sign on the front of a different building that read "Modern and Ancient Engineering." He hurried inside.

CHAPTER 22

STANDING IN the atrium of the building, Starion experienced the view of a gorgeous Earth woman with long brown hair who he thought appeared a little younger than he was, at least in Evion years. He recalled the discussion back on Evion about whether there was a difference in lifespans of the two planets.

She was wearing a light blue skirt with a yellow and blue blouse. Starion noticed her enhanced eyelids, along with her very red lips. He could see thin gold rings attached to her earlobes. He also detected a slight sensuous scent.

She asked Starion with a coy smile, "Are you here for the symposium on new possible energy sources?"

Starion was surprised by the question. He should have asked about the braydium exhibit, but he felt powerless, like he had in England with the other young woman. He was instantly enamored. He nodded yes.

She motioned to him. "OK, follow me."

While following her up the stairs, he observed her seductive legs and hips stare back at him. He applauded her ability to climb the stairs with her strange, dangerous-looking shoes with small pointed heels.

Once in the room, he sat in a chair in the back watching her set up the class for her teaching session, trying not to look like he was staring. He didn't want to be called a creep again. He watched as the class filled up with students. Most were wearing their see-through face-panel IS units strapped onto their heads. He was happy to see a variety of other older humans arrive. For some reason, their IS units were around their waists. Some of the oldest even carried theirs in a bag, pulling them out and plopping them on top of their laps.

The radiant teacher began the meeting. "Today we will be discussing Earth's present-day as well as possible future energy sources and their uses. Hopefully this will inspire some of you to be the next generation of inventors. If you are wearing your I-panels, you can view in 3-D; otherwise, you will have to see it 2-D."

Starion listened to the discussions on coal, oil, natural gas, nuclear power, windmills, solar energy, and rocket fuel. Occasionally, the nagging feeling of guilt overwhelmed him again. Were his fellow Evions OK? Even though his people had been spared of the flare he had seen, there may have been another.

Behind the teacher were 3-D images that included the current uses of energy. Starion read the caption below each. There were images of coal power plants spewing large amounts of smoke into the sky, oil well pumps, nuclear power plants, home furnaces and water heaters, windmill farms, automobiles, planes, and rockets, including a space shuttle.

"As you all know, someday we will run out of oil. Hydrogen split from water seems to be the next source…but even water is limited on this planet. We will need to consider other types of energy, too."

She used a remote control clicker to change slides.

Interesting… Starion thought.

"Here is some old history of energy and its uses, as well as a warning of what can happen if energy is not properly studied. These rockets are from one hundred years ago, near the end of the first Industrial Revolution in 1963. Coincidentally, this was also the infancy of the Computer Revolution."

She showed the class the first rockets invented and followed up with the history of the large boosters. Then she changed the slide to a tragic image of a rocket ship bursting into flames at a launch.

"This is what can happen if new types of energy are not

carefully studied and tested," she stated sadly. "This was Apollo I." Starion remembered the horrific tragedy Deon had shown: the elders of the humans testing atomic power in an aircraft. He had knowledge that this would occur in ten Earth years.

"But we did figure it out—here is a successful launch of Apollo II," she said, showing a rocket spewing vast amounts of hydrogen vapor while it traveled up and out of the Earth's atmosphere. "And not long after that, we landed a man on the moon."

Starion remembered the reference to Apollo from his memory-scanning of Greek mythologies. *Interesting . . . they named this rocket after one of their Greek gods. I like that.*

Afterward, the woman displayed a view of an awkward-looking v-breaker with its large rocket booster on the launchpad. It was spewing liquid hydrogen and oxygen.

"Thank God, we started up our space shuttle program again after thirty years at the Kennedy Space Center. Propellants used in these rocket boosters for space travel are still being invented as we speak. Someday, they will be extremely important for space travel. Right now and ever since the Apollo program, liquid hydrogen combined with oxygen is the main mixture used. As far as our automobiles and smaller planes, there is much work ahead before we could convert to hydrogen engines, for example."

Starion scanned the presentation, storing it in his mind. He was especially interested in the information regarding hydrogen. He couldn't help but think of Evion's ancient hydrogen technology and his own ancient engines he had acquired for keepsakes. He didn't know if any of them or his ancient water splitter still worked.

"Now, everyone, let's talk about our oil supply," the teacher said, changing the subject. "How many years do you think we have until we run out of oil here on Earth? And, by the way, we are presently losing about one hundred million barrels of oil per day. Anyone?"

One student shouted, "Fifty years."

Another yelled, "Thirty-five."

Starion analyzed the data he had scanned in from Deon's S-ray at the Earth presentation, along with the other data he had scanned when he visited the bookstore in England. He also remembered the depressing fuzzy broadcast he had seen just before leaving for Earth of an imminent attack.

"Twenty years," Starion mumbled.

He apparently hadn't been quiet enough, because the teacher heard him. "What? Did I hear you say twenty years?"

Starion nodded.

She leaned toward him. "How did you know that is exactly what I believe?"

"Just a lucky guess," he replied, repeating a term he'd learned in his recent study of Earth's lingo.

The class laughed. The teacher smiled, looking curiously at Starion a little longer than she should have. She fumbled with her notes then finally came out of her trance.

"If we are successful with hydrogen power for everything, not just for our rockets, after our petroleum runs out, how long will that last? In other words, how long will our water last?"

"About fifty of your Earth years," Starion blurted out again while the class snickered.

"What will we use when that runs out?" she asked the class.

Two students yelled out "Nuclear power" and "Electric." One more student yelled out "Solar."

"Yes, star power," Starion offered.

The class laughed again.

"Why would you say that?" the teacher asked with a look of admiration on her face.

"Well, it makes sense…just look at that large star out the window."

The class was now hysterical.

"OK, everyone, class is over," the teacher announced.

After the last of the students left, Starion started to get out of his chair. Like the beautiful teacher, he was in a trance, too. He was frustrated. He didn't know what he should do.

The teacher spoke up first. "I was very impressed with your twenty-year answer on oil. And your fifty-year answer regarding hydrogen and water—may I ask how you arrived at those?"

Starion was nervous. He couldn't think of a good lie. He panned the room. He found the Earth's periodic table on a classroom wall. "Do you think any of these elements mixed together could produce alternative energy sources?"

"Well, I don't know. Maybe someday...but that would probably be a long way off. I admire your passion on the solar concept for after we run out of oil and water," she proclaimed, raising her thumbs at him.

"How come braydium isn't in your periodic table?" Starion asked, puzzled by her gesture.

"What is braydium?"

"It's a very strong and resilient element. When added to water, it is like glass and aluminum combined."

"Never heard of it," she told him.

"I am doing research on it, and I was told that Berkeley had a traveling exhibit twenty of your years ago...I mean, recently...that included it." *Oh, no—I did it again.*

"Ha—twenty years of 'our' years? You sure are an interesting fellow. I can check with our administration office, if you like."

Starion nodded yes, watching her walk into a nearby office. There she picked up a strange-looking device and started to talk into it.

"Hello, this is Amelia in Engineering...I was wondering if you could help me out. I need to know if there was an exhibit by us here at Berkeley that included an element called braydium."

Starion thought how closely her name sounded like his wife Aphelia's.

There was a pause before she spoke again into the device. "Oh...not till tomorrow morning?...OK, thank you."

She set the device back down and turned to Starion. "She will check on it, but she won't know until tomorrow morning."

"OK," Starion said. Disappointed, he started for the door.

"Wait—how about a drink?"

"What?" he asked.

"How about a drink over at my place…unless you have other plans?" she said seductively.

Starion looked into in her eyes; her smile was erotically inviting. He couldn't refuse. He nodded yes, unable to think clearly.

As they headed out of the building, the gorgeous teacher interlocked her arm with Starion's. He concentrated to keep his gliding in sync with her walking.

"What's your name?" she asked.

"Starion."

"That's unique."

"What's your name?"

"I'm Amelia. Should we take my vehicle or yours?"

"I glided…I mean, walked and took the magical aid…I mean, and old wooden boat over here from downtown," Starion informed her.

"OK, we'll take mine."

Just before getting into a red surface vehicle with a metal exterior and black rubber tires, she popped open the hood. Starion thought he had seen this before. Then he remembered the red surface vehicle he had shown Aphelia.

"So you think hydrogen is the answer…I like these old antique cars, by the way. This one is almost one hundred years old."

Starion stared deeply into her eyes, using telepathy by instinct. She trembled briefly, shaking her head from side to side for an instant. He suddenly stopped. Worried, he hoped he hadn't sent an image of the Evion hydrogen engine he'd been thinking about. He had to hope she hadn't connected.

"Hmm," she muttered, putting her hand up to her chin while shaking her head. "And you think someday we will use solar power, huh?"

He desperately wanted to tell her, but the council's reminder not to interfere with Earth's history kept ringing in his ears.

His slip moments ago, along with his other slips in judgment, now bothered him.

"Speaking of hydrogen, I really liked your discussion on the rocket boosters," Starion said. "Where is this Kennedy Space Center?"

"In Florida."

"Oh…on the other side of the continent," he concluded, closing his eyes for a second. Upon opening them, Starion noticed a new look on her face. He was learning how to interpret expressions, and he could tell she was confused. She shut the hood and they both hopped into the car.

Riding along, Starion curiously observed all the knobs, lights, and gauges as they drove over the bridge to downtown San Francisco. She turned on the radio and Starion heard a woman sing seductively, "*When cupid shot his dart he shot it at your heart…*" He looked over at this attractive Earth woman steering this ancient type of vehicle. His mind was not working. He felt his body taking over.

"What do you do for a living?" she asked, the song playing in the background.

He forced himself to answer. "Well, I guess you could say I am looking for more new energy for my people."

"How about family? I can't see your ring finger because of your gloves…I assume you're not married. If you are, I will drop you off immediately," she informed him with a sly smile.

"I am not married. My wife recently died."

"Oh, I'm sorry. I am so sorry."

"I have two children back at home," Starion continued, ambiguously enjoying her company while trying to fight off his desire for her.

"Oh, how nice. And where is home?" she asked.

He paused for a moment. He had to lie, but he didn't want to. "I am from England."

"Oh…how wonderful," she said, trying to remember if she had heard this accent before.

They drove over to her home and went in, arms locked. He saw more of the 2-D pictures he had seen at the gold exchange. Next to them was a large wooden bookshelf full of books on energy, including petroleum, nuclear, hydrogen, and solar. He scanned them instantly with his back to her.

"Would you like wine, beer, or liquor?" she asked.

Starion didn't have a good experience with the hard liquor. He shrugged his shoulders.

Starion watched as she poured a glass of red wine for him and for herself.

He took a sip. She kissed him on his lips. He was powerless.

CHAPTER 23

THE NEXT morning, back in her office at the college, Amelia was on her communication device. "Let's see if they have an answer for you."

"OK. Thanks," Starion uttered.

She turned to Starion after putting down the device. "It looks like all the information on this exhibit originated in New York at the Museum of Natural History. I'm sorry."

She kissed him on his cheek.

"Maybe we can see each other again," he asked instinctively.

"Good luck in your search," she said while starting to get things ready for her morning class.

Disappointed and rejected, Starion started for the door, but for some reason he felt compelled to give her something. He reached into his pocket, then handed her the extra copy of his favorite book, *Anciente Evion Adventura~Hero*.

He saw a surprised look on her face as she examined the cover. She set it down on top of several other books.

Starion felt rejected again and headed outside. Then he remembered the book he just gave her was in Evionish. Should he go back? He decided he shouldn't. It might create suspicion.

On his way toward his v-breaker, this time he wasn't able to enjoy the scenery. He had too much on his mind. He was really starting to feel the pull of human culture. And he now knew the truth of Ardia's statement: the life force of love was very powerful. His mind was cloudy and he felt terrible. He also felt guilty.

He thought about Aphelia and his mission. He had to be

much more careful around these Earth women. He had other things he needed to do. He had to try to force himself to avoid them.

He passed by another digital newspaper stand, where he read, "Strange Occurrences Continue: This time clothes made from fabric never seen before were found in England; some say incidences a Hollywood hoax." And below this, there was a second headline: "Renowned Scientist Leonard Vincy Urges Colleagues to Move Faster on Alternative Energy Sources; 'Time is limited,' he says." On another line, he saw: "On a related subject, there is much discussion on who will be the last country to have oil deposits in the years to come. Will it result in war?" Lower he read, "Two Dead from I-jet Flyer Collision: Flying while drinking suspected." And finally he observed. "More Incidents of Gas Station Robberies; Thieves stealing gas and I-jet tanks, not money."

Loneliness overwhelmed him. He missed his wife and children. He was beginning to question if braydium was really on Earth. And if so, how could Deon have made such a mistake by using that planet-net recording of where and when braydium was found on Earth? Were his people OK?

All the new Earth-induced emotions were getting to him. *Yes ... these Earth people are much more complicated than I thought. No wonder they need all those art forms.*

Just then he swore he saw the same man with the hat again. This time, the man was wearing a blue suit and hat. Then a bright light shone from his face panel.

Starion instinctively took off faster than he should have. He left a glider imprint on the concrete sidewalk while zigzagging in and out, avoiding the many people. He hit a red traffic light stumble-gliding out into the street. He heard and then saw a large surface vehicle heading right at him. He jumped over the vehicle, landing on the other side and smashing into a man wearing a black uniform, a hat with a visor, and a gun.

He had to get out of there as fast as he could.

The man pulled out his gun, but he was too late; Starion was gone.

When Starion finally arrived back at the v-breaker, he made sure no one was near or above him. Calming himself from the recent incident, he guided the ship out of the ocean and climbed in as fast as he could. He pulled out as many 4-D images of his family, Evion, and his people as he could, just as he had when he left England.

He shot up to his nine-e-mile zone, hovering where he hoped it was safe. Then, unexpectedly, two aircraft flew by him but then turned around. They were heading right toward him.

He aimed the ship straight up then jettisoned out into Earth's orbital space. The Earth aircraft chased after him until they couldn't go any farther.

He sat there floating in Earth's orbit, feeling lonelier, guiltier, and more confused than ever. He decided he would fly farther away from Earth, over to the dark side of the moon. There he would be completely safe. He would gather his thoughts again, and then figure out if he should go to this New York. He needed to decide if finding this braydium was hopeless. Maybe he should put all efforts toward trying to find other energy to get home instead.

Starion hovered above dark side of the moon, trying to gain his composure. He needed to decide what he wanted to do. He was beginning to seriously consider trying to find another type of energy to get him home.

"*Low on energy...Low on energy,*" the IS unit announced.

At that particular moment, he saw Earth rise up over the moon's surface. Then he happened to glance down at the seat, where he had left his original tattered copy of his book. It had now been jostled open to the chapter with the title *"Adventura~Denial."*

He looked over at the navigator with the 4-D I-spacer of a globe-looking image of Earth. Curiously, he read the words "New York City" highlighted brighter than the rest. His scientist mind tried to figure out why this might be. Then he remembered the old stories, his mentor Ardia, the old philosophers, and the old men and women in the Earth cave.

Be open to fate.

Inspired again, he raced over to Earth and then dropped down to the nine-e-mile mark. He pointed his hand spacegazer at New York City then slightly north. He located a possible place to land and hide his ship. He was aware that it was quite a distance to the city; he would just have to glide speedily and hope no one noticed him.

Then he saw the gauge was even more dangerously low.

"Dange—"

Without warning, the IS unit went dead.

He opened the compartment where the star-power cells were. He shook them. Luckily, he could see the needle on the gauge climb just barely.

He descended and landed next to a long river. This time he grabbed his last copy of his favorite book, the one Bria had put back together for him. He put it in his pocket. He also felt compelled to take Aphelia's ashes this time.

He decided he had enough money without finding a gold exchange. He hid the craft in the water again. Soon after, a squadron of twenty aircraft raced across the sky. He started toward downtown New York, the late morning sun shining its glorious rays at him from his left. He was happy to need to squint.

He felt rejuvenated while taking in all the fresh air and sites he could. As he traversed along the countryside, he found himself gliding down a quiet, hilly road through rolling fields and pastures. He observed tall trees and green vegetation, just like he had seen in England and San Francisco.

Then he saw the same fighter aircraft squadron fly above him again. By instinct, he hid underneath a tree beside the road.

When he was sure they weren't coming back, he started on his way again, but two surface vehicles drove past him, one slowing while the occupants stared at him. After they were out of sight, he decided to glide into a vast meadow of tall grass instead of the road.

It was a day with a slight breeze blowing the air with a variety of enticing smells. From his memory of Earth's yearly orbit and its turning on its axis, he figured this was the growing season on this part of Earth.

He took off his gloves; he wanted to feel everything he could. He reached down and pulled out a handful of grass. He smelled and even tasted it. He left one of the long blades in his mouth. It hung out, blowing in the wind. He liked the fresh taste.

Nearby, a small animal hopped into some bushes. Then he saw three deer bounding along in the distance like he had seen in England. He decided to take off his gliders so he could feel the grass with his six toes and feet.

After traveling some distance, feeling the sun on his face, he was tired. It had been a long time since he had walked manually, but he felt like he had accomplished something. He stopped when he reached a shady area under a large tree. He saw a red small animal he figured was a squirrel scurry its way up into a branch above him. Then it jumped over to another nearby branch to hide.

Suddenly, he heard a new sound. Near him was a small, clear, bustling creek. The water was racing and zigzagging down its path on its way to some unknown place.

He took out the pouch of Aphelia's ashes and softly sprinkled them in the green grass underneath the tree next to the creek. He stood there remembering his wife's last words. "Nothing is impossible…and you will find love again. I want you to go to this Earth and save our children and our people. That is my dream. It is not impossible…and find a good Earth woman. Please, fulfill my dream."

He looked up into the floating clouds in the blue sky. He swore one cloud resembled his wife. He recalled the dream he had about her the night before. A tear rolled down his cheek.

He had to get going. He put his gliders and hat on again and headed on his way, briskly heading down a steep knoll. Not paying attention, he stumbled, and he laughed to himself as he fell to the ground. His facial muscles hurt.

"Earth will work...I know it will," he shouted, not caring if someone heard him.

CHAPTER 24

STARION FINALLY could see the tall city buildings in the near distance. He could see surface vehicles and people hustling about. Then he saw something up in the air between him and the starshine. He held his arm up to block the sun. He heard and then witnessed four humans drop down, softly landing near him. They were wearing I-jet flyers. Starion saw four very elderly Earth people, two men and two women. One noticed Starion and yelled, "Good morning."

Starion shouted back, "Good morning to you, too."

Starion entered the large city limits. He was amazed with the tall different-shaped and colored buildings of steel, glass, brick, and concrete.

He couldn't believe the massive amounts of humans in the streets, along with the noise from thousands of surface vehicles and several I-jet flyers. Because these single-person flyers were above all the chaos, Starion could see them zip above the streets and around the tall buildings with ease. He witnessed several land in what he figured were designated I-jet landing areas.

Still careful of stumbling and trying to make sure he walked like a human, he took in the different-looking ethnic races, hairstyles, and body features, including painted images on their bodies. He knew for sure he would never be found out here. After he'd recently learned the word "strange," he figured he was as strange as anyone else.

One man noticed his ease of walking and said to him, "Hey, man…you must really be in good shape. It doesn't look like you have to force your legs forward. Cool."

Starion nodded yes to him but didn't feel comfortable replying. Moving on, he found himself entering the busy street on a red light. Suddenly, a large black surface vehicle rushed toward him. He panicked. His eyes wide open and terrified, he instinctively jumped over it like he had done in San Francisco.

Several humans rushed over to him, looking around.

"Where's the camera?" one man yelled.

A young boy yelled, "Superman!"

His friend yelled, "No, it's Spiderman!"

An adult lady surmised, "Iron Man?"

"Well, it's *some* kind of movie production..." another man conjectured.

Starion decided he had better get lost. He hustled away into the crowd, mad at himself again. He had just promised himself he was going to try harder to be inconspicuous.

He glanced back several times to see if anyone was following him. He noticed one man wearing a black uniform suit with a hat running and chasing him—it was the same man that he had seen before in London and San Francisco. Starion was no match for him again. Starion scurry-glided two blocks, taking a right turn at each. Finally, he stopped and waited.

He was safe for now.

Just then an elderly short gentleman with a long grey beard and a cane walked by. Starion asked, "Do you know where the Museum of Natural History is?"

The man pointed down the street.

Starion, leaving, looked back to thank the man. He was mysteriously gone.

While he waited for a traffic light to change, Starion marveled again at the different sizes, colors, and shapes of humans. They all had different hair, different heights, different facial expressions.

He listened to several conversations at once and witnessed their eyes and emotions. He felt invigorated and inspired. His synopsizes of the old stories were firing away again. He sadly remembered when he had unsuccessfully looked for inspiration back on Evion from fellow Evions eyes before he had left for Earth.

To the right of him, two more humans on the wooden boards he had been seeing somehow stopped without any physical effort. *These people aren't so far behind us*, Starion decided.

Continuing on his way, he saw another building similar to the one he had seen in England that apparently sold gasoline and I-jet tanks. Suddenly, two I-jet flyers landed, carrying some type of guns and empty bags. The two wearing masks ran inside the building and back out with full bags, and then flew up and away. Just then another I-jet flyer with a bright red flashing light and a siren followed the two while yelling and shooting some type of gun at them.

Starion had second thoughts about whether the humans were far behind them.

A little shaken, he headed down the sidewalk again. Just then a large red surface vehicle drove by with its loud siren. It stopped just ahead of him, where he witnessed a building burning. He watched several humans nearby run to the house. Two young men ran inside. Starion couldn't believe it. What were they doing? They could burn instantly, like he had seen too many times on Evion.

Four other humans with strange uniforms ran out of the large surface vehicle dragging long hoses. Two of them hauled out a ladder, dangerously placing it against the building, and started climbing up.

Then two young men ran out, coughing and carrying a woman in their arms, finally falling on the grass. All three were gasping for air.

Moments later, the two in uniforms who had climbed the ladder carried a small child down, also coughing and gasping for air.

Starion couldn't believe it. It was obvious these people didn't know each other, but yet they had risked their lives. A small tear ran down his face.

Then he saw another man wearing the strange uniform rush out carrying another woman limp in his arms. Hacking uncontrollably, he laid her down in the grass. Two other humans raced to help. One pounded on her chest, while the other placed his face and mouth on hers intermittently. They stopped and then tried again several more times. They were unsuccessful. More humans gathered around her with their heads down and hats off. Someone said something but he couldn't hear.

Just then another surface vehicle with a loud siren stopped nearby. It sadly reminded him of his own planet's v-ambulances, like in England, and he ached of guilt and loneliness. Were his people OK?

Continuing on his way in shock, he glanced down at a digital newspaper stand. There was a story that read, "I-jet flyer dead from running out of fuel. Pronounced dead on the scene, the man's flyer emergency chute didn't deploy and he crashed to the ground."

Underneath was another alarming headline: "Is there a connection between the UFO sightings and unusual activity in San Francisco and London?"

He felt more remorse than ever.

Suddenly, he felt his arms being pulled behind him hard. He instinctively jumped up and out of the arm lock. When he landed, he looked back. It was the man with the hat again, this time yelling into a clear face panel while chasing him. "Who are you? Stop!"

Starion took off around the corner, trying the best he could to glide-walk instead of glide-run so as not to attract attention. A few moments later, he heard an enticing iron bell. He followed the sound until he saw an interesting-looking building with an adorable steeple. He entered through the large arched door, where he was immediately drawn into the warm, peaceful atmosphere. He concluded that this was an Earth religious building.

He sat down in a back wooden bench. He occasionally looked

back to the door. Starion was fascinated with the stained glass windows, the high ceiling, and the architecture. He loved all the décor, the peaceful smells and sounds. He listened to a middle-aged man in front wearing a shroud. He was speaking about someone who had forgiven another country and its people, even though they had almost taken his life as a young man.

The man in the shroud introduced an old man with two prosthetic legs, who hobbled up to the pulpit and said, "One must forgive in order to be one with God...whether it is as large as forgiving a whole group of people or as small as just one person, you must forgive in order to move forward with life. And you must forgive yourself, too." The old man looked vaguely familiar.

Soon after, he heard the first man request. "Let's pray for the heroes who have given their lives for us." Starion witnessed everyone bow their heads, some with their hands together.

Leaving, he walk-glided by an old building he recognized as another religious building on one block, then another on another block, then finally another. After that, he glided by a long fenced-in area with a large brown brick building beyond. In between were several humans in white clothes sitting outside in the late afternoon sunshine.

"I know these buildings are important," he quietly mumbled to himself. "This is something Ardia was very concerned about."

Observing some of the humans in the white uniforms move about, he contemplated how best to further learn about these Earth customs and practices. When he turned to leave, he observed a sign on a building across the street. It read "Institute for Comparable Religious Studies."

At that moment, someone yelled from behind the fence. "Hey—hey!"

Starion turned back and noticed a man skipping toward him. When the man arrived next to the chain-link fence between him and Starion, he stared down at his feet. He was a weathered-looking man with long grey hair and dark green eyes.

The man looked up, and for one brief moment he stared deeply into Starion eyes. Then he looked back down at his feet. "Good to see you again."

Starion's hair stood up on the back of his neck. This man's eyes were eerily blank. The glance reminded him of a look he had seen before on Evion, but he couldn't place it.

He didn't know what to say, so he answered the man, "Same to you."

The man skipped away.

CHAPTER 25

STARION DIDN'T know what to think, but he turned his attention across the street again, toward the Institute for Comparative Religious Studies. He hoped this would be a good place to ask about the Museum of Natural History—and maybe he could get some answers to his questions.

He glided over to an old yellow building, similar to the large red one he had seen in San Francisco, then glide-hopped up the stairs. Above him was a human on a ladder painting the building. The young paint-stained man had a book sticking out of his back pocket, just as the man in San Francisco had. Starion shook his head. *Didn't I see this before...?*

When Starion stepped through the door, he encountered a pretty young brunette woman sitting behind a large wooden desk. She had a similar panel in front of her face he had seen on many humans. She was talking softly, as if to no one, while looking down at several ancient, tattered books. There was a hallway with several offices behind her.

"Can I help you?" she asked.

"Is the leader of this institute here, and can I speak with him or her?"

"We don't have a leader, but Mrs. Thompson is the president of our nonprofit organization."

"Can I meet with her?"

"Do you have an appointment?" she asked.

"What?"

Just then, an attractive woman who he guessed was about the same age as he was poked her head out of her office door. She wore a long blue dress, and had long red hair and a seductive smile. She appeared very diplomatic. She didn't have any type of technology hooked onto her.

"May I help you?" she inquired.

"Yes…I was wondering if you can help me with a question." But he found it difficult to continue; he felt the same powerless attraction to Mrs. Thompson that he had felt in England and San Francisco.

"I'll try," she said.

Starion tried to fight off her beauty. He turned away for a moment, trying to block the attraction.

With all he could muster, he told himself he was going to ask where the museum was. But when he turned toward her again, he was struck by her bright green eyes. They reminded him of Aphelia. He rationalized; Ardia's orders were to learn.

Starion manifested his best leadership qualities by fighting off his interest long enough to ask, "Well, I just walked by four of your religious organizations and one of your psychiatric hospitals, and I was wondering why they are all in separate buildings."

Starion noticed a confusing look on Mrs. Thompson's face. "Come into my office," she tentatively stated.

Starion followed Mrs. Thompson. Like in San Francisco, he couldn't help but notice her curved hips and seductive walk.

Once inside, she left the door three quarters open, and they both sat down. From behind her desk, she said, "I have never heard it put quite like that before. I guess I don't know what you mean."

Starion was mesmerized by this woman's beauty, plus the fact that she was an expert on Earth's religions and philosophies. He stuttered, "Well, I—I am interested in the interrelatedness and history of these religious traditions, and how they compare to the analytical study of the human mind. In other words, does one help the other and vice versa?"

Mrs. Thompson hesitated. She looked out the window across the street at the fenced-in area he had just come from. She glanced back and forth a couple of times, inspecting Starion and his clothes.

Starion was aware that he might have confused this poor lady, so he changed the subject. "Can you tell me where the Museum of Natural History is?"

She peeked at her watch and then back at Starion as if to size him up again.

"I am going down there right now to give them a few of our books. I can show you."

"OK."

They headed out of the building down the stairs to the sidewalk. She had two books underneath her arm. Starion noticed that the young man he had seen on the ladder was now lying on the grass, reading a book page by page.

Mrs. Thompson spoke first. "Have you ever been to the Museum of Natural History?"

"No, I haven't."

"You will really enjoy it. I take it you are not from here?"

"No, I'm not."

"What's your name?" she asked as they headed down the sidewalk, looking a little more comfortable being with Starion in a crowd. He also was getting used to syncing his gliding to a human's stride.

"Starion," he answered.

"Are you married?"

"No, my wife died recently."

"Oh, I am so sorry," she said. After a pause, she asked, "Any children?"

"I have a boy and a girl," he answered.

"How wonderful!" she exclaimed.

"What's your name...and what about you?"

"My name is Mary...and my husband recently died. As far as children, I never had any."

"I am sorry, too."

"Why the gloves?" she curiously asked.

"Oh, I just prefer to wear them."

"What do you do for a living, where are you from, and why are you in New York?" she asked in a rush.

Looking into her compassionate eyes, he blurted out without thinking, "Well, I am from another planet and am looking for a mineral called braydium in order to save my people."

Mary burst out laughing. Several people walking nearby turned to see what had happened. She laughed so hard she had tears coming out of her eyes and had to stop walking.

Why can't I stop revealing why I am here?

When she finally gathered her composure, she commented, "You are quite the interesting fellow. By the way, that question about why all the religious buildings and the mental hospital were separate—what did you mean?"

"Well, let me put it to you this way: would aliens be welcomed into Earth's religions?"

Mary started to laugh but could see Starion's serious demeanor. "Would aliens be welcome into Earth's religions? Hmm…" She pondered for a moment. "Well, the ultimate message of most religions is to help move the human race forward with a vital, peaceful, and spiritually healthy society. If the aliens' intentions were to help this occur, then I see no reason why any religion would reject them."

Starion smiled the best he could. "I have heard that before."

"From whom?"

"A very wise woman from where I come from."

Mary responded with clear intentions: "Was it your wife or girlfriend who said it?"

Starion picked up on her intention, too, and replied, "No, just a friend."

Continuing on their way to the museum, the two passed by a window front. The sign read "Download Music from Our Music Pods." Next to these words was a type of fruit with a bite out of it.

Starion couldn't resist. He hurried inside, while Mary

curiously followed. He found several vertical circular pods seven feet high and about four feet in circumference. Above the thin entrance door of each pod was a sign: "mPod."

He entered and closed the door, leaving Mary outside the pod. In front of him was a screen with thousands of songs listed. He chose one. Sound filled the small circular pod, reverberating in his body and soul. He heard the singer sing.

"*... They slip away across the universe ...*"

"Hmm..." he said to himself while scanning all the songs, "Another art form."

Suddenly, he remembered leaving Mary. He hurried out, and luckily, she was still there waiting for him.

"I'm sorry," he told her. Remembering what Ardia had told him, he said, "Music is the soul of the universe."

"That's OK. I admire your passion."

Outside and continuing on their way, he observed through a window a 3-D image of a human man wearing something on his neck, talking into it by moving his mouth slightly toward it.

There was a sign above it. "Coming in 2061: The much-anticipated voice-activated miniature neck iPod."

Next to this store, inside the glass window, there was another animated 3-D image of an Earth woman speaking into a small clear face panel. She was running. He read the sign, "Who needs an iPod when we can have it all?" Next to these words was an image of some kind of an orange fruit with a bite out of it.

Moving on toward the museum, Starion and Mary passed by another store displaying a sign that said "3-D Ultra-High-Definition Flat-Screens."

Starion heard a live newscast from one of the screens. The newscaster reported, "These odd sightings and behavior in New York, London, San Francisco, and around the world is being blamed on Hollywood...especially the strangely designed clothing found in London. The fabric is unknown. Hollywood denies any involvement."

Afterward, the screen displayed an interview of one of the young boys who had seen Starion jump over the surface craft. "The man jumped over the car and easily landed on the sidewalk on the other side," the boy stated.

"What did he look like?" the news reporter asked.

Starion turned away before he could hear the boy answer.

CHAPTER 26

"HEY, LET me buy you a cup of coffee," Mary said grabbing his arm and pointing to a small table against a brick wall. "I'll be right back. What do you want?"

"I'll have what you're having," he answered, anxious to get to the museum.

Soon she came back carrying two hot cups of black coffee. The two sat, while Starion sensed Mary was sizing him up. He really didn't know what to say. She didn't offer any conversation for a few moments.

Sipping nervously on his coffee and suddenly feeling wide awake, he watched and listened to the humans interact. He witnessed and experienced their variety of expressions and voice inflections. He kept glancing at this attractive lady, not wanting to stare. He heard song lyrics in the background.

"Some call it magic, the search for the grail..."

He loved the melody and lyrics, as well as experiencing the lively patrons as they argued, laughed, cried, yelled, sneezed, and coughed with different facial expressions. Starion remembered the elder meeting when he had imagined what it must have been like long ago on Evion to see and hear a smile or a laugh.

Mary suddenly saw someone she knew. She left briefly, holding up her index finger to Starion. He was worried she had left him for good, but she stopped just a few tables away. She gave him the one-finger gesture again and he got the message.

Next to him were two young men. Just then, one of them blurted, "High-five." Then he saw them each lift up one hand and slap each other.

On the other side of him, Starion heard a young couple talking. He heard the man say, "What do you call a crazy alien from outer space...an astronut!"

Starion didn't understand. He turned his attention to Mary and her shapely body with gorgeous hair hanging down her neck and back.

Suddenly, she turned around and came back. "Are you ready to go?"

Starting on their way again, Starion felt like he could glide forever after drinking his coffee, and he had to fight off his gliders.

"There it is," Mary noticed, pointing to the museum a block away on the same side of the street.

Starion glanced directly across the street. The man with the black uniform and hat was glaring at him through his face panel.

Starion gripped Mary by the arm and hustled her through hundreds of humans walking on the sidewalk over to the museum. Once inside the entryway, Starion peeked out the window to see if the man had followed. Luckily, he had been caught in the crowd.

Starion followed Mary to a back office, taking in the large, mysterious Museum. It reminded him of his own Audiseum. He felt at home—but he conjectured why there wasn't a glass dome and spacegazers.

When they reached the back office, Mary handed the two books she was carrying to an elderly lady with long grey hair and a cane. Starion looked closely at the woman. He swore it was the same woman he had seen at the London Museum. "Thanks, Mary. We are always looking for more ancient books to add to our library room."

He hoped she might be able to help him, so he spoke up. "Can you tell me if the museum has ever had a mineral called braydium in any of your exhibits?"

"I will have to check for you and get back to you. Can you give me an hour or so?" she said with a mysterious smile as if she knew something.

"Thank you," he answered, learning proper etiquette.

Mary took his arm in hers and led him away.

They toured all the exhibits, including birds, reptiles, and amphibians; fossil halls, human origins, and cultural halls; the Rose Center for Earth and Space, which included the Hayden Planetarium; and the Discovery Room, which was for children to explore the Earth's vast history.

Starion memory-scanned everything he could.

He was especially interested in the ancient bones and skulls of humans. When he noticed the dates on some of the ancient bones, he couldn't believe it. Some were from ten thousand of their years ago, some from a hundred thousand years ago, and some were even from one *million* years ago.

"Are these dates correct?" he asked Mary.

"That's what our scientists say."

"Hmm," he pondered, trying to fathom it. There hadn't been any ancient bones found on Evion past ten thousand of their years.

Then he saw a whole separate large room with a sign on top of the entrance that read, "Two Hundred Years of Oil So Far—what's Next?"

He couldn't resist and urged Mary into the room. He reveled at the ancient surface vehicles, internal combustion engines, and large oil well pumps. There was a large sign on one pump that read: "In Use: 1906–2049."

Starion was aware that his own planet had used up its oil in similar fashion, in two hundred of their years. He wished he could warn Mary about what would happen in twenty years.

Next to this was room with a sign above its entrance: "100 Years of Computer History."

Mary nudged him out of the exhibit and into the Hayden Theatre, where they watched a 3-D video on a very wide and tall semicircle screen. At one point, the video panned the Milky Way Galaxy. "The Milky Way Galaxy is trillions of miles across," the narrator explained.

Suddenly, the view focused in on one of the arms of the galaxy. It was hauntingly familiar. Starion instinctively and unknowingly pointed his focus finger at it. The film stopped. Starion noticed everyone turn look around while hearing someone utter, "What's going on?" Still unaware of what he was doing, he tried to pull the image out to a 4-D view with his hand.

Finally, he saw Mary look over at him, and he realized he was holding up the film.

"What are you doing?" she asked.

"Oh...I am just exercising my arm," he quickly justified, releasing the video to continue.

Then he heard a couple of young men talking next to him. He overheard one of them say, "Wow, this is awesome. Do you believe the big bang theory?"

"No, I don't," the other replied.

"I do."

Starion turned to Mary. "What is 'awesome'?"

She laughed without saying anything.

"Do you believe in this big bang theory?" he asked.

"I don't know...I guess it doesn't matter to me. I like to think about the future as often as I can."

Starion squeezed her hand in approval. He wondered what holding her hand would feel like without the glove.

Starion knew the answer to Earth's big bang theory, but he felt this wouldn't be the appropriate time to discuss it with her. "The universe is much more complex and interesting than you can imagine, Mary."

"Are you an astronomer?"

"I guess you could say that."

"Do you think the universe has all the answers?" she asked.

Starion pondered for a moment. "I used to think so, but now I'm not so sure."

When the film was over, Starion stood up, noticing the few audience members seated behind him. There was a lone figure of a man with the same hat he unfortunately came to recognize.

The man quickly put a brochure up to his face to read, obstructing Starion's view.

On their way out of the theatre section, Starion told Mary, glancing behind them, "Wouldn't it be interesting if your museum had a large glass planetarium dome so hundreds of Evions—I mean, humans—could sit in an Audiseum on bleachers—or, I mean, an auditorium—that sat on a large round slab? You could have spacegazers—I mean, telescopes—next to each person so they could view space while the Earth rotated on its axis."

Mary burst out in laughter again, grabbing ahold of his arm. "You have the best imagination and sense of humor of any man I have ever met. How did you know how to get to my heart?"

Starion was confused again. "Why would I want to do that?"

After another round of laughter subsided, he continued, "Believe me, Mary—it is important for your people and especially your children to learn about your local solar system, your section of the Milky Way Galaxy, your sun, and especially your planet. Never allow them to become complacent," he warned her seriously.

"How come you talk as if you are not from here? Like I said, you sure have a good sense of humor. Maybe you should go into acting," she continued, squeezing his hand again.

"What?" he asked as they headed over to where they had left the elderly lady. He also panned the room searching for the man, but didn't see him.

Just then the old woman came toward them. "Sir, we did have this mineral you call braydium here a month ago. However, there wasn't any interest in it. This was one of many items included in the exhibit. The exhibit was from Thomas Edison's lab over in Menlo Park…apparently, Thomas Edison was made aware of its existence near Roswell, New Mexico, between one hundred fifty and two hundred years ago. A scientist named Leonard Vincy found his notes in a mysterious container a year ago. He wanted see if it was considered important by introducing it to other scientists and to the public, but again there was no interest."

Starion was confused, but sensed the old woman was pushing him forward somehow with a compelling look.

CHAPTER 27

WHEN THE lady left, Starion asked Mary, "Where is this Roswell?"

"It is in the southwest part of the United States."

On their way out, they passed by an old bookshelf containing many tattered books. On top was a sign: "From Thomas Edison's Personal Library." Some titles included *Fundamentals of Electricity*, *The Combustion Engine*, *The Steam Engine*, *Earth's Elements*, *Calculus*, *Physics*, *and Engineering*.

Admiring the old books, Starion observed something he couldn't believe. He looked again and again. He put his hand up to his chin. He pulled the book out of the top shelf and read it aloud. *"Anciente Evion Adventura~Hero."* It had the same mythological creatures on the cover as his own book. He opened it. It was in the Earth language.

Starion anxiously panned the room, bewildered. How had it gotten there?

"What's wrong?" Mary asked.

"This book is not supposed to be here."

"Why—what's it about?"

Starion noticed a security guard standing near the door looking sternly at him, along with the man in the hat.

He put the book back while grabbing Mary's arm. He guided her out the door and swiftly through a large group of students, then around a corner.

"What's wrong?" she asked.

"Someone is following me."

Mary burst out laughing. "Let's have dinner."

"OK," he answered quietly, hurrying her along after a glance behind him.

Once at the restaurant, Starion's mind was racing. Now he knew where the braydium was, but since he couldn't make a new magnifier or new cells, how was he going to get home to help his fellow Evions? And he still couldn't figure out how the book could have gotten into Earth's famous inventor's bookcase. Finally, who was this man chasing him?

There was one thing he did know: He was falling in love with Mary.

After the wine was brought and they had ordered dinner, Mary asked, "So where do you come from again?"

Starion started to think of another lie but couldn't anymore. He reached over to hold Mary's hands. "Mary, I have a secret to tell you."

"OK, what?" she asked.

He took a deep breath. "Do you remember when I told you I was from another planet?"

"Yes."

"Well…it's true."

Mary's expression changed from a loving look to a more serious one. "This isn't funny anymore, Starion," she told him.

"Please believe me; I need to tell someone on Earth. Please believe me."

Mary seemed to recognize how serious he was. "OK, what planet are you from?"

"I'm from the planet Evion."

She continued to listen but took her hands away. She took a drink of water. She looked around as if to make sure she wasn't alone. "I'm listening," she said.

Starion thought she believed him and continued quietly, "Mary, my planet's sun is dying…I traveled back in time to find the mineral braydium, which is necessary for our people to store energy. We ran out of it. I need it so I can save the last remaining Evions from extinction. There are probably only a few thousand of us left. There was another massive flare and quake when I left. It destroyed the farthest planet...how that is possible, I don't know. But thankfully my children, friends, and the rest of my people are still OK. I was going to use Earth's braydium to create more power so I could travel back to Evion with new energy, and then bring our people here to Earth...if we would be welcome."

Starion felt like a load had been lifted from his shoulders. He couldn't quite interpret what Mary was thinking...

Starion decided to take off his gloves and hat. When he did so, he saw a surprised and frightened look on Mary's face.

Staring at his six fingers and odd ear shape, she commented, "How interesting, Starion...you are a very unique person. How wonderful." She began to inch away from him.

"Look at this, Mary," he said, pulling down his collar to show her his DTI implant.

"How nice...I have to go the restroom," she told him, leaving the table.

Starion felt the urge to use the restroom, too, so he walk-glided back to the men's room at a more leisurely pace. On his way, he heard Mary's voice when another lady walked out of the women's restroom. Curious, he opened the door slightly and heard her talking on her wrist phone.

"Please come over here to the restaurant. This man needs help...Put it this way: he thinks he is from another planet."

Starion hurried into the men's bathroom before Mary could find him listening. Inside, he felt devastated and humiliated. This beautiful woman believed he was crazy. Now what was he going to do?

As Starion paced the bathroom, he finally decided there was only one thing to do. He hustled back out to the table, but instead of sitting down, he leaned over and whispered, "Mary, I know what I told you was a shock, and I'm sorry...in your circumstances I would have been skeptical too."

Holding out his hand, he continued, "If you will trust me

this one time, it will completely blow your mind about everything...your planet...your sun...the universe. Please," he pleaded with her, remembering the term "blow your mind" in his scanning of something called "The Turbulent 1960s."

"OK, but let's finish up here first," Mary lied.

"No, I know you have someone coming here. I overheard you on your Earth phone."

Starion took out his watch and put it on. She looked bewildered at the small protruding image of Earth. He stared deeply into her eyes, attempting to use telepathy even though he knew it wouldn't work. He kept saying softly, *Please trust me...please trust me...we have a lot to offer...*

He sent an image of the v-breaker and his large dying planet. He didn't know if it worked or not.

She finally succumbed. "Alright."

Starion and Mary leapt into a cab outside, the waiter running after them. Starion guided the driver as close as possible to where Starion believed he wouldn't be seen maneuvering his craft out of the river. He told the driver to stop, then handed him seven hundred-dollar bills. The driver saw the watch. "Hey, is that a Rolex or an I-watch?"

Starion stepped out of the car, along with a reluctant Mary. When the cab sped off, he led her down the bank of a river.

Starion made sure no one else could was near, then pointed his two fingers, pulling the v-breaker up and out onto the grassy bank.

He could see Mary was in disbelief, as if she could not comprehend what she was seeing. All of a sudden, her knees buckled, and she fainted.

Starion caught her to break her fall and laid her down softly. He glide-ran over to the water, cupped some in his hands, then splashed it on her face. In a few moments, she came to and sat up, glaring at the glass-looking spaceship.

"Is this a movie?" she asked.

Starion replied, "No, it isn't. I'm sorry to say this is real."

Mary stood up, staring at Starion in a way she had never

looked at him before. "You *are* from a different planet," she said, trying to catch her breath.

He took her reluctant shaking hand. He guided her into the v-breaker. Once inside, Starion threw the gloves and hat over onto a seat. He didn't want to wear them anymore.

Then, looking through the clear ship, he suddenly noticed an I-jet flyer traveling fast toward them.

Starion could see it was the man who had been following him.

CHAPTER 28

STARION SHOT up immediately with his silent v-breaker, leaving the man in pursuit behind.

Mary appeared mesmerized by the panoramic view out the clear spaceship as it jettisoned upward. She watched her New York City home, along with that part of America, gradually become smaller.

"This is incredible," she burst out. "Our space shuttles must create enough g-force to break out of the atmosphere, but you do it so easily."

Starion took her on a brisk orbit around the Earth. Mary viewed her planet from a completely foreign perspective. She witnessed the brilliant stars and nearby planets through the ship's clear exterior.

"This is simply amazing, Starion...simply amazing. How can your ship's exterior withstand the zero gravity?"

"It is made from braydium."

"Oh, I see—that element you are looking for."

"Do you want to see your moon up close?" he asked, glancing at and disregarding the low gauge yet again.

"Well, of course...but how much time would that take?"

"I'll have you back for the dinner you missed—how about that?"

"OK," she answered, moving close to Starion and putting her hand on his shoulder.

Starion, happy with her touch, traveled around the moon twice, glancing down to happily see the signal booster still flashing its small green light. This reminded him of Deon and his discovery of the hyper-asteroid that would pass nearby Earth in twenty years. Should he mention this to Mary he wondered? Since Deon believed it would safely miss, he decided not to.

Each time they came around the moon and could see Earth, Mary shook her head overwhelmed.

Starion raced back above Earth. He stopped one hundred e-miles away, avoiding any s-rovers. The two of them stared at the magnificent, slowly revolving blue planet. Mary, to Starion's surprise and satisfaction, reached over to hold his hand. Starion looked out in the opposite direction. "That must be the next planet closest to you."

"Yes, that is Mars," she told him. "It was named after a Greek god. There are many old stories about Mars."

"Yes, I scanned in some of your old mythical stories of gods, goddesses, and heroes—I mean, I read them. Do you like to scan—I mean, read—the old mythical stories?" he asked, catching himself.

"Yes, I do."

"Do you believe them?" he asked.

"Well, as far as historical fact, I didn't used to, but now that I am with an alien in space looking down on Earth, I am not so sure. But I can tell you, if the story has a positive metaphorical message, I believe it."

Starion proudly replied, "Yes, I know what you mean. I was recently introduced to many of our ancient stories. I don't know about your people, but ours have lost the ability to catch the meaning of a metaphor…if I could entice my people to read the old stories instead of scanning them, I think I could bring them out of sleep-mode."

"Bring them out of what?" she asked.

Changing the subject, Starion asked, "Speaking of that, you never did answer my question—why are your religions and psychiatric hospitals in separate buildings?"

"Well, that is hard to answer," she said, scrunching her face in deep thought. "I guess part of it is because we have evolved so rapidly in terms of technology and population growth, along with the sudden expansion and introduction of different cultures to each other. The religions or traditions passed down through many generations offer some comfort and therefore serve a vital function in our society. These old passed-down stories were and are necessary to help us through these changes throughout different stages of our lives."

Mary paused for a moment, looking at Earth, but then continued. "For some people, life's struggles have been too hard to live with. Therefore the old stories don't work for them, so they need professional medical help. Like the mental institution across the street from my institute."

"I've noticed your culture has many different art forms. Are they all necessary?"

"Why, yes...it is the ultimate task of the artist, the writer, the teacher, the mentor, the philosopher, the hero in the stories, or for that matter every individual on Earth—"

"You mean in the universe." Starion interrupted.

"Yes—to delve deep inside themselves. There, he or she must face difficult problems, clarify them, then somehow eliminate them, or at least learn to live with them. And if he or she ultimately wins the inward battles, there is a renewed fresh new perspective view of life. Then it is the responsibility of the person to tell everyone about it through philosophy, religion, psychology, and the art forms. Then, hopefully, the message can help people live a life under any circumstances."

"That's it—and then dreams can be realized," Starion agreed, remembering his wife's last words. He also finally understood the messages of the Earth books, music, movies, and paintings. "You Earth people sure place a lot of importance on your art forms—but maybe you should think about combining your psychiatric hospitals, ancient stories, and religions. Maybe one can help the other."

"Interesting..." she pondered for a moment. "I can tell you what I have found in my own inward journey. The most important virtue of them all is forgiveness. When my husband and several family members died of cancer, I had to forgive God. And I had to forgive myself."

Mary, beaming at the large swirling blue planet, continued. "What are your dreams, Starion?"

"Mine are the same as my wife's. With her dying breath, she told me to bring my family and people here to Earth. I want my children to be able to follow their dreams."

Starion asked. "What are your dreams, Mary?"

"Well...I have many, but my main dream is for my people to cure cancer. Cancer has taken not only my husband, but my father and my brother. Then my next dream would be raising a family. I would like to have a child, even though I know that's impossible. I have been told I can't conceive."

With a discouraged look, Mary changed the subject. "By the way, Starion, why were you so surprised by that book at the museum?"

"Because it is from my planet—and to my knowledge, no one from Evion has ever visited here. Deon, who is the head of my research team, did just recently visit, but I know he would not have left it here. Anyway, he was here twenty years from now."

Then, while putting his sixth finger and his thumb up to his chin, something dawned on him.

"The only possibility would have been if Vincion had visited here about one hundred Evion years ago, or two hundred Earth years ago—our days on Evion are longer than yours—but I studied all of his research notes, and there isn't any record of him visiting this part of the galaxy. It couldn't have been him."

"Who was that?" she asked.

"He was one of Evion's greatest inventors, scholars, forward-thinking scientists, and philosophers. He was the first to recognize the signs that our sun was dying, but no one believed him. Without permission, he started looking for another planet to emigrate to. After looking for several years, he mysteriously vanished. I was able to analyze some of his manual writings of his search results, which helped me and Deon search for a viable planet. But I never found anything related to a visit to Earth."

Starion gazed out into the universe then continued, "He was also misunderstood about other ideas and concepts. For example, he created a way for people on Evion to view live signals from our space engineers using their DNA. He was also trying to create the fifth dimension, which would have allowed us to interact with live signals and broadcasts. I felt a lot of kinship with him, because I feel like I have been misunderstood my whole life as well."

"You will fit right in on this planet," Mary comforted him. "Wow—your people are way ahead of us."

"I'm not so sure of that, Mary. As in the old stories, we are missing something."

Mary changed the subject again. "You have seen Earth twenty years in the future—can you tell me what it will be like?"

"Well…" Starion remembered just before leaving for Earth, when he'd heard the newscast of the imminent attack. He couldn't bring himself to tell her. "I am forbidden to change history. That is a promise I made to my fellow Evions," he declared.

Starion took the v-breaker to Mars, circled it twice, and then stopped above the large red planet. They both visually inspected the mysterious surface.

"Has there been any life on this planet?" Starion asked.

"As I said, there have been many stories, but scientifically, we don't know yet. We can't travel around as easily as you can. We have sent probes here, and four years ago, two men landed, then returned to Earth. It took them over three months to get here and another three months to get back. In their research, they found no evidence of life."

"IS bank, analyze the surface of this planet and tell me if there has been any life in its planetary history."

The IS unit performed its analysis and had just started to reveal its results when Mary put her hands up to her ears. "I don't want to know—I don't want to know!" she exclaimed.

"IS unit, stop...I'm sorry."

Starion moved closer to her, held her face in his hands, and gently kissed her.

To Starion's dismay, the IS warning blurted again. "*Energy low . . . Return to Evion.*"

"What is that?" she asked.

"Oh...nothing to worry about," he lied.

Within moments, he flew the ship back above Earth's orbit again. Starion stopped so they both could watch the blue planet slowly turn while using minimal energy.

"She sure is beautiful," Starion said.

"She sure is," Mary answered.

"I hope you all know how lucky you are," Starion told her.

They sat close together in two of the passenger seats while gazing out.

Starion motioned with his hand to an e-screen on the side of the craft. Mary watched in bewilderment as he brought up the image of Evion and its dying sun in the 4-D elliptical format. Then he brought up an I-spacer image of the ancient healthy Evion right next to it. Both protruded out toward them.

"How did you do that?"

He beamed. "That's nothing—watch this," he said, grabbing the two images while expanding and twirling them.

"This I-spacer image shows present-day Evion, and the other one is our old, healthy, vital planet. This is what will happen to your planet when your sun dies or if you don't take care of it," he told her, pointing to the present-day Evion I-spacer.

Then he created another I-spacer on a new e-screen of the anticipated trajectory of Evion he had shown everyone back home.

"This is what will happen to Evion within three Evion days, when I get back...*if* I can get back," he told her sadly. "That is, if Evion is still there. Logic says I am back in time twenty Earth years, and therefore time is not moving on Evion...but it has been hard to use logic in these circumstances."

"You can't and shouldn't suppress your emotions, Starion."

"What?"

"Twenty Earth years…do you mean you know the future of Earth?" she hinted again.

"Yes, but I can't tell you anything. It is forbidden by Evion law."

Starion brought up another I-spacer while he moved the two others of Evion over so they were hanging in air. Again, Mary was astonished. This new image was of Aphelia and his two children.

"This is—was—my wife…and here are my children," he wept.

"What a nice family. Your wife is so pretty," Mary said tenderly. "How did she die?"

"There was an Evion solar flare quake and she died in my arms at the hospital."

"I am so sorry. At least you were able to say good-bye, like I was able to do with Charlie."

He closed up all the images and turned to Mary. "Mary, I feel so guilty and selfish. It's all my fault."

Mary comforted Starion with hug and a kiss. "You are only human…I mean, Evion," she corrected herself.

Starion pointed, starting up a song from his new library of Earth music. He chose a song about two lovers at sea.

Unlike his encounter with Amelia in San Francisco, Starion felt this was different. He was in love. He felt like he had found his soul mate—a new term he had learned on Earth.

The v-breaker hovered above the blue swirling Earth with the song still playing in the background.

Starion gazed into her clear green eyes, wondering what she was thinking. His desire for her was overwhelming. In a passionate kiss, with bodies locked together, they fell to the floor.

CHAPTER 29

SEVERAL HOURS had passed. Starion noticed the Earth had rotated farther than he had planned.

"I'm sorry, Mary—your sun's rays are way beyond New York."

"That's OK."

The two sat together, gazing at Earth. "Look at that mystical blue planet," Starion said, treasuring the moment, and he remembered the ancient book he had been reading back on Evion with the similar title.

Mary put her head on his shoulder.

Starion started to think that if he couldn't leave Earth after all, it might not be so bad starting over here. Ardia had been right. The universal love and life force is very strong.

But then he remembered the I-spacers he had just seen of his family and Evion.

At that moment, he heard the familiar annoying beeping and monotone voice: "*Energy low . . . Final warning.*"

"I need to find enough energy to get back home," he confessed sadly to Mary.

"Yes . . . I know," she sadly answered. "Do you have any ideas?"

Starion stood up and pace-glided the ship. Mary was fascinated by the ease with which he was able to move. He put his hand up to his chin. After a few moments, his eyes lit up. "When I was in San Francisco, I was introduced to Earth's energy sources—specifically hydrogen, which is used in your rockets. I was told there were hydrogen rocket boosters at what is called the Kennedy Space Center."

"I thought this braydium would help you," she asked.

Starion pointed to the pile of glass-looking pieces near the side of the ship. "The braydium mold-casts to create a new magnifier and new cells were destroyed on the way here, along with the old magnifier."

Starion pointed to the four nearly empty star-power cells in the energy compartment of the v-breaker.

"How do these derive their energy?" she asked, touching one gingerly.

"From our sun…and from your sun, too. I had hoped, anyway."

"Can't you manufacture new molds?"

"It took our scientists five hundred years to perfect the cast long ago. The schematics were destroyed in a mass deletion of our IS banks."

"And you think one of our rocket boosters might get you home?"

Starion shrugged his shoulders.

"You will succeed, Starion. I know you will."

"How can you be so sure?"

"Call it a sixth sense."

Starion began pacing again. "This will be a huge risk for you as well."

"I like the word 'risk,' Starion. Don't worry about me."

"Can you show me where this Kennedy Space Center is?" he asked, pointing to the I-spacer of the Earth-globe.

Admiring the floating image, she said, "Of course. By the way, you're lucky we started up the shuttle program again. It was stopped for many years."

"Why?"

"I don't know…I don't know…"

"We will have to be careful…someone knows I'm here, Mary."

"Oh—you're the strange occurrence I have been reading about in the paper?"

"Yes…and remember that man with the black hat?"

Mary nodded, looking uncomfortable.

"Also, many of your aircraft have been after me."

Starion accelerated at a direct angle to Florida, keeping a keen eye on the airspace and the gauge at the same time.

He flew above the southern and southeast part of Florida until they found the large launchpad with a shuttle ready for launch. They hovered safely above it, as the sun had just set on that part of Earth.

He pulled out his spacegazer and found two large buildings he hoped were large enough to house rocket boosters. Next to these, he saw large amounts of spewing liquid hydrogen from a vertical standing booster. It had a v-shaped aircraft attached to it.

"I wonder if they have a spare."

"I would think they would."

"I feel bad that I am going to take it. And I don't want you to get in trouble, Mary."

"I pay my taxes. Don't worry about it."

"What are taxes?" he asked.

"Good question," she responded. "What's your plan, Starion?"

"I think we should land and find a booster. If there is one, hopefully we can latch it onto the bottom of the v-breaker. If we can do that, I will bring it to the moon, strap it on more carefully there, and then use it to get home."

Mary kissed him on his neck, just missing his DTI. "What is that?" she asked.

"That's for data transfers and communication."

"When you come back, you will have to hide it when you introduce yourselves to our leaders. And speaking of your return, if I am still here in twenty years, find me and I can help you."

"You will be here ... I know it, Mary," he vowed, hugging her tightly. "And by the way, it will be twenty years for you. For me, if we make it back, it will be only a few days."

Then, without warning, they felt the craft slowly being pulled downward. Starion opened the floor and took each of the four star-power cells out. He shook them again as before and then placed them back. He felt the ship stabilize. "Whew…that bought us some time."

He descended and landed. Hand in hand, they quickly searched both hangars, checking carefully to make sure no one was around. Finally, in the second building, they found a large rocket booster lying horizontally on a large V-shaped metal holder with a sign labeled "Spare."

"This will work," Starion shouted.

"Look—this roof opens up," Mary yelled back as she pushed an "Open" button she had found on the wall.

"OK, all we need now is something to help strap my ship on top of it."

They searched the large warehouse for a short time without success. They stood there in frustration, trying to think of other possibilities. Then Starion took a closer look at the booster. He noticed the large, cylindrical booster had two L-shaped hooks on it where the shuttle hooked on.

He pondered for a moment. "Yes…I think it might work."

"What?" Mary asked.

"I think I can latch it on the bottom hatch that was used long ago for us Evions to bring our luggage on long trips."

Starion ran outside. "Open the roof, Mary!"

Mary opened it while Starion hurried outside. He maneuvered the v-breaker down into the hangar, hovering just above the rocket. It was at least eight times longer than his v-breaker and as wide as the ship's body. He guided the ship down so the L-hooks on the rocket were now just inside the bottom hatch. He closed it.

"Let's get out of here," he hollered, hoisting Mary up and in over the cylinder.

He transported the booster up out of the large hangar. Glancing below, he saw a brightly lit area that stored ten-foot sections of steel girders. He figured these long metal pieces were used to build the vertical launchpad of the shuttle.

He softly landed the large and long booster in a horizontal position, with his v-breaker sitting on top. Mary watched in amazement while he opened the back hatch and then jumped down. From several feet away, he used two fingers to guide each large, heavy steel girder back into the cargo bay. They were so long they reached up near the front of the spaceship and almost touched the v-panel.

When he jumped back up, Starion noticed Mary's mouth hanging open. He knew he had to say something.

"We have a thing with metals."

"Oh."

Without warning, a man with a different hat and uniform stumbled upon them. "Hey...hey! Stop!"

CHAPTER 30

STARION CLOSED the hatch, then hauled the heavily loaded v-breaker straight up into space and over to the moon.

He landed on the surface next to the signal booster. He unlatched the rocket booster and then landed the v-breaker next to it. He turned on the v-air threshold so Mary had ample air. Putting on his suit over his Earth clothes, he guided the large steel girders out through the back hatch. He hurried back in, taking off his suit.

At that moment, the gauge beeped again. "*Star-power energy empty.*"

Starion shook the four cells one last time, hoping it would help. The needle moved slightly.

"Take me home, Starion. You are running out of fuel…and if you're going to leave; do it now or else it will be too painful for both of us."

He was saddened. He had to leave his new love. He didn't want to lose her. He also could only hope he had enough energy to travel to this Roswell to load up on braydium.

He flew the v-breaker directly above the New York coast.

This time, he landed farther north than where he had landed before. He was worried the man with the hat could still be lurking around.

It was dark, but the sky was lit up with galaxies, stars, and planets when he parked the craft on the beach. They stepped out hand in hand.

"Are you going to be OK, Mary? Will you be able to get home from here?"

"Yes, I can call a cab from my wrist phone."

They hugged and kissed. Mary turned to leave. "I love you, Starion, and I know your dream will come true...I will see you in twenty years."

"I love you, too, but remember—it won't be twenty years for me. It will only be a short period of time. It is only you that will have to wait...and I hope your dreams come true, Mary."

"Are you going to have enough power to get to Roswell and load up some braydium, and then travel to the moon?"

"Yes," Starion answered, hiding his worry.

Mary started to leave.

"Wait an Earth minute," Starion said, pulling a copy of the book his daughter had put back together back home, *Anciente Evion Adventura~Hero*. He handed it to her.

Remembering Mary's dream she had just told him regarding curing cancer, Starion stared intently into her eyes, concentrating on the image of body S-ray. Mary trembled from his penetrating thoughts, but he couldn't tell if she had connected. Then Starion decided, as long as he was at it, he would try to send her another message: he was going to send her information on the hydrogen engine and the imminent attack in twenty years.

He understood he wasn't supposed to interfere with Earth history, but if he were to connect with her telepathically, he decided it would be all right. The humans didn't know how to perform telepathy, so it would be just like the old stories, when the hero was inspired by a magical aid.

Am I a magical aid now?

He tried again, and this time, he knew for sure nothing happened. He couldn't sense any connection. He shook his head. Maybe his new emotions including his love for Mary were affecting his ability? After all, his people back home only recently obtained the ability due to circumstances.

He had also wanted to tell her about the nuclear test flight disaster ten years from now that Deon had found out about. He tried again, but it was no use.

Just then, he heard through the hatch, "*Final warning. Two minutes to shut-down.*"

He couldn't try to connect anymore; he had to leave. Mary was still dazed as they kissed and embraced for a few more moments. Starion turned her around, pointing her on her way while she remained slightly hypnotized.

Starion sadly watched her walk away, suddenly sneezing. He watched her vanish into the darkness. He thought a quote from his Earth scanning: "She vanished like the substance of a dream."

When he started on his way back to the ship, he heard a constant beeping. He had only a short time. He hopped in, opened the compartment, and shook the four cells again. The gauge needle didn't move at all this time.

He had to turn his attention to the task ahead. He needed to load up with braydium at this Roswell and then head back to the moon.

He quickly found Roswell on the Earth globe and flew there instantly.

While hovering a mile above, he shouted, "IS unit, locate braydium."

Within moments, an I-spacer exposed a brown substance within the image.

"Land near this element."

The IS unit analyzed the surface below then landed the ship. Even though it had been dark when he left Mary, this part of Earth still had a hint of light on the horizon.

Starion hopped out and opened up the back hatch. He grabbed a shovel and heaved as much braydium inside as fast as he could.

Breathing heavily from his refreshed but still malnourished lungs and lack of physical labor, he suddenly heard the roar of aircraft above him.

He hopped in and launched upward, but the limited power slowed him down. The sleek aircraft were right behind him.

This time they fired at him. He felt several shells hit the ship, but luckily they bounced off without inflicting any damage.

With all his might, he shook the four cells again. Nothing happened. Unknowingly a small amount of braydium dust fell from his hands onto top of the cells. The needle moved. He was able to propel instantly out into Earth's orbit, but he still heard the worrisome beeping.

There he could see the frustrated squadron circling as high as they could below him.

On this trip to the moon, Starion traveled by the orbiting satellites. He spotted a large object. He pulled out his space-gazer and could see the emblem "International Space Station." Then he saw a face inside a small window looking his way.

When he reached the moon, he landed on top of the large white rocket booster. He hooked on, admiring the NASA emblem on the side this time.

He hauled the booster up a few feet and hovered there. He put on his space suit, turned on the v-air threshold, opened the back hatch, and then jumped down onto the surface, where he maneuvered the steel girders underneath the rocket. He stopped for a moment, deciding where to point them. He moved over to the signal booster and turned on the laser ray, like he had done when he placed it there. Then he eyeballed the same direction the signal booster ray was pointing out into the galaxy toward Evion, while adjusting the steel girders. When he had matched the ray the best he could, he lowered the v-breaker and booster on top of the girders.

He jumped back up over the large cylinder, climbed inside, and shut the hatch. He was just about to order the IS unit to shut off the v-air threshold when everything went dead. He felt the ship adjust slightly.

He had to hope the ship was pointed in the right direction.

Then, suddenly frustrated, Starion hit his hand against his head. "Ouch! Son of a ..." he exclaimed, repeating something he'd heard a man say on Earth.

He had forgotten to figure out a way to launch the rocket.

He sat there in the dark. Even though the tank was full of fresh compressed Earth air, the hyper-fan stopped pumping. And because he hadn't shut off the v-air threshold in the back bay area, which still had the vacuum, he had even less air than normal.

No. This can't be the end.

He had accomplished so much. All he needed was a spark to ignite the rocket boosters—but how?

He peered up into the sky for inspiration. Searching, he found the constellation Prometheus, which he had learned was an Earth myth about a man who stole fire.

Then he remembered the book of matches he had put in his pocket at the bookstore.

He pulled them out and stumble-glided past the empty passenger seats, bumping into them in the dark. He climbed on top of the braydium he had loaded and opened up the hatch. All air in the ship had now vanished. He stood at the back edge of the ship, where he could see the bottom five booster fuel holes.

He realized the matches wouldn't work in a vacuum, but he had to try. He figured, if he could just keep a match lit after throwing it near one of the rocket fuel boosters, maybe he could perform a miracle—a new word he had learned in his readings.

He tried for eighteen of the twenty matches. No luck. There wasn't any oxygen to burn.

Down to a few breaths left, Starion closed his eyes in the deepest meditation he had ever performed in his life. His concentrated deep into his newly found soul. He thought about everything at once: his family, his planet, the old Evion stories, Mary, and Earth, along with Earth's old stories and art forms. He made a wish like some of the heroes did in the old stories. He opened his eyes. He threw the lit match down into the fuel holes. It ignited the rocket, startling him. He quickly closed the back hatch in happy amazement and then glided up to the front.

The ship accelerated while his instruments somehow lit up.

The inside filled up with Earth's air from the internal air tank and pump. He didn't fully understand how this was all working, but it didn't matter.

As Starion had done when he left Evion for Earth, he held his finger on the screen to fool the IS unit into surpassing the speed of light. It worked. The craft gradually sped up to twenty times the speed of light. He had to hope the Earth's rocket had enough power, and that he was on the right course.

Now, all Starion could see were streaks of light. And everything now depended on fate.

He wished he could have connected with Mary or anyone on Earth about the impending energy problem they would encounter. He should have given them the necessary hydrogen and solar technology. He had also wanted to inform them of the nuclear disaster in ten Earth years.

Suddenly, he had an idea. If he were successful in creating new star power and persuading his fellow Evions to migrate to Earth, he would come back in time again. *Why would it matter when I come back?*

Streaking across the galaxy, he was now in the stage of the ancient stories when the adventurer returned with a new or forgotten message of the life force. But what were these mysterious life force clues—and did he have one? He also remembered Ardia saying there were other types of adventures. One was redemption. Was he trying to redeem himself for failing to save the sun? Maybe it was both redemption *and* finding a life force revelation?

Missing his Earth clothes, he took off his suit, exposing them again. He pace-glided the v-breaker floor thinking about everything. Along with all his new emotions, he felt both cold and hot at the same time.

CHAPTER 31

A SHORT while later he started to see familiar star systems and nebulas. He prayed with his hands with his head down that his children, friends, and fellow Evions were still safe, just as he had seen the congregation in the church do, along with the small vigil at the burning home.

First, he saw the plasmic sun, still spewing out solar flares. Then, when he traveled closer, he searched for the farthest of the planets, Sagion. But then he remembered it had exploded while he was on his way to Earth. Then he saw Galion with its red rings. Hope crept back.

Please be there…please be there…

Finally, his eyes as focused as possible, he could see his old and devastated planet Evion. Nearby was its eerily reddish moon. He was so happy he was beside himself. His heart raced. He performed the new Earth gestures he had learned. First he did the thumbs-up, then, seeing a reflection of himself on the outer shell, he held his arm up and slapped his six fingered hand against the reflected hand.

"Awesome"…"Cool!"

First he would see if everyone was safe, and then he would use his orbit tester. If he was right, he would still have three days to persuade everyone to emigrate to Earth. But before that, he would manufacture a new magnifier and star-power cells from the only remaining braydium mold-casts at his house. And even though he had fresh braydium, he had to hope the dying sun's rays were powerful enough. But he figured at least he wouldn't have to keep trying to pump different gaseous mixtures into the upper chamber anymore.

Starion believed Evion appeared the same from this distance, but he wouldn't feel comfortable until he was able to talk to his children, Ardia, and Deon.

Just then, the annoying warning sound started beeping again. He hoped he had enough power to land safely with this large Earth rocket booster he was hauling. If it should run out of fuel, he would be dead in the air and pulled into Evion's surface. He thought how ironic this was. Only two Earth days ago, he had wanted to crash-land on Earth, but now he felt rejuvenated. *We have a good chance to succeed.*

He sped by the red lit-up moon. He knew long ago it was the first destination his people traveled to beyond Evion. Passing by, he could feel it's lonely gravity tug.

When he was one hundred e-miles above Evion, he noticed a strange form floating ahead of him. It looked like a person, but when he examined it closer, he could see it was an IS-man. *Hmm...I wonder how that got here. It must have been an IS-naught, used long ago for certain space tasks.* Even though he realized it was a robot, he felt sorry for it.

When entering the thin Evion atmosphere, he was struck by how different it was from Earth's thick atmosphere. However, he believed the thinner air would allow the craft to travel much easier and quieter, and therefore use less energy. It made him feel better that he could expect to make a safe landing.

Approaching his home, he hoped no one could see him with this large rocket attached. Then, he saw the whole east side of Alexon had been destroyed. There was a large crater-looking hole with smoke billowing up from it. He felt terrible. His heart sank.

This is what must have happened when I left...my children.

His worry erupted, and even though he was desperately low on energy, he headed toward his new home, still carrying the booster.

Fortunately, he could see his home still intact. He wanted

to land and go inside, but he knew he had to hurry back to the e-center.

He did the next best thing, calling his children on his DTI. "Contact e6218 and e6008, please," he spoke into his DTI.

Much to Starion's surprise, both children answered right away, but the sound was full of static.

Bria was the most enthusiastic about her father's return, while Dustion sounded glad but didn't display as much emotion.

"Hello, Dad!" Bria beamed. "What's that beeping noise?"

"Hello," Dustion answered in a quiet voice.

"Hello, my children. How are you two?" Starion grinned happy to hear his children's voices as well as the Evion language again.

"We are fine," they both replied in unison.

"I missed you two so much," he said with a tone he didn't recall ever using in front of his children before. "I will be home shortly, OK? I love you both very much."

There was a pause, but then his daughter finally reciprocated. "I love you too, Dad."

Dustion didn't say anything.

Starion circled above the e-center and called Deon. "Deon, I'm back. Open the dome."

Deon replied immediately. "Got you, Starion; we have been waiting for you. What is that thing you are bringing with you?"

Starion brought the ship in for a landing after the dome opened up. He realized he couldn't land normally because the thrusters of the rocket were propelling him. He pointed the front of the ship down at a forty-five-degree angle and flew down into the e-center hangar. Then he had to make two spiraling 360-degree turns to land. He hit hard, skidding on the ground. The thrusters went dead.

The Earth rocket was lying horizontally on the ground with the v-breaker on top. Deon closed the roof.

Starion sighed while bringing up an I-spacer image of Mary and Earth on one e-screen, along with his children and Aphelia on another. But after a short moment, the ship went totally dark. He had run out of power. But then his watch lit up the small protruding image of the Evion from the moon.

He sighed. *Whew—not a moment too soon.*

Starion was as happy as he could be. He grabbed a handful of braydium and put it in his pocket. He also took his orbit tester, but left his shroud. He jumped down over the curved rocket cylinder to the ground. He immediately glide-ran to Ardia and Deon, hugging them so hard he surprised them. He nearly knocked them off their gliders. They had never been hugged like that before.

Starion was aware they were staring at him with his Earth clothes and hat. Also, Deon couldn't stop looking at the large, long, white, cylindrical rocket booster.

Ardia telepathically asked, *Are you OK?*

"Yes, I feel good…a little tired, but my lungs are much stronger from breathing in all that fresh air—but they need much more," Starion acknowledged, looking around like someone who hadn't seen his home for a long time. "How long was I gone? And what happened when I took off for Earth?"

"You have been gone for about four hours. Zealeon believes we were very lucky. But the whole east side is gone. He thinks we might be down to only five hundred of us left."

"Yes…I saw the devastation and could feel the thinner air when I landed."

After taking two deep breaths, he continued, "From a population of five billion one hundred years ago to a million a year ago…and now down to five hundred today? Why isn't it clear we need to get out of here?" Starion proclaimed and continued, "Oh, you two…I wish you could have seen what I witnessed and experienced. I know we could survive on Earth. I just know it. And by the way—thanks for the message. How did you do it?"

Deon was still inspecting the large rocket booster. "I was familiar with the electronics of the signal booster. So I plugged in the same coordinates I gave you to travel to Earth, and I tricked the IS unit here on Evion to send the message twenty times the speed of light back in time to that part of the galaxy."

"Why didn't I think of that?" Starion said, not telling him that he had done the same with the v-breaker.

"Tell us about Earth," Deon inquired. "Did you find any braydium?"

"Yes...I did," he said, pulling some out of his pocket, "and the rest of it is in the back of the v-breaker. But when the solar explosion hit Evion along with the whole solar system on my way out, my ship went into a tailspin and the braydium mold-casts along with my magnifier were shattered. Luckily, I have the last pair at my home."

"What is that big cylinder for?" Deon asked again.

"What about the humans?" Ardia added immediately.

Starion sniffled, feeling the curious sensation of his nose beginning to run. Deon and Ardia didn't seem to notice.

"This is what I had to use to get back here to Evion," he told Deon. "Ardia, the humans are much more vibrant but also more complicated than I imagined; however, I truly believe we could cohabitate with them."

"Did you like their music like I did?" Deon asked.

"Oh...I loved their music, Deon, and all their art forms."

Starion pulled out his orbit tester and pointed it at the sun. After a short moment, he blurted out, "Oh, no—it looks like our g-force is up to *nine* now...I thought we would have three days until we reached the point of no return, but now it looks like it is down to two days or less. We'll have to hurry."

"We have a couple of major problems, Starion," Ardia informed him.

"What?"

"First of all, Glenion, who traveled with Deon to Earth is sick and in the hospital. And whatever he has, Judion's wife caught, too. They are both bedridden. Judion is awfully upset. He thinks it is something Glenion brought back from Earth."

"How can he be so sure?" Starion asked, sniffling again.

"I don't know."

"What else? You said a couple of problems."

This time Deon answered. "When you left, Judion must have seen you fly out into our solar system...and then he noticed the v-breaker was missing. When he inquired, we had to tell him...we're so sorry."

"You couldn't help it. But it doesn't matter. Judion won't stop us now."

Then without warning, two Evion men entered and held Starion's arms. His orbit tester fell to the ground.

Ardia yelled, "What's the meaning of this?"

One of the men demanded, "We are arresting Starion and bringing him over to the Audiseum for trial."

While on his forced way out, Starion turned to Deon.

Get the braydium mold-casts from my home and create a new magnifier and star-power cell from the braydium I brought back, then bring them over to the Audiseum.

CHAPTER 32

THE TWO men forcefully brought Starion across the devastated surface and glidewalks to the Audiseum. Without his shroud and hood, Starion felt the blast of hot air heat up his head and body.

Once inside the hot building, the two guided him in front of the sloped seating area. Then they stood near him to guard him.

The hyper-air flow system had stopped working. All three of them started sweating.

Starion watched Evions arrive one by one. They sat down in the steep Evion Audiseum seats scattered all over. Starion noticed it was very quiet. No one was talking. Most went immediately into sleep-mode. From the rest he felt cold stares while the sweat poured down. Some lucky Evions still had their hypercoolers intact. He tried to figure out how Judion had been able to connect with them when he himself couldn't a few days earlier.

Starion didn't know if they were looking at him or at the strange clothes he was still wearing. None peered through their spacegazers upward out the large glass dome.

Still looking at their cold, sullen faces, he started wondering if he should introduce them so suddenly to the human interactions and emotions he had witnessed.

Starion looked for Judion, but he was nowhere to be seen. He searched for his allies, Ardia and Deon, but they were nowhere to be seen, either. Moments later he saw Valkia, her husband Keon, and Quarion arrive together. They sat down in the front row to his left. He was aware the eldest elder, Quarion, along with the tired Valkia from the elder meeting, would still be against him. He didn't know about Valkia's husband or the rest. But there was no sign of Judion yet.

There were now about three hundred Evions scattered throughout the two-thousand-seat bleachers of the Audiseum. It was still eerily quiet. Starion stared sadly at the empty seats, recalling the two giant solar flares, explosions, and quakes that had wiped out the north and east sides of the city.

Finally, Judion glide-ran into the Audiseum carrying an Evion shroud. He pulled back his hood and took off his gloves. Starion and all the Evions watched as Judion glided up to the podium. When he passed by Starion, he didn't even look at him.

Starion asked softly when Judion passed by him, "How's your wife?"

Judion ignored him, proceeding with the meeting. He motioned the two guards to take their seat.

"Everyone, thanks for coming. We will keep this as short as possible in order for you to get back home before it gets too hot...I asked you all here to judge Starion on his treasonous actions by using up valuable energy traveling to Earth."

Judion turned to Starion and threw the shroud over to him. "Put this on."

Moving behind a wall to change clothes, he wondered where Ardia and Deon were. While changing, he glanced at several of the oldest Audiseum's rooms across from him. If he recollected correctly, these rooms housed old artifacts of ancient tools, IS units, and surface vehicles. It reminded him of the museums he had just seen on Earth. When finished, he moved back.

Happily, he saw Deon and Ardia rushing in. Ardia was carrying several tanks of Earth's air. Deon was hauling a brand-new shiny arched star-power magnifier, along with a new uncharged cell. He also had something in his pouch. He almost dropped everything as they set the items down in front of their seats. They briefly glanced at Starion.

Judion continued the meeting, shouting, "Starion stole and used up all our remaining star-power cells to travel to this Earth and back again, bringing with him who knows how many diseases…and I believe he, Ardia, and Deon should be banned."

The synopses of both the ancient Evions stories, along with the human's stories, fired up and gave him strength. Starion decided to put up a fight. "Wait a minute—Ardia and Deon were forced *by me* to perform certain tasks. They are not at fault," he yelled to the crowd.

Ardia and Deon stood up and moved over to Starion, flanking him. Deon carried the magnifier and cell under his arms and managed to reach into his shroud pouch. He handed Starion his orbit tester who put it in his own pouch.

Ardia spoke over Starion and the audience. "That is not true, Starion. Deon and I are on your side. We believe we should migrate to Earth, too."

Both Deon and Ardia gave Starion pained smiles, while a tear came to Starion's eye. He knew that friends coming to one's aid; was prevalent in most of the hero stories.

Judion took control again and glared directly at Starion, even though he was addressing all three. "All three of you are charged with treason. Starion—you purposely ignored the council's voting rights and then visited Earth while using up our remaining energy cells in the process. Is that correct?"

Starion was outraged. "Judion, I have not been stealing the cells…and I have a feeling it has been you all along."

There were several gasps from the audience. A few stood up and yelled, "How could you do that, Starion?"

Starion observed that some of the audience had started to talk to one another. Most, however, had put their heads down while closing their eyes in sleep-mode.

The politically savvy Judion ignored Starion. Holding up his arms to calm the audience, he spoke loudly, "Hold on, everyone…as Evion law states, the accused are allowed to explain their actions."

Starion moved over to the podium, bumping into Judion on purpose. Ardia and Deon followed and stood next to him.

To Starion's left, he noticed the vertical lever that was used long ago to start the large circular metal plate underneath the bleachers. He remembered this allowed the audience to follow the night sky as the planet turned. He reached down, pushing then pulling it back and forth twice. The plate jolted slightly each time. Some Evions opened their eyes, some didn't.

"Wake up, everyone. Wake up. We only have two days left. We must leave Evion now…I may have acted impulsively, and maybe I should have gotten your approval first, but I can tell you I have no regrets. I traveled to Earth to find more braydium."

The old bald Quarion fired back, "Did you find any?"

"Yes. I did. But my magnifier and cell braydium mold-casts, along with my magnifier, were smashed on my way."

Judion raised his head, seeming to sense victory. "A likely story—just like those old mythical stories you keep bringing up."

Deon piped up. "Starion *did* bring back braydium, and here's the proof. Also, we should all try some of Earth's air from these two tanks."

Deon placed the new magnifier in front of the bleachers. Then, looking up through the large glass dome, he adjusted it to the best angle to pull in the dim sun's rays. Then he put the new star-power cell beneath it and adjusted it.

Moments went by. Nothing happened.

Deon adjusted everything again while looking up, trying to match the dim sun's rays. Again there was nothing. Not even a faint yellow ray. Starion found the lever to open the dome. He pushed it. The half-sphere roof opened up so the sun was now shining directly into the magnifier's convex lens. Still there was nothing.

Judion shut the dome.

Starion was devastated. He should have had Deon bring the many flasks of gases to try. *Maybe he could have pumped a gas mixture into the top chamber that might have helped.*

Suddenly he felt a rumble while a woman shouted, "What does all this have to do with our survival here on Evion?"

"Everything, if you still believe the universal life force is in all of us—like I still do, and like my wife did before she died. We must survive! Earth is our only hope. Our trajectory path will fling us into the dying sun within two days," he implored, fighting for air.

Now there was much commotion and chaos while several others came out of sleep-mode. Starion pointed his two fingers and brought up a 4-D I-spacer of the elliptical simulation that anticipated Evion being pulled directly into the sun.

Judion immediately took hold of it and tossed it at a wall, where it broke into specks of light. He brought up his own simulated elliptical path again of Evion slinging around and then safely away from the dying sun. "Nonsense, everyone…we will safely make the elliptical turn away from the sun."

Ardia hustled up to the podium. All Evions were aware of Ardia's wise elder status. She was able to calm them down when she put up her hands. Several of them awoke.

"Please let Starion explain. Please…he's right…can't you feel it? We are hurtling our way into the sun."

Starion observed many could not handle the stress and went into sleep-mode again. Starion threw Judion's image at the same wall he had just done with his image, scattering it apart. Angrily looking at Judion, he brought up the 4-D I-spacers that had been shown in the elder room several days before, of the views of Earth and Evion in relation to each other in the galaxy.

Starion moved the image of the galaxy and then hung it in the air next to the left of the audience. Then he enlarged the I-spacer of Earth and its sun then moved it to the right side of the audience. Finally he created an I-spacer of existing Evion along with its dying sun. He left it on the I-screen but pulled out the 4-D holographic image until it touched the first row of seats. He pointed to the I-spacer to the left with the galaxy view.

"Everyone, this is where Earth is located in relation to Evion." Then, pointing to the right-side I-spacer of Earth and its sun, he yelled, "This is Earth and its healthy powerful sun." Starion increased the size so it was very bright. The Evions in awake-mode had to put up their arms to block the bright light.

Judion yelled, "All right, Starion—what are you trying to do, blind everyone?"

Starion decreased the image and light from Earth's sun while increasing the size of Earth. He articulated, "Can't you see, every-one? This planet has a healthy sun with plenty of vegetation for food and water. I *know* we could survive there. Look at our planet and sun, then look at Earth and its sun...I know it would work."

Quarion stood up from his seat in the audience, turned around, and yelled, "Starion, it doesn't matter; it is too far away. We don't have enough energy to migrate all of us there...especially now that you have used up our last supply of star-power cells. Even though you brought back braydium, it looks like we can't charge new cells."

"*I* didn't use up our supply." Starion slowly shuffle-glided, deep in thought. "Besides, I believe I have a solution that will still allow us all to travel to Earth."

Starion recalled and proceeded to show the image he'd seen at Berkeley of the space shuttle riding out of Earth's atmosphere on the large rocket. "We can use hydrogen fuel technology to bring us all safely to Earth," he concluded.

"Starion," a man yelled, "we trusted you once, when you claimed you could save the sun. Now you think the ancient hydrogen engine can save us? Ha!"

"You disobeyed Evion rules by traveling to Earth...you can't be trusted. You and your hope," a woman scoffed.

Chaos erupted again in the audience. More awoke from their sleep-mode and left the Audiseum. Judion stood nearby with his arms crossed. He strutted up to the podium giving Starion a triumphant glower. "We won't be using our valuable water supply for this crazy, hopeless notion."

Starion's optimism sank. Deon and Ardia looked like they were in stunned disbelief.

Quarion chimed in, "And anyway, hydrogen technology is ancient. That old fuel wouldn't have been powerful enough."

"Yes it would—I used it to travel back from Earth on one of Earth's rocket boosters. Come take a look, everyone…it's down at the e-center!" Starion yelled as loud as he could through the chaos.

Judion countered, shouting, "Everyone, we don't have much more time this morning—it is getting dangerously hot outside. In order to be fair to these three, I want to show you several live views from Earth and also random views from its past. Deon left a spacegazer camera—or what Starion and Deon call their I-mooncam—on this Earth's moon."

Starion trembled, remembering the broadcast of an imminent attack he and Deon had seen just before time traveling to Earth. He expected to see Earth at war with itself, while the 4-D I-spacer appeared with the word "live" in the upper left. He and Deon exchanged worried glances.

Surprisingly, when Judion zoomed in and out, then around the whole planet, Starion couldn't see any sign of trouble. He glanced back to Deon, who shrugged his shoulders.

But when Starion looked back at the image, he realized there *was* something different. He noticed that all the bodies of water—oceans, lakes, and rivers—had less water for some reason.

Judion showed a live view of a large city. Thousands of surface and aircraft vehicles were traveling above and in between the large buildings, with thousands of humans walking the glidewalks.

"Look at this mess, everyone."

CHAPTER 33

STARION EXAMINED the Earth image more closely. He put his six-fingered hand up to his chin. He could see a clear liquid dripping out of the exhaust of one of the surface vehicles. *It looked like . . . water.*

Then he noticed a pumping station like when he was on Earth. This time he saw a sign: "Water: $3.98/Gallon." And another sign: "I-jet Flyer Tanks: $5.78/Tank."

Starion sat back casually, hoping Judion hadn't noticed his reaction. Somehow, he knew the humans had perfected the hydrogen engine before their oil ran out. Earth's history had changed—but how? He believed he hadn't connected with Mary when he tried to show her the hydrogen engine.

Judion changed the subject. "We were able to view Earth's past from the I-mooncam. By the way, Starion and Deon, you are to be commended for your technical expertise . . . this view is much better after you placed your signal booster on this Earth's moon."

Judion twirled his hand counterclockwise one hundred and forty times extremely fast. When he stopped, there was an I-spacer from a violent world war on Earth, with strange-looking green tanks and surface vehicles. Green aircraft dropped bombs and shot bullets. Starion looked closely, noticing the aircraft were very similar to what he had seen at the museums on Earth.

Starion glanced over at Deon, who shrugged his shoulders again. Deon telepathically whispered, *Starion, after you placed the signal booster on Earth's moon, Judion must have realized he could view Earth's past because it is outside our solar system.*

"This Earth war is from only one hundred forty Earth revolutions around its sun," Judion pronounced.

Then Judion, his hand shaking angrily, motioned toward the large e-screen, and then fast-forwarded by twirling his hand clockwise a little under eighty times. "And here is a view of one of Earth's largest cities almost eighty Earth years ago."

The Evions witnessed two large passenger aircraft crash into two tall twin buildings. Judion exposed the aftermath of the injured along with tremendous amounts of ash permeating the city. Then he showed people running to escape the area, their faces and clothes full of blood and ash.

Then Judion brought up a view of another war. "This war was only seventy of Earth's orbits ago." Judion revealed a roadside bomb blow up, killing several soldiers. One was barely alive and missing both his legs. He zoomed in on a young man in his early twenties.

Starion looked closely at the young man; he appeared awfully familiar, but Starion couldn't place him.

The Evions still present and awake gasped. Several gave Starion the evil eye as more of them started to leave. Starion put his head down.

After that, Judion pointed to Earth and zoomed in on the same location Deon had at the elder meeting.

"The Earth people had a major disaster only ten of their orbits ago when testing nuclear power to power their aircraft," he pronounced to everyone.

Starion and Deon held their breaths.

Judion finally zoomed in on where Deon had. He zoomed in and out, then around the area. It was normal. Judion looked puzzled at first but then turned angry. He expected to see the Earth's nuclear disaster.

Starion was relieved. He gave a puzzled-looking Deon a thumbs-up. Deon was even more puzzled at the gesture. Starion almost smiled.

"One more thing, everyone," the disappointed Judion yelled,

putting his head down. "As we speak, both my wife and Glenion, who visited Earth with Deon, are sick with an unknown illness over at the hospital. I know it was brought back from Earth. I know it for a fact."

He instantly created an I-spacer image of the two lying in hospital beds.

Starion now knew for sure Judion hadn't seen what he and Deon had witnessed before leaving for Earth. And he hadn't caught that the Earth people were using hydrogen now. Judion also didn't figure out why the view of the nuclear devastation was now gone either, and he didn't catch the difference in land-to-water mass from the elder meeting to this new view of Earth.

"Who is favor of banning these three from the council?" Judion yelled as if proving there was plenty of air.

Every Evion who was still left, including those in sleep-mode, put their hands up.

When Judion glared at Starion with his black, dark eyes to inform him of his lost position, Starion remembered the poor soul back on Earth in the fenced-in yard of the mental asylum. That man had the same look in his eyes that Judion's had, Starion now realized.

Everyone left except for Starion, Deon, and Ardia.

"I'm sorry I got you two into this."

"That's OK," they both consoled him.

"They didn't give us a chance," Ardia protested.

"Maybe if we would have been able to get them to try Earth's air …" Deon offered. "Or, if I would have brought some flasks of different gases, we could have tried to pump them into the magnifier."

"You two had better get out of here. It's getting late," Starion warned sadly.

Deon answered, "I don't have anywhere to go."

Ardia offered, "You can stay at my place."

"That's OK, Ardia; there are plenty of empty homes I can use."

Deon glanced over at an Audiseum room out of the corner

of his eye. Trying to cheer up his mentor, he pointed up at the speakers in the Audiseum while bringing up an Earth song.

They all heard, *"In the year 2525...If man is still alive..."*

Deon half-glided over to the room, yelling back. "This is where I put those Earth musical instruments, Starion. Maybe you want to see them."

But when he opened the door, a crestfallen look crossed his face. He shouted back, "They're gone...they're gone."

Starion didn't care.

Deon left, scratching his head in confusion. He took the magnifier, the cell, and the two Earth air tanks with him.

Ardia offered her wise support to Starion. "Starion...keep the faith. We still have two days. There must be a way...the spirit of the life force will guide us. Don't you remember the old stories?"

"Ardia...I am tired. You heard Judion—they won't let us use any of our water supply...I could never persuade them...never. How can we continue without any star-power cells or the technology in the e-center?"

"Starion, the heroes in the old stories never gave up—never—and you just said the Earth people haven't, either. I'm going home for a while to try to think of something. You do the same, OK? Open up your mind to fate, Starion, and listen...listen to the whispers of these ancient heroes from our ancient past. Their messages are there for the taking."

"OK," Starion said, nodding out of courtesy to his mentor. But he realized he was done. He had failed. He could no longer compare himself to anyone in the old stories. His eyes drooped with exhaustion.

After Ardia departed, Starion was the only one left in the Audiseum. He shut down all the I-spacers still hanging in the air with a defeated swipe of his hand. He left a live view of Earth up on the big screen while sitting and staring in disbelief. He couldn't understand why his fellow citizens were so against him.

Again he thought of the evil forces in these old stories. *Maybe they have won,* he conceded.

Starion felt extremely depressed. He felt like all the energy in his body had been pulled out of him. He was more tired than he had ever been in his life. He sneezed again. He felt his hot forehead with sweat dripping down. He sat for a moment on the bottom row of the Audiseum, looking at the live view of Earth. He glanced back up the stairs to his left. He saw Vincion's ritualistic ten spacegazers. He started to glide-climb up there for inspiration but then decided, *What for?* Two days would not be enough time. Anger built. He reached for the image of Earth with both of his hands. He heaved it at a wall, where it burst into large specks of light.

He realized he had to leave for his new uncomfortable home. He pulled up his hood and put his hands in his pouch along with the orbit tester. Then he headed out the door into the torturous heat and dead air. He could feel the temperature had steadily increased all morning.

What was he going to tell his children?

CHAPTER 34

WHEN STARION started for home, he happened to glance through his drooping hood across the street at the I-mover. Like the other day, he noticed the same mysterious blue light shining through a window. He wished he could escape back in time by watching one of the old Evion I-mover films he had always heard about, like those he'd seen in theatres on Earth.

Suddenly he had a major brainwave—or, from what he had learned in his Earth scanning's, a "revelation." He went into deep thought, closing his eyes. His eyelids glowed bright blue.

He flipped back his hood and spoke into his DTI. "Deon…Deon…"

"What is it, Starion?"

"Deon, even though we were ousted from the council and the e-center, we still have the right to go get our belongings, right? Grab all of your items and mine and then meet me at the I-mover as soon as you can."

"Why?"

"Please just do it. I'll tell you later."

"OK…but that I-mover hasn't been used for over one hundred E-years."

"You let me handle that."

"OK," Deon answered with limited confidence.

"Can you find just one more star-power cell with any power? Look everywhere, Deon. Then can you get Zealeon and Curion to haul water?"

"Anything else?" he asked.

"No. Not for now," Starion said, ignoring the sarcasm in his friend's voice.

Figuring out what Starion was up to, Deon asked. "Will that one large cylinder, hold enough hydrogen to power a v-breaker with five hundred Evions onboard to Earth? If so, we would need a tremendous amount of water to split out the hydrogen."

"Yes...if we can create a launchpad of some sort and set it on our moon, I think it will work. And as far as water, Valkia professed before I left that a new reservoir was found, right?"

"We'll have to find the old formula somehow, so we know how to compress the gas after the water is split and at what temperature..." Deon surmised.

"I have the ancient splitter at my home—if it still works, anyway. I think I have one of the old books that have the hydrogen energy properties and functions, too. We can figure it out."

"Will we have enough time, Starion?"

"I don't know...I don't know. Oh, don't forget to bring the star-power magnifier and cell you just created, along with the old mold-casts. Also, bring any old empty star-power cells, along with my gas bottles and flasks."

"Why? We are using hydrogen technology to get to Earth!"

Starion ignored him and contacted Ardia. "Ardia, come on down to the old I-mover and bring your things. We are leaving for Earth."

"That's the confidence I was looking for, Starion," came the response. "I knew I could count on you."

"Can you pick up Bria and Dustion on your way?"

"We will be there shortly," she told him.

With renewed energy, Starion hustled over into the I-mover. He inspected the hazy, dark, and hot old building. His eyes adjusted slowly to the dim lights that lit up the lobby area. He was startled for a second when he came across a silver and black IS-man in a stationary position. The robot had its face-paneled head tilted down. It was holding a broom. *Why didn't I see this the last time?*

As with his previous visit, he could smell the musty air and he could see the dust that had been stacking up on the floor, red chairs, and small wooden tables next to each chair. It was very hot and sweat ran down his face.

He located the basement door and climb-glided down the stairs to find the hyper-airflow exchange unit. He found a light switch on his way down. He pointed, turning on the lights. He saw the jungles of hydraulic cylinders that at one time were used to move the entire building according to the movie director's intentions. He noticed the cylinders were all covered with dust. He understood there was a room somewhere that had been used by the I-mover director to perform the building's movement, along with a special IS unit, but he didn't have time to look for it now.

He searched through the maze of tall cylinders until he finally found the hyper-airflow exchange unit. He flipped the switch and, to his surprise, heard it fire up, but it didn't sound very healthy. Cool air began to slowly permeate the room, replacing the hot air.

On his way back out, he was surprised to see that the walls of the basement were made of wood from the large Evion trees of long ago. The smell reminded him of the trees he'd encountered on Earth.

He glide-ran back upstairs. His main concern now was to make sure the large white I-screen was intact and could display the 4-D holographic image. If he could get this working, he could use it to study Earth more while deciding how and where to land. That is, if they were successful in migrating there. He also hoped he could somehow entice his fellow Evions to the I-mover. If he could, he would show them more about Earth while Zealeon and Curion hauled water.

He hurried down the aisle and felt the enormous I-mover screen with his hands. It was sublime. He swore he almost could feel the long history of images that had appeared on it over the thousands of years it was active. He looked up at its large, elliptical shape. He didn't see anything wrong, but he wouldn't know for sure if it worked until he brought up an I-spacer. He reveled again at the large red embroidered curtains on each side and the stage below the screen, along with the ancient style of décor, including the mythological creatures forged into the wall above the screen.

He hustled back up the thirty rows of chairs toward the back seven v-rooms, feeling the air slowly cool. As with his previous visit, he remembered these rooms allowed Evions to view, stop, rewind, and fast-forward the I-mover in order to study it further. Many had been used for the elite Evion population to use long ago.

When he glided into one of the rooms, the light came on automatically. Inside, there was a wooden desk, an old e-screen unit on top of it, and a large ancient white IS tower next to it covered in dust. He decided this would be his v-room.

Still checking things out, he headed into the v-room next door. There he observed five old e-screens hanging from the ceiling, full of dust, as well as several large data storage towers he believed had been used to store I-mover films from the past. This was the control room for the I-mover I-screen. This was where he and Deon would need to reestablish the connection from the signal rovers on the roof to the Earth. He hoped they were still being sent; Starion didn't know what Judion had done after ousting him.

There was one more room he was interested in checking out. He hustled down the narrow back slanted floor to his right, feeling the metal slab on the bottom of his gliders. He imagined again what it must have been like to be sitting in the I-mover long ago, when the whole building lifted up, down, and also side to side following the action of the I-spacer.

Once inside the room, to his happy surprise, he found what he wanted: a small domed glass skyroid. The v-room had been used for writers of films and teachers to be able to view an I-spacer along with the heavens at the same time. There was a two-way mirror that allowed someone to view out into the I-mover while working in the room, therefore not interrupting the dark ambiance. Looking upward, he expected to see through the glass below the spacegazer, but he discovered a layer of dirt and dust distorting the view of the massive dying sun. He realized he would have to clean off the inside and possibly the outside of the glass before he could use his orbit tester.

He stood on a desk and reached up to clean the inside of the warped skyroid glass. He pointed his orbit tester up at the sun. It didn't register.

He hurry-glided to the front lobby, where he found a stairway to the roof. Climbing up, there was a trap door at the top. He pushed hard to unjam it. When he did so, the dangerous and scorching hot air entered the room, burning his face and hands.

Starion growled in pain, quickly wrapping his hood tightly across his face. He put his hands in his pouch. He wished he had a copy of his book.

Outside on the roof, he found three large s-rover dishes attached to a flat metal plate pointing up into the sky. Two of them were melted, while one was very close to being destroyed. Starion located the half sphere of the small v-room skyroid he had just cleaned below. He hurried over then used his right arm's shroud to clean off the glass the best he could. He glanced over at the large galvanized glass domed roof, which encompassed the main part of the I-mover. He imagined what it must have been like long ago, when the dome was open during a crisp, clear, starlit night while the I-movergoers watched a film.

He hustled back over to the stairs, climbed down, and shut the door. He felt his face burning from the brief exposure to the sun. He grimaced as the pain began to set in.

He scurried back into the skyroid and then pointed his orbit tester at the dying sun. It worked this time.

Oh, no—down to less than a day!

He spoke into his DTI, "Deon, any luck finding another cell? And with Zealeon and Curion?"

"I found a very old cell in the Audiseum. It looks very strange, but it gives off a slight blue glow…and Curion and Zealeon just took off for a load of water. But do we have enough time, Starion?"

"I don't know. I just used my orbit tester and I think we are down to less than a day. But I have a plan. Come down here— we need to intercept the signals from Earth so they are piped directly to the I-mover. Thankfully, I think one of our s-rover dishes is still intact…grab our things and hustle down here."

"I will do my best. I'll bring the O-scopes, too…but why do you need the star-power magnifier?" he inquired again. "Aren't we going to use hydrogen to escape?"

"I want to show Mary and Earth's scientists when we get there—at the proper time, of course."

"Who's Mary? And, Starion, if we get to Earth, we can't change their history…right?"

Starion ignored him again and then moved back to the v-room he had chosen for his own. He wiped away the dust from a chair. He did the same to the desk facing the large I-screen through the v-room window. He pointed at the IS e-screen on top of the desk, which was still connected to the large old tower. Now there was an older D-box he had never seen protruding out toward him.

Some of the options in the dropdown box included "Evion Planet-Net," "Medical Information," "Documents," "Space Games," "Help," and "Archival Information."

From the last category, there were subcategories: "Evion Inventors," "Evion History," "Space Physics," "Evion Elements," "I-Spacer DNA Molecule Link," "Fifth Dimension," and finally, "I-Mover Antigravity."

CHAPTER 35

WHEN STARION discovered all these options, he had to look twice. His heart and emotions were racing.

This IS tower had not been affected by the tragic virus that had destroyed all the information in Alexon a year earlier. Why hadn't he thought of looking here when the virus occurred? It wouldn't have all the missing data, but it would have helped repopulate the IS banks across the city, along with each Evion's home.

He was so excited he didn't know what do to. He couldn't wait. He now had found a possible way to answer something that had been nagging at him ever since he arrived back home from Earth.

He asked the IS unit, "Help."

"What is your request?" it answered back, sounding very different than his home or v-breaker IS units.

"Give me the archival information."

"What subcategory would you like?"

"Evion Inventors," he said. Soon after, an alphabetical listing of all the great Evion inventors was displayed.

He scrolled down to the name "Vincion" then pointed at it. Instantly an I-spacer protruded out, startling him as the light encompassed half his body. He moved it closer to the e-screen and adjusted it to a more reasonable size. He noticed that like the IS unit's voice, this was different, too.

He heard a thump from below; it had to be the hyper-airflow exchange unit. He was right; he could feel the damp, hot air start to permeate the building again.

The I-spacer began to play a 4-D biography of Starion's dead mentor, Vincion, as a child. Starion had seen this biography when he was younger, but now he was more interested in his hero's later life. He fast-forwarded.

Now, on the 4-D image, Vincion was speaking to the interviewer over one hundred years in the past. He was about sixty E-years old. He had smooth, long, grey hair combed back and a white beard. His eyes were a piercing blue. His demeanor resembled Ardia's; he also had read all the ancient stories. Furthermore, he was a solar and star system traveler.

The interviewer asked Vincion, "What do you have to say about your theory that the sun is dying?"

"As you know, most scientists don't believe my theory. I believe our sun will slowly grow larger and larger, thus pulling Evion into its surface at some point in the next one hundred years. And as everyone knows, I have been traveling around the galaxy, looking for a suitable home."

Starion listened intently as the interviewer continued, "As you know, Vincion, most people think our sun will revert back to its original size and our elliptical orbit will continue safely as always. And some people think our orbit will adjust even if the sun remains large. But I am curious—have you found any new possible planets yet? And why don't you allow us to view your missions from your I-spacer molecule DNA technology? That way we could follow your exploits."

"I don't think the signal from my DNA would work because of the astronomical distances we are traveling. And no, I haven't found a suitable planet yet, but I have hope for our next mission. I—"

Suddenly, the interview stopped. Starion tried to rewind several times, but it wouldn't play any further. He asked, "IS unit; is this the end of the I-spacer?"

The IS unit paused and then answered a few moments later, "No, there is another two minutes."

"IS bank, the I-spacer has stopped before the end. Please analyze and advise."

Starion heard the data storage unit rapidly analyze the data. It answered back in a monotone voice, "The code is damaged and cannot be repaired."

"IS bank, please provide the code."

The computer instantly provided the code:

"10111000100010101000100111101000000001011110100 10010101010..."

Starion recognized the error and fixed it immediately, now sweating up a storm.

"IS unit, please continue."

The video continued on with the interview. "I will be traveling to an area of the Milky Way Galaxy called the Optim section. My reports show a small blue planet that looks promising."

"Ah-ha—Vincion *was* there," Starion confirmed aloud. He stopped the I-spacer.

Starion now knew his mentor had been on Earth two hundred of Earth's years ago, or one hundred of Evion's.

But did he really provide specific technology information to this Thomas Edison guy? And if he did, why didn't he give him more information about things like energy and medicine...and why wouldn't he have told Edison how to use the braydium?

The interviewer changed the subject. "I understand you also are working on other inventions, such as developing a way for I-movergoers to join in with the 4-D image and interact with it?"

"Yes, that is correct; it would be called 5-D. But keep in mind my main reason to invent this is to help us easily divert future deadly hyper-asteroids. I was very close to succeeding, but ever since our atmosphere's gas composition changed due to the sun's sudden change, I have been having difficulty. It seems like the gas composition of twenty-two percent oxygen and seventy-eight percent—"

Starion shut off the interview. He was sweating, sneezing,

and coughing from deep in his lungs. It hurt. Furthermore, he was tired.

He now understood: Vincion had visited Earth but had only given Edison enough clues for inspiration, along with the ancient Evion book. He had not given the man the actual invention designs, theories, or schematics.

Starion pulled out his last copy of his book. He opened it to the chapter, "*Magica~ Aid.*"

He smiled a little, noticing that his facial muscles didn't hurt as much as before.

At that moment, there was a flash followed by a rumble. The whole I-mover shook, along with his desk and chair. He hung on while the quake slowly subsided.

Deon stumble-glided into the I-mover lobby carrying several items. He yelled, "Hey, Starion—I have your last old mold-casts, the new star-power magnifier and cell, and your flasks of gases outside."

"Hi, Deon," Starion yelled, pointing to the main I-mover control room. Sneezing again, he continued, "Put your things in there…and by the way, do you have any more of Earth's air tanks? We may need them."

"Just one. I gave the other one to Zealeon and Curion."

"How are they doing, by the way?"

"They just started hauling the water, Starion. Hey, it is really hot in here." Deon wiped away sweat with his shroud arm.

"Good. They sure are a couple of good men. How did you talk them into it?"

"It was easy—they had been testing this green weedy thing, and that stuff called beer I brought back. They have also been listening to Earth music…and when they sampled Earth's air, they jumped at the chance to help us get there."

Deon stumbled and fell, but then saved an O-scope.

"I'm sorry, Starion."

"What are you sorry about? You will make lots of mistakes

on Earth. That's how we learn. But just one tip: don't get angry when someone laughs."

When hauling in his own items, including the new shiny star-power magnifier, Starion lamented, looking at the top clear empty chamber, "I wish I could have found the right gaseous mixture."

"We won't need it now, with the Earth rocket we are going to fill with hydrogen," Deon yelled back from the control room, where he was setting up his things.

Starion decided to store all of his magnifier items and flasks in the skyroid v-room, along with several dead cells. While setting down the many flasks of gases, he told Deon in a raised voice, "For the last eight years, I just couldn't grasp the gaseous arrangement necessary to magnify the Evion sun's rays...I tried every combination of gases. Most recently I had been using a mixture of oxygen, helium, hydrogen, and argon. I tried all possible combinations, but I just couldn't seem to get the right one... I hope hydrogen fuel and one Earth rocket booster will work!"

"Well, at least you tried, Starion...who could fault you for that? You are only Evion."

Starion smiled, remembering Mary telling him the same thing. He glided over to the main control room. "Thank you, my friend," he said, looking up at the large I-mover screen. "We're going to succeed, Deon...we're going to make our people understand. I can feel it. I don't want to leave anyone behind...I was elected president to lead and save everyone."

"I hope so, Starion...I hope so."

"Well, Deon, let's hurry. Let's see if we can pull in Earth's signals—we need to figure out how and where to introduce ourselves when we get to Earth. Also, we need to try to somehow get our fellow Evions down here. We need to show them important aspects of Earth while we wait for Curion and Zealeon to finish."

"I wish I had your optimism, Starion...I would have quit by now, if it weren't for you."

Starion sneezed again. "You should read our old stories as well as Earth's instead of scanning."

Deon grimaced when he witnessed Starion wipe his nose with his shroud. "What's wrong, Starion?"

"I have caught something…maybe even from Earth, like Kircia and Glenion have."

CHAPTER 36

"**DEON, LET'S** hurry and set up a direct link to Earth's signals with the one good s-rover dish on the roof...at least, I *think* it is still good. Also, Judion and his group might have cut us off from the e-center, so we need all signals from Earth to be direct."

Deon started to set up the I-mover system's IS banks to receive the signals from Earth while Starion pace-glided the back row in between the last row of seats and the v-rooms.

Deon turned on the switches with a swipe of his hand while setting up his O-scope. Panning the room, he discovered the main IS tower, like Starion had seen in his v-room. He yelled, "Hey, this is very old."

"Yes, I know...it even has some of the old options, such as the 'I-Spacer DNA' option and Vincion's invention of the fifth dimension."

Now in the back row, Starion used his full hand to pull out a large protruding 4-D empty image. It encompassed the whole I-mover.

Starion pointed his two focus fingers at the big screen and brought up a D-box on the lower left startup view.

"Wait a minute, Starion," Deon yelled.

"You mean our minute or an Earth minute?" Starion asked, trying to lighten the mood.

Just then, Ardia and Bria arrived. Starion noticed his daughter's large blue curious eyes light up. She climbed up and down the aisles without her gliders. Ardia also looked around, nodding in approval.

"Where's your brother?" Starion asked Bria.

"He left just before Ardia came."

Starion yelled into his DTI, "Dustion...Dustion!"

There was no answer.

"Be careful in here, Bria." Starion told her sternly. "Where's your air tank?"

"I forgot it. When do we go to Earth?" Bria shouted, running through the lined rows of chairs.

"What's the plan?" Ardia asked.

"Zealeon and Curion are hauling water so we can split it into hydrogen. Then we will use the Earth rocket booster to power us back to Earth."

"Yes...and this seems impossible," Deon yelled from his new v-room.

"Have faith, Deon," Ardia bellowed back, standing next to Starion in the back row.

"Faith can't move planets, Ardia."

"Oh, yes it can...yes it can."

Starion continued, "While they haul water, Ardia, we are going to pull in Earth's signals so we can decide on where and how to introduce ourselves when we arrive. We also need to somehow send and show the good aspects of Earth to our fellow Evions if we want to entice them to glide over here from their homes."

"Why only the good aspects? We need to see your full visit, including your interactions with the humans. Did you transfer it?"

"No...there were some things that weren't very good. I think we should show them the beautiful scenery on Earth, Ardia, and that should be enough," he said, then changed the subject. "How was your travel over here?"

"It's getting more precarious by the moment, Starion," she answered, her expression making it clear she was aware of Starion's reluctance to keep discussing his Earth visit. "By the way, I saw your neighbor, Ripeon, who must have just arrived home from the e-com. I told him to come down here and help us with our plan to go to Earth...unfortunately, he just twitched twice and went back inside."

Deon shouted, "OK, Starion, you should have options in the startup menu."

Starion brought up a D-box: "Evion Planet-Net," "Earth's S-Rover Video," "Earth's S-Rover Audio," "Earth's I-Mooncam," the "Evion EBS," "Starion's Adventure to Earth," "I-Spacer DNA Molecule Link," "Fifth Dimension (5-D)," "I-Mover Antigravity," and finally "Unknown."

When Starion saw the "Unknown" link, a strange feeling came over him.

Enthralled, Deon yelled, "There are some old options, like you said...but I wonder if they work."

"Yes, Deon, apparently the I-mover was spared the mass deletion virus...but why did you create this unknown option?"

"There is a signal on the O-scope from Earth, and I don't know what it is."

"All this technology...ancient or not...will it save us?" Starion mumbled to himself, and then chose the option for the I-mooncam first.

After a few moments, a live view of Earth gradually projected a few feet out in a 4-D image.

"Yes—awesome! The signal booster I placed on the moon works perfectly!" Starion shouted.

Even though Judion had utilized it at the Audiseum, Starion wanted to test it himself. Using both hands, he opened up his six fingers as large as possible. Then he grabbed and pulled the image out directly over the I-mover seats. It displayed a high-level view of Earth slowly rotating. The word "live" was displayed on the upper front part of the large holographic image.

"Isn't she beautiful?"

"She sure is, Starion," Ardia told him.

Starion thought of a better word than "live." He poked his head into the main control room. "Deon, can you change the word 'live' to 'life'? It seems more appropriate."

Ardia nodded in approval.

They both stared at the lively vital blue planet.

Starion commented, "If we ever have time, I would like to go way back in Earth's time and see the full history of its life from the I-mooncam."

Deon joined them in the back row. "Sorry Starion. I wish I had caught that ability to view back in time before Judion did. Seeing those awful Earth images from its past was apparently the last straw for most of the Evions at the Audiseum."

"It's not your fault, Deon. I should have figured it out too. Judion won't succeed, my friends...he won't win."

"By the way Starion, how come things on Earth look a little different? And why weren't they at war? And furthermore, why couldn't Judion find the accident of the nuclear devastation I discovered."

Starion shrugged his shoulders and zoomed in on San Francisco, along with the bay he had ferried across to get to Berkeley. He could see that the water level was lower. While happy they had found the benefit of using water, they seemed to depleting it quite fast. Zooming in further, he saw the old wooden boat he had taken to get across. He remembered the many synapses of the old stories and the magical aid he had pondered about at that time.

"Hmm," he mumbled.

I will have to return the favor somehow once we get there.

"The zooming function works," he acknowledged, hoping no one had caught his thought. He chose a different link. This time he chose the Earth s-rover audio option.

Once displayed, there were several subcategories like he had witnessed in the music store on Earth. He scrolled through the Earth songs with his philosophical memory filter then chose the song "Across the Universe," which he remembered listening to in the mPod on Earth.

Leaving the song playing, he chose another option. Now, up on the screen was an Earth news broadcast. Starion turned up the sound by rotating his finger. The interviewer was asking a middle-aged paraplegic, "How can you win races even against normal healthy people? It's amazing...it's absolutely amazing...and you have been doing it for twenty years?"

The broadcast showed the man in a two-wheeled chair when he was young. Starion, looking closely at his face, realized this was the man he had given his extra gliders to.

"Oops," Starion blurted out.

CHAPTER 37

STARION CHANGED to another broadcast, where a woman newscaster explained, "Still no success on finding any information on the stolen NASA rocket booster twenty years ago...but the government, Hollywood, and the Pentagon still deny any cover-up. Some think this was related to the hoax when someone jumped over an SUV in New York and also to the strange clothes found in England."

The anchorwoman turned to her fellow anchorman and said, "Most still think it was Hollywood trying to drum up publicity for the movie *Species XXI*."

"Ahh..." the man responded. "But what if it wasn't?" he asked, raising an eyebrow.

On one more broadcast that didn't come in very clearly, Starion noticed a woman who looked vaguely familiar. She was saying, "We have to look for other sources of energy. We are running through water at a fast rate."

"What are our options?" the interviewer asked.

"I don't know...solar maybe," the woman explained.

Starion didn't know what to choose next. "Deon, make the I-mooncam view of Earth the default view."

"OK, done."

Ardia telepathically stared at Starion. *Starion, you need to transfer your visit,* she insisted.

Still ignoring her, he brought up an animated film with characters flying inside a strange-looking aircraft with a glass bubble on top of it. Just as he was going to change it again, Bria blurted out, "Hey, I want to watch that."

Starion motioned her into one of the back rooms and started it up there. Once out in the I-mover again, he changed to another fictional film with live human characters in spaceships this time. One character wearing strange white clothes said, "The Empire will never win!"

All of sudden, there was a flare and quake. The I-mover screen shook as dust fell from ceilings. The image on the e-screen in Bria's v-room and all of Deon's e-screens flickered and went out. It was dark, and they felt the floor rumble.

Starion tried his son Dustion again on his DTI. "Hello, Dustion. Hello, Son...are you there?"

There was no answer.

Starion pace-glided the back of the I-mover with worry. The quakes got worse. He covered his daughter with his body to protect her from falling objects.

"Hold onto something, everyone," he yelled.

This was the worst rumble Starion had witnessed. It was pitch black. Dust and debris infiltrated the I-mover again while they gasped for air. He felt the floor shake and crack while hearing buildings crumble outside. Finally the rumble subsided, and the I-mover defaulted back to a live view of Earth.

"That was a long one. I think the I-mover building is now tilted," Deon yelled after things finally calmed down.

"Yes, they are getting longer and stronger now. We have to get going! Deon, see how far Curion and Zealeon are...I have to find Dustion somehow," Starion shouted from Bria's v-room.

Deon put his hood up and left.

Starion was just about to leave also when he noticed Bria's e-screen start up again after the quake.

Just then, the broadcast stopped. But another totally different I-spacer started that exhibited a large ship full of humans on the water on Earth. It was cruising along a long and wide shoreline on a sunny blue day. Right after that, another showed a smaller, hairy, miserable, human-looking animal with a red nose at some type of store. The sad-looking animal looked up at a human with a scarf wrapped around his neck.

"Hey, Ardia," Starion yelled, pointing up at the live view of Earth. "I am going to create an I-spacer of Earth to show our fellow Evions. Then we can try and pipe it to all Evion homes, along with any remaining city speakers still intact via the emergency broadcast system...if it works this time. Then maybe they will join us."

Deon awkwardly rushed in from the lobby, short of breath. "Starion...Starion, Zealeon and Curion are about half done."

Starion pace-glided the floor again. "We need to start splitting water now...I will see if Dustion is home and pick up the water splitter."

Suddenly, another massive Evion quake shook the I-mover even more than before. Now they were coming fast and furious. The I-mover shook with so much force this time they all fell to the floor. They each clung desperately to whatever was near them while a large crack formed on the domed roof. They felt the floor shift at a slight angle. They couldn't see anything while struggling to breathe.

Starion yelled to Bria, "Are you OK?"

"Yes!" she shouted.

"I'll be right back," he told her, scrambling toward the lobby, bouncing off the walls. The large I-mover image protruded so far back it lit up a small portion of his shroud and body. He saw a young man in a spaceship talking to an older man with a grey beard who was wearing a black shroud.

He couldn't waste time. Starion struggled to open the door, the I-mover was sinking. He headed outside, where the air was so thick with debris he couldn't even see across to the Audiseum. Traversing over sinkholes and crevasses, afraid of another flare and quake, his gliders were in full force. The shoes sensed his desperation; he made it home in record time.

Once there, he searched while yelling for Dustion. There was no sign of him.

He grabbed the water splitter, which was heavier than he

remembered. Then he found one last copy of his favorite book, *Anciente Evion Adventura~Hero*.

He glide-ran over to his neighbor's house carrying the water splitter.

"Ripeon—any sign of Dustion?"

Ripeon shook his head no while twitching twice.

"Come with us, Ripeon?"

He shook his head no with another twitch.

Starion visually searched the other homes, speaking into his DTI. "Dustion...Dustion..." There was nothing.

Discouraged and gasping, he headed back to the I-mover but decided to bring the splitter to the e-center first. When he entered, he was glad to see Zealeon and Curion pumping the latest load of water from the v-breaker into the old water tank. They were occasionally putting the mask on from the small Earth air tank.

"Is the water holding in that large old tank?" Starion asked, setting the splitter down.

"We think so," Zealeon told him.

Starion felt compelled to help. He hopped in as the ship flew up and out of the open dome with them.

Starion searched for any sign of his son below—and for any Evion, for that matter. As they flew over the devastation to the underground water supply, they passed by the foothills of the mountain Starion had tried to crash his ship into as a young man. The terrible recollection of that time, along with the guilt of failing to save the sun, overwhelmed him. He put his head down in shame.

But when he lifted up his head again, he saw a dim light flickering on the side of a mountainous incline.

"What a minute," he told the two men. "Fly over near that flickering light."

When closer, all three could see the dim light through a small opening on the side of the mountain.

"Land as close as you can, Zealeon," Starion ordered.

"I thought we didn't have much time," Curion reminded him. "I'll just be a minute."

When Zealeon landed, Starion zigzagged up a path. Just before he reached the cave entrance, he felt a rumble; he hung onto a nearby rock for life. The rumble finally subsided, and he finally reached the entrance. He struggled to catch his breath and smelled smoke. He hurried into the cool, damp cave.

There was a flickering light coming from around a jagged rock wall. Turning the corner, Starion noticed a fire in the middle of a rocky room. He panned the fire-lit room but didn't see anyone. Then he heard a faint groan coming from a dark corner. He moved closer and could just make out the figure of a man wearing an orange shroud. The man was lying on a blanket on the ground, his back to Starion. He was having difficulty breathing.

Starion carefully knelt down, looking to see who the man was. He pulled the shroud's hood away from the man's face. He saw a very old man with a long white beard. He could see right away that it was the leader of the philosophers who had first found him when he crashed here, long ago. Starion picked up the frail old man, gently threw him over his shoulder, and then started carrying him out of the cave. The old man mumbled, "My books...my books." He pointed over to a makeshift bookshelf near where he had been lying.

Starion set him down while he gathered ten old books into an empty bag he found nearby.

When he struggled back to pick up the man again, the old philosopher gently muttered, "Starion, you have done well. You have done well, my son. My name is Phileon...now please get my staff as well."

Starion gently lifted him over his shoulder, taking the bag of books and a long wooden staff. He hauled him out and down the path and into the v-breaker. He gave the man some of Earth's air.

"Take us to the I-mover while you two continue on with your intended...or I mean *unintended* adventure?" Starion told them.

They both shrugged their shoulders.

Zealeon navigated the ship over to the I-mover and then helped Starion and Phileon out.

"Hurry, you two...and good job," Starion told them, giving them the thumbs-up.

"What's that, Starion?" Curion asked.

"That means good job."

"No one has told me that I did a good job in my whole life," Curion said just before the door closed, and the ship took off.

When Starion approached the door carrying Phileon, he was startled by two Evion bodies lying on the ground nearby, burning. He looked closer and found, to his horror, that it was his neighbor Ripeon and his wife.

Starion hurried inside. He carried Phileon and his staff, along with the bag of books, back to one of the v-rooms. Ardia, Deon, and Bria followed him.

"Who is this?" Bria asked.

"This is Phileon. He helped me when I was a young man."

"Oh...like in the old stories," she concluded.

Yes, that is right, Ardia answered.

CHAPTER 38

NOW BACK inside but depressed after seeing his dead neighbors outside, Starion saw that the fictional space movie from Earth now displayed a scene of a young man staring out into the magnificent desert at two sunsets, with a look of wondering where his life would take him.

Starion found a bottle of Earth's water Deon had brought. He hurried over to Phileon and helped him to drink some of it. Starion motioned Deon to follow him into the lobby.

"Deon…the bodies of my neighbor Ripeon and his wife are burning out there."

"Where are we going to put them?" Deon asked after a short pause. "There's nothing we can do for them."

Starion, with a raspy voice and plugged-up nose mumbled, "Every time I do something, I seem to mess it up. I am doing the best I can…like in the old stories, something or someone must not want me to succeed."

Starion sat, exhausted, in a chair in the main seating area toward the back. He reached down and adjusted the lever like he had when he stopped by the I-mover before he left for Earth. He chose the prone position and was now lying flat on his back. He tossed his book on a table next him.

Phileon, apparently feeling better, struggled to his feet with his staff. He had heard Starion and shuffled over to him. "Starion, anger doesn't do any good…it only distorts the truth."

"But every time I try to help someone, I seem to mess it up somehow."

The old man put his hand on Starion's shoulder. "If your deed is something you believe in, then this is part of the universal life force…and fate will help you."

"Yes, that is what Ardia keeps telling me…but what about losing my son? Is *that* part of the life force?"

Ardia, overhearing, moved closer. She tried to comfort Starion, too. "He's fine…I know he is. You know teenage boys."

Starion wasn't so sure. He was exhausted and depressed. He coughed then sneezed. "Dustion…Dustion?" he spoke hopefully into his DTI. Again, he received no reply.

Starion pulled the lever next to the chair again. Now he was sitting up in his chair. Ardia pulled him up with both hands, forcing him to stand, and put his favorite book back in his pouch.

Just then, there was another enormous quake. The domed ceiling cracked again as Starion felt the building sink further. This time it was almost like an explosion. They felt the floor shake and tremble. Starion believed this might be the end. He hurried over and covered Bria again, yelling to everyone, "Take cover—take cover!"

Finally it subsided. They could hardly breathe, and they couldn't see in front of them. Starion was gasping along with everyone else.

"Deon, quick—come with me. We need to fly the v-breaker I took back from Earth over here into the I-mover. There is a tank of Earth's air inside it."

The two hurried to the lobby, forced the door open, pulled up their hoods, and jumped up three feet onto the dangerous terrain. Looking up at the sun, Starion could see that it was suddenly almost twice as large as when he last viewed it. They didn't have much time.

Starion's heart leapt into his throat when he discovered that the buildings near the I-mover were completely destroyed. The Audiseum, the e-com where he had planned to use the Earth's air tank, the hospital across the street—all gone.

"Dustion...Dustion..."

They glide-ran over to the fallen hospital. Starion could just barely make out a figure of someone digging through the hospital rubble. As he came closer to the figure, he knew it was Judion.

"Kircia? Kircia!" Judion was yelling.

Just as Starion reached him, Judion passed out.

Starion picked him up, lifted him over his shoulder, and then hurried back over to the I-mover lobby. Catching his breath, he continued into the back row of the main seating area and into an empty v-room. He laid Judion down on the floor and fast-glided back outside. He and Deon combed through the rubble, looking for more survivors.

Suddenly, they heard someone cry out. They found Glenion, gasping for air, while coughing and sneezing. Deon helped him over to the I-mover while Starion kept looking for survivors. Soon he noticed an arm protruding through the debris. Removing several pieces of the melted debris, he found it was Judion's wife, Kircia. She was dead.

Starion gently picked her up in his arms and carried her back to the I-mover. He laid her down in a v-room next to Judion. The rest of the I-mover occupants followed, watching with sadness.

Starion motioned to Deon to head outside. They hurried over to the e-center. They searched the rubble where they figured the hangar was located, gasping for air. They heard someone crying out faintly.

"Help...help."

They managed to clear away the broken melted glass. Underneath was Curion, badly injured. He had cuts and bruises, a broken leg, plus a broken arm.

Deon lifted him up and carried him out onto what was left of the glidewalk, then underneath an overhang of a destroyed building.

Starion kept searching. Suddenly, he discovered a hand sticking up through some debris. He frantically removed pieces of melted glass, where he sadly found Zealeon. He was dead inside what was left of the v-breaker he and Curion had been using.

Starion was devastated. Zealeon had been instrumental in keeping Starion and the elders up to date on the planet's condition. And he had just heroically volunteered for this adventure, just like in the old stories.

Starion, remembering the ritual on Earth, wanted to say something, but there wasn't any time. He put Zealeon's hands on top of his stomach, knelt, and lowered his head for a moment. He placed his hands on top of Zealeon's hands. Just as he was about to stand, he felt something in Zealeon's pouch. He reached and found a tattered, rolled-up scroll. Starion put it in his own pouch then climbed out of the v-breaker.

To his left, he discovered that the large water tank nearby had been demolished, too. The water Zealeon and Curion had hauled was now spread all over the debris and quickly evaporating away.

Next to this, he found that his water splitter had also been destroyed.

Oh, no . . .

Grief-stricken, he searched for the v-breaker he had taken to Earth. He hoped the air tank was still intact, and he wanted to see if the Earth rocket booster was still intact, too.

He finally located the v-breaker, discovering it was badly damaged. Next to this, he found the Earth rocket booster in pieces. Clearing away rubble, he hopped down inside the v-breaker to visually inspect the air tank.

Deon hob-glided back from safely dropping off Curion.

"Any luck finding Zealeon?"

"He is dead, Deon. And I was the one who asked you to persuade him," Starion said, putting his head down as a small tear fell. "The air tank in this v-breaker looks OK," he observed, shaking his grief off the best he could while a sinking feeling told him it really didn't matter anymore. "Deon, see if you can find the star-power cell from the destroyed v-breaker Curion and Zealeon were using . . ."

Deon hurried over to a section of demolished glass, while Starion continued to inspect the v-breaker he had taken to Earth. He found several holes on each side and on top.

"I found the cell and it looks OK," he heard Deon yell moments later.

Deon hauled Curion back. He laid him down on one of the back chairs. He also brought the cell, along with the tank of Earth's air Zealeon and Curion had been using. He shook it. "I think there is some left."

Starion took the cell and installed it in the floor compartment, then moved up near the front v-panel. He tried to manually fly up, but it wouldn't move. "We need to clear away the debris," he yelled.

Deon and Starion hurried outside. They tossed pieces of glass and rubble away from the v-breaker and then climbed back in. Finally, the ship managed to fly up and out. With the holes in the ship, the three were now exposed to dangerous air and sun. Luckily, they had the tank with some of Earth's air left. They passed it back and forth, each taking deep breaths.

Starion glanced upward. He saw a terrible sight: the moon had succumbed to the gigantic sun's gravity. The small sphere was now imbedded in the fiery surface.

It was in flames. He noticed that his watch was dead.

Adding to his concern, while flying to the I-mover, Starion witnessed the terrible destruction below. He did the best he could not to think about his son.

By the time they landed, the small tank of Earth's air they had passed between them was empty. Starion urged Deon with a monotone voice, "Hurry inside and into your v-room. There is a lever that should open up the domed roof."

"That hasn't been used for over a hundred years."

"I know...give it a try."

Deon rushed in after jumping down and squeezing in the door. He hurried into his v-room, found the lever, and then pushed it. There was a large squeaking sound. Dust fell from the dome celling as the metal cover started to open from the center. Everyone turned their attention upward with concern, gasping for air.

Once Deon thought it was open enough for the v-breaker to fly through, he stopped.

Deon and the others, fighting for air, watched Starion first hover above the dome and then it slowly descended through the opening above them. It slowly lowered down to the left of the building while hovering over the I-mover seats.

"Everyone be careful and stand back," Deon yelled as he returned to the control v-room. He pushed the lever back, allowing the dome to slowly close. Deon hurried back out to guide Starion down.

Starion, also struggling for air, steadily lowered it onto the left side of the sloped seats. Several seats and the tables next to them were instantly crushed from the weight, while others held as the front of the v-breaker pointed slightly upward.

Finally, the v-breaker came to standstill.

He opened up the windows and skylight, and then manually turned a knob on the large tank holding Earth's air. The Evions in the I-mover all heard and felt the fresh air permeate the room. They hurried down the aisles to get closer.

Starion carried Curion to the back and on top of the braydium pile from Earth. He opened the hatch then hopped out with Curion. He brought him up to the v-room where Judion was laying.

Starion was exhausted and depressed. He looked for Dustion.

Ardia, catching his eye, shook her head side to side at him.

Starion stumbled over to a back chair, sneezing and shivering even though he was sweating like everyone else.

"You brought that air just in time...what happened, Starion?" Ardia asked as she, Phileon, and Deon followed him.

"That last flare and quake pulled the moon and most of our remaining atmosphere into the sun," Deon answered.

Starion lied down in an I-mover seat while lowering it with

the lever. With one eye half opened, he spoke to the rest gathered around. "We aren't going to make it…now there isn't any way to travel to Earth…our plans to use hydrogen and Earth's large rocket won't work now…everything has been destroyed."

CHAPTER 39

THE OLD philosopher, Phileon, gripped Starion's arm. He opened his book to a chapter: "*Adventura~Denial.*"

Despondent, Starion noticed it was in a different language. He tried to see the cover of the book, but Phileon closed it and put it back in his shroud pouch before he could.

"This isn't the time to quit," Phileon urged.

Ardia nodded in agreement. "Yes Starion—and what about your son? There are Evions out there who might still be alive...we need to try to get all the remaining Evions to the I-mover. Otherwise, they will suffocate," Ardia pronounced.

"If anyone is still alive," Deon spoke up.

"Do you think our EBS system will work?" Ardia asked Starion.

Starion just shrugged his shoulders.

Deon answered instead. "Judion may have erased the code, Ardia."

"While you were away, Bria and I created the hologram-cast you suggested...have faith, Starion. Let's try it."

Ardia pointed at the big screen, where the old space movie was still showing. "I feel a presence I've not felt since—"

Ardia pulled out the D-box to the category "EBS" and highlighted that option. The monotone voice stated, "Input your message."

Ardia chose an icon labeled "Hologram-Cast" and highlighted it. Then a monotone IS voice filled the whole I-mover.

"Message sent."

"It worked—it worked!" Bria yelled.

"*This is an emergency. This is an emergency,*" the monotone voice bellowed while a 4-D I-spacer of Earth protruded out from the I-screen. It startled everyone, even those in the back row and back rooms.

The e-sound started up with Ardia's voice. Starion opened one eye. He viewed her inside the I-spacer standing next to an image of Earth.

"Please, everyone, we don't have a second to spare. We must leave Evion...take a look at this planet. It is called Earth. Please take a look at it and consider it your new home. We don't have much time."

An Earth song began to play.

"*To dream the impossible dream . . .*"

Inside the image, Starion's orbital simulation of Evion's demise appeared on the lower right.

Astonished, Starion pushed the lever and sat upright in his chair. Hopefully his people would see this. *And if they do, they would have to feel something from it! But then again—as before, when he had tried to connect to his people before leaving for Earth—maybe this hologram-cast wouldn't be sent.*

The I-spacer was now a view of Earth, its moon, and the bright yellow sun. Then the image revealed the comparison of Earth to Evion, both present and past, as well as the comparison of Earth's sun to Evion's sun in the present time. It displayed Earth's oceans, rivers, mountains, and green vegetation, along with the fresh air that blew the grasses, crops, fields, and tree branches around. It showed a rain shower, and after that, cities, small towns, and farmhouses.

Ardia appeared again on the elliptical 4-D hologram-cast inside the image. "Please, take a closer look at Earth. There isn't any more time. Look outside at our sun now. You can tell it is growing larger and nearer."

Ardia pointed to the simulation next to her in the image and continued, "And here is what will happen less than a day from now. Please come down to the I-mover to view even more aspects of Earth. Please come down to the I-mover…now!"

Ardia wanted to show and tell one more thing. She created another hologram-cast on the spot and then sent it. In it she announced. "We also have fresh air!"

Starion lifted his head up. "Good job you two…good job," he praised them, giving them a thumbs-up. "Let's hope our people received and viewed it or heard it on city e-speakers, if there are any left. Then let's pray they come down here."

"What?" Deon asked.

Now standing, Starion looked for Bria. He saw her safely in the v-room watching the animated Earth I-spacer.

But how are we going to get off this planet now? Starion telepathically asked Ardia.

Like I told you before, open up your mind to the universe and listen.

Meanwhile the large I-mover image changed from the hologram-cast to a default live view of Earth from its moon.

Starion glided down to the lobby. Hopefully the hologram-cast was received by his fellow remaining Evions and they were inspired to come take a look. He frantically searched for survivors outside, especially Dustion. He also tried to think of a way to get his people to Earth. He struggled to open the door, which had sunk a foot more below the surface. He gasped for air.

It's impossible for anyone to still be alive, he tragically contemplated.

Pace-gliding the lobby, glaring outside, he suddenly saw several Evions above him, covered with their shrouds and fighting for air. Luckily, there was just enough room for them to safely jump down. Starion opened the door, squeezing them inside. When they pulled back their hoods, he counted six of them. There were four adults, two very elderly, and two children. He was at least happy to see Kelleria, a teacher, and hugged her. None was Dustion.

Soon, seven more jumped down at once, including Valkia and Quarion, who was limping. Starion noticed that his glider electronics were exposed. Starion desperately looked at everyone to see if any were Dustion. Two more of them were children, and two more were elderly. None was Dustion.

"Everyone up into the I-mover near the large tank of Earth's air," he ordered. "You children can join Bria in one of the back rooms."

He paced for several more moments and, and he was just about to go get some fresh air along with everyone else when suddenly four thinner and shorter Evions jumped down in front of the lobby door. They were carrying strange-looking objects. They were all gasping as they threw back their hoods. There were two young men and two young women. One was Dustion.

Starion helped them inside and hugged his son. Dustion reciprocated just slightly.

"Where were you?"

"We were practicing," he told his father, pointing to the strange-looking devices.

Starion recalled Deon trying to cheer him up by showing him Earth's musical instruments when they were ousted. He wanted to admonish his son but knew it wasn't the time. "All of you, up to the I-mover to the large tank of Earth's air."

He pulled out his orbit tester, held his breath, stepped outside, and then pointed his orbit tester at the sun.

His short-lived hope took a dive. "Oh, no…we're out of time."

Starion followed his son and his friends into the main seating area. Deon and his friends found their own back room, apparently already breathing easier.

Starion pace-glided the back row of the I-mover, back and forth, trying to think of some way to save his people.

He hurried down into the v-breaker. He pulled out the star-power cell. It had a dull blue glow. He could tell it was nearly dead. It wouldn't be enough anyway.

He zigzag-glided each row of the I-mover, deep in thought. Eventually he found himself in the back row again, where Quarion was tending to his right foot. Quarion had badly damaged the glider on that foot. Quarion stood up, trying to move, but with one good glider and one bad one, he couldn't sync his walk. Finally he took both gliders off and wiggled his six toes. "At least they still work," he said.

Quarion looked at Starion and continued, "I suppose you think you were right, Starion?"

"No, I don't, Quarion. Who could have predicted this would happen so fast?"

"Well, you were right. But Deon tells me your plans to use hydrogen are now gone."

"That's right."

"What are we going to do?"

Starion didn't know what to say. He wandered over to the sky-roid, where his new magnifier, new star-power cell, and several dead star-power cells lay next to the flasks of gases. He looked up into the glass dome. He could see it had been warped even further. He could see the sun was just starting appear through the edge of the domed half-sphere.

He put his hand up to his chin, contemplating anything that popped into his head. Soon after, he looked back up at the magnified warped glass. More of the sun was visible. He had to squint. He hadn't needed to squint for most of life.

He was inspired. He had a brainwave. "Maybe—just maybe—this new skyroids shape can help magnify the sun's rays so we can charge a new star-power cell."

Starion removed the spacegazer below the small dome to make room. He strategically placed the magnifier and cell in its place. Then he waved his hand at the e-screen on the desk. He brought up a large list of combinations of gases. Quarion struggled in behind him, along with Phileon, Deon, Ardia, and a couple of the new arrivals.

"The only chance we have is to keep trying to fill the mag-nifier chamber with possible gaseous mixtures. Then maybe we can charge a cell. The sun should soon be near its peak strength through this skyroid."

"You have been trying for eight years, Starion…do we have

enough time?" Quarion blurted.

"I don't know—but I would rather die trying," Starion told them all, preparing a gaseous mixture in a flask.

Deon joined in the negativity. "But even if you are successful, what about the v-breaker, Starion? It has all those holes."

· "One thing at a time, Deon."

Phileon and Ardia didn't have to nod this time.

The air was getting hotter and thinner by the moment. Starion and the others were sweating profusely. No one was wearing a hypercooler.

Starion started creating a new gas mixture in a flask while viewing out the two-way mirrored window. He could see the large live 4-D image of Earth protruding out over everyone. The v-breaker lay tilted on the left side. He observed many Evions slouched over in sleep-mode. Others shook their heads from side to side in disapproval.

"So it has come down to this," Starion observed, looking at Quarion, Deon, Phileon, and Ardia, who were standing near the skyroid doorway. "Our race, which numbered in the billions only a few generations ago, is now down to the last twenty-three Evions. Nine are children...unless by some miracle more show up..."

Then, Starion remembered something.

"Oh, I forgot—we need to count the two in the envoy you sent to the other side of the galaxy. Have you tried to contact them, Deon?"

"Yes, but I still haven't received anything from them."

"It's amazing the signals are still coming from Earth. I wonder why?"

Maybe it's because you're open to it, Starion, Ardia telepathically told him.

"We need to show our new arrivals the beauty on Earth. Ardia, can you zoom in? Show them the blue skies, the green prairies, the mountains, and the oceans."

What about the Earth people? We need to show if they are living out the quest, she implored.

Starion ignored her while he finished his preparations. Then he pumped the gas into the magnifier and adjusted the cell beneath it.

"Let's try that," Starion said. "If it works, we should see a strong blue glow."

"When?" Deon asked.

"That my friend is the trillion-dollar question," he replied, seeing the confusion on Quarion and Deon's faces. *They'll learn soon enough.*

Nothing happened to the cell.

"Let's try more helium," Starion guessed while trying another mixture.

Ardia gave Starion an unhappy frown at his lack of response about transferring his visit. She zoomed in on the oceans, mountains, and vast plains of one of the continents. Then she revealed a long river that zigzagged north and south.

Starion noticed the teacher, Kelleria, glide by. He yelled, "Can you teach the children about Earth in one of the v-rooms?"

"Of course, but what should I teach them?"

"Teach them about Earth's geography, the atmosphere, and its chemical, mineral, and gaseous elements. Deon, can you give her an Earth disk to use?"

"I would be happy to," she replied, gathering up the children and herding them into an empty back v-room.

Ardia gave him another disapproving mentor look.

Unexpectedly, they heard a loud voice yell from the back of the I-mover, "What's going on here? What's going on?"

Starion could tell it was Judion's voice. He had awoken and was stumble-gliding down one of the aisles.

"Deon and Quarion, can you keep trying different mixtures?"

"But which ones?" Deon asked.

"Take a guess," Starion panted, hustling to confront Judion.

244 (JIM EVRY

Quarion shrugged his shoulders. "A guess...that's not very logical."

When he caught up to Judion, Starion sneezed twice, then said, "Calm down, Judion. We are alive in this I-mover thanks to Earth's air. And we are charging up a star-power cell over there to take us to Earth before it's too late."

Judion glanced around the I-mover, in obvious shock from what had happened. Then he saw a woman's legs lying just inside one of the v-rooms. He rushed inside and knelt above her, weeping. "Oh, Kircia...Kircia..."

Ardia moved over and shut the door quietly, so as to let Judion grieve in private. They all sadly turned back to the I-mover view of Earth.

Starion headed back to the skyroid v-room, where Deon and Quarion had just tried a new mixture. There was still no sign of success.

Just then, Judion ran out of the room where his wife lay dead. He yelled to Starion while everyone turned their attention to him.

"Starion, you killed my wife just like you killed my brother...and now you want to kill the rest of us while we get stuck between Evion and that planet Earth."

Starion told Deon and Quarion, "Keep trying different combinations. I'll handle this." Starion hurry-glided back out and followed Judion down to the front, trying to calm him. Judion's eyes were lifeless.

Starion tried his best again. "This last flare and quake took our moon along with most of our atmosphere and air with it, Judion...and now our orbit has shifted, too. Look around. We are the last of our race...we don't have any more time. Deon, Quarion, and I are trying to create a new energy cell, right over there in that back v-room, so we can migrate to Earth. We must hurry before this tank of Earth's air runs out. Help us, Judion."

When finished, Starion sneezed again. Judion blocked it with his shroud arm.

Judion was clearly unstable with both his thinking and his coordination. He stumbled and shouted, sweat running down his face. "There was a vote, everyone. And you lost, Starion. We are not going to Earth. And finally, you are risking all of our lives. You have the Earth disease."

There were several gasps.

Judion viewed the large I-mover, which was still showing Earth Mountains and a serene lake. He rapidly twirled his hands counterclockwise, changing the image. Suddenly they all witnessed two planes crashing into a building on Earth.

Many in the audience gasped again.

"See, everyone, we can't survive there," Judion explained while twirling his hands clockwise very fast this time. He displayed the same scene of the war he had shown in the Audiseum with the roadside bomb. They all witnessed the young man who lost his legs. "This was only seventy of Earth's orbits ago," he told everyone.

Judion finally showed his sick, bedridden wife again. Starion could see his eyes turn dark and cold.

Judion glided down an aisle on the left side of the I-mover next to the v-breaker. He stopped halfway down.

"Starion, you killed my wife," he yelled again, then broke down weeping. A little more than half of the Evions hurried down to support and console Judion.

Judion sat down in despair but continued by bringing up his version of the orbital clock. "And we are *not* being pulled into the sun … we will safely travel around, and then everything will start to revert back to normal. Then we can build a new greenhouse and e-com."

One of the Evions who, like Judion, had dark cold eyes, shouted, "I agree with Judion—we couldn't survive there."

Starion, in the back row, watched each Evion now choose sides. Those with Judion moved over to one side. Those on Starion's took the other.

CHAPTER 40

VALKIA, WHO was still in shock, chose Judion's group, along with Glenion, still sniffling. And then six more adults, plus the four elderly Evions, also joined Judion.

Some in Judion's group took advantage of the adjustable chairs and were lying in a prone position.

Curion, who had seen Judion rush out of the v-room they had just shared, managed to struggle out into the last row to join Starion's group.

Concerned, Starion told him, "Curion, you need to rest."

"I'm OK."

"Judion, you're a doctor. You need to help Curion," Starion shouted.

Judion ignored him.

Still standing in the back row, Starion counted the thirteen who were now on Judion's side. Thankfully the four other children had joined Bria in the back v-room. Starion sat down in a chair while holding his head down. If by some miracle they were successful and left Evion, Judion's group would perish. Ousted or not, he'd been elected president, and he felt he was responsible for all Evions.

Ardia and the frail Phileon witnessed everything. Phileon shuffled up next to Starion with his staff. Starion felt his firm grip and looked up at his old wrinkled face.

"Starion, I knew you were the one who could lead Evion to survival when you were a young man. You should be proud of all your accomplishments…now is not the time to give up. If one ever gives up on his enemies, there is no hope."

"But I have done everything I could," Starion protested. "Even if by some miracle we are able to create enough power and fix the v-breaker, we have exposed to our fellow Evions everything I could about Earth. We showed them the sunshine, the blue skies, the vital green rolling hills, the rain. They are breathing Earth's air as we speak…and the majority still doesn't like humans and Earth. If they want to stay here, that's up to them."

Phileon pulled out his tattered copy of the book again. He whispered, "Starion…you have revealed Earth's outer aspects, which are fabulous. But you have forgotten something."

"What?"

"That is for you to ask yourself my son; when you were on Earth studying the people, did you find anything you felt our fellow Evions were missing, besides the fresh air and beautiful planet?"

"What do you mean?"

He held up the book. "Every story in this book has a standard motif: The heroes, at some point in their lives, felt something was missing…and not just food, water, and air."

Starion couldn't think of an answer.

After a long pause, Phileon smiled. "You told me you liked the Earth people. Why?"

Starion paused for a moment. "They had strong emotions of love, compassion, competitiveness, anger, jealousy, and passion, along with dreams and wishes…most lived an adventure every day while confronting tough situations constantly. Most of them seemed to keep pushing forward, no matter what…"

"How did you come to learn this?"

"I saw it on their faces. I heard it in their voices. I saw the pain in their eyes. I scanned in their literature, I-spacers, music, and paintings. I experienced their despair when a fellow Earth person died tragically, and how they held vigils. I also discovered hope in their eyes as they walked by me on the street, even when their circumstances were not good."

"So are you saying something is missing here on Evion?"

Starion pondered for a moment—then he saw Phileon point a five-fingered hand at the large screen. Starion stared in surprise.

"Show us what we have been missing," the old man told him.

Starion stood up. "But not all is good...and their emotions are very strong."

"There cannot be good without bad. There can't be tragedy without comedy, there can't be life without death, there can't be light without darkness."

"Yes," Ardia added, "and if the humans are living out the story of the quest, they must have these emotions."

"Show us your visit, Starion. Highlight their emotions while Deon and Quarion keep trying to charge a cell," Phileon suggested.

Starion nodded reluctantly and moved over to the skyroid. "Quarion, keep trying. Deon, follow me," he said, hurrying over to the control room while Deon followed. Ardia also came along to make sure Starion transferred his visit. She stood behind him while he transferred a blue stream of data into an IS unit.

"Hmm..." Ardia said.

"Link this download to the D-box you labeled 'Starion's Earth Visit' and start it up," Starion told his friend, noticing Ardia behind him. *Just wait, Ardia.*

"Download?" Deon asked.

"Yes, that is what they call it on Earth."

While Deon worked on this task, Starion streamed another ray of data.

"Create a subcategory to that link, Deon, and call it 'Earth Human Emotions.'"

Ardia nodded in approval.

Deon instantly linked both downloads. When finished, out of the corner of his eye, he saw the strange unknown signal on the O-scope oscillating more.

Starion and Ardia moved out into the I-mover. Starion pointed at the large screen. He brought up the D-box and chose "Starion's Earth Visit."

Now on the screen was an I-spacer of when he had taken off for Earth. He, along with everyone else, viewed the terrible solar explosion he had believed destroyed Evion.

Judion yelled while stopping the broadcast with his finger. "What's going on here...what is this?"

Ardia clearly had enough. She moved halfway down the middle aisle and sternly told Judion's side, "Everyone, this is Starion's visit to Earth. If you don't want to come with us, that is fine...but please, let us perform some research to find out where *we* should land and how best to introduce ourselves."

Ardia's credibility still worked. Most nodded to Judion that it was OK. Judion angrily motioned and started the visit back up.

Starion started back to help Quarion, but on his way he felt something suddenly pull at his emotions.

Deon suddenly interrupted his thoughts. "Hey, Starion...this unknown signal is pulsating even more."

"We don't have time to see what it is, Deon," Starion told him.

Deon's curiosity took over. He pointed his finger at the signal anyway and pulled it out toward him. Inside the 4-D image on the O-scope were other signals, too. "Hey—there are three signals imbedded in it."

Deon's scientist brain couldn't let him leave it alone. He quickly labeled them "Signal 1," "Signal 2," and "Signal 3." He chose "Signal 1" and put it up on the large I-mover screen, replacing Starion's visit. Then a fuzzy image slowly started coming in clearer and clearer.

The Evions and Starion, who was just starting a new mixture, observed two young men on Earth near a large brown brick building. The two were standing over an old red Earth surface vehicle. It sure looked familiar to Starion.

Starion felt something overpower his reawakened soul. He stepped out from the skyroid into the back row for a better view.

The two young Earth men inside the live image opened up the hood and peeked inside. The Evions saw a small thin engine with a black solar magnifier panel on top of it. Then Starion recognized a similar panel on the hood itself.

The word "life" was in the upper back left of the floating image.

Ardia looked keenly at one of the young men. Then she glanced back and forth between him and Starion.

"What?" Starion asked her.

"This young man on Earth is yours, Starion."

There was a loud gasp from the other Evions.

Starion zoomed in on the young man. He twirled his hand and the bright sun was now in the background. There were trees with bustling green branches and leaves.

He zoomed in further. He could see the young man was tall, skinny, and had red hair—and six fingers.

"Oh, no," Starion mumbled.

"Ah-ha!" Deon blurted. "Starion, the I-Spacer DNA link is somehow working from this old IS unit."

Moments later on the screen, three other young Earth men walked by; the sound of humans filled the I-mover. One of them yelled, "Edison…you will never get that damn solar engine to work…you have been working on it for eight years!"

"Yes we will!" the young six-fingered man yelled back. "Won't we, Nikola?" he asked his friend, who also was skinny, had black hair, and wore a pair of black plastic glasses.

His friend nodded yes. "We will present this at the symposium on new possible energy sources at Berkeley."

"Now we know what you were doing on Earth," Judion bellowed.

All the Evions were startled by the sound of the young humans.

Judion shouted, "Ha—just like his father, he can't invent something worth anything."

Starion put his head down and glided back into the skyroid v-room.

Deon chose the second of the three signals.

Up on the screen was an image of a young Earth woman

dressed in black standing next to a long wooden box. There were thirty others, along with another older woman. The background was of a dark, cloudy part of Earth. Again, the word "life" was displayed in the upper front of the image.

Starion poked his head of the skyroid room. "Deon, we don't have time for this!"

Starion finished a mixture then tried it. But after glancing up at the screen again, he couldn't resist. He stood with one leg in the back row of the I-mover and the other in the skyroid. He glanced between the cell and the large new image on the screen.

Again, Starion noticed Ardia look between the young woman and him.

"Oh, no ..." Starion uttered while zooming in on the young woman. She was very attractive with long blonde hair. After seeing her resemblance to an Evion, he examined her hands. Luckily, he could see only five fingers. His emotions skyrocketed.

"Quarion, you try a different mixture," Starion requested, turning his head toward the skyroid room and then back to the I-mover screen again. He wanted to check this out more diligently. He twirled his hand counterclockwise, and the word "life" changed to "rewind."

Starion stopped when he found an older, very frail man sitting with this young woman. He was flipping through a family album. Starion saw several 2-D pictures of Mary at different ages holding babies. "But I thought she couldn't have children," he mumbled quietly to himself.

Suddenly, the Evion audience was again startled by the man's voice and different nuances. "Dea, you mustn't give up on your dream of a body S-ray that can help us view inside ourselves to help prevent cancer—never give up."

"But I have tried and tried and can't figure it out," the young Earth woman explained.

"You told me you had this image imbedded in your mind ever since you can remember. Don't give up now!" the man implored while coughing from deep inside his lungs.

252 (JIM EVRY

Judion interrupted the playback. "Ha—your daughter can't invent anything either, Starion."

Starion again put his head down. Ardia glided over for support.

"Ardia...all of a sudden, I have these extreme emotions," he confided.

"Yes...Starion, you are feeling your Earth children's emotional signals."

"This far away?"

"Yes. A parent's love for a child is the most powerful force in the universe, as I have told you before. Any kind of love is the ultimate life force."

They heard someone sniffling down in Judion's group. And then they saw a woman tear up.

Suddenly, there was another massive solar storm. A solar flare hit the small skyroid dome. It was so bright for an instant that it blew up the cell underneath. *How ironic,* Starion thought. *The giant sun's rays weren't strong enough anymore to charge cells, but this flare blew up a cell.*

Starting to reach for another old cell, an I-spacer he had scanned on Earth flashed through his memory. Then he pondered, *what if he were to somehow harness the energy of one these single flares, and then filter it into a more manageable stream of power?* If he could do that, maybe he could charge a cell. But then he realized there wasn't enough time. And he would never know where or when a flare would occur.

Several massive quakes now followed the storm. Starion could feel the whole I-mover shift and sink as the Evions held on for dear life.

CHAPTER 41

"THIS FLARE storm and quake will pass just like the rest," Judion declared loudly.

"No it won't," Starion yelled back. "And Deon, stop these unknown signals—it's too difficult for me to concentrate."

Phileon countered, "Look Starion...Quarion is still trying...and these broadcasts of your Earth people seem to be affecting Judion's group."

With a wink, Ardia nodded at Deon to continue.

Starion tossed the blown-up cell over in the corner then placed another older cell below the magnifier. He reluctantly looked on while Deon chose the third signal. Now, up on the screen were two scraggly young men with long hair sitting on a sidewalk with their backs against the wall. One was strumming a stringed instrument Starion had seen on Earth. It was also similar to what his son Dustion had brought with him. There was a hat with some bills and change inside it that sat between them.

Starion noticed Dustion and his friends poke their heads out of the back room.

Again, the Earth sound caught all of them by surprise.

Starion was angered by Deon's insistence on showing these new Earth signals, but he couldn't refuse the protruding image. He moved out of the room again and zoomed in. To his dismay, he saw six fingers on the young man with the instrument.

"Who is *this* now?" he quietly murmured, rewinding it like before. Finally, he recognized the young woman he had met at the gold exchange in England. She was carrying a baby. She dropped it off at a place that had a sign: "Dickens Orphanage."

Starion forwarded back to the live view. The I-mover audience observed an Earth man rush out of door and yell, "Wayden, get out of here, you creep."

"I'm not a creep," Wayden said, standing up. He continued, "Let's get some wine, Alan."

The two took the money out of the hat; Alan put it on his head. They both walked into a store, and then walked out, each a carrying a tall green bottle.

When they started to drink it, standing on the sidewalk, the signal faded and the image gradually turned to static.

Again, Judion yelled, "Ha—another one of your Earth children, Starion. Now we know what you did on Earth. You weren't trying to save us."

Suddenly Starion could feel a different and frightening type of rumble. He felt his equilibrium change. The I-mover sank and tilted even further. They heard the hyper-fan in the air tank inside the v-breaker slow down.

Judion reassured everyone, "We are fine…that is the shift in our orbit I was talking about. We will now swing safely around the sun and then our atmosphere will replenish itself."

Full of new emotions and trying to handle them, Starion hurried into the skyroid. He mixed up a brand-new mixture, but before pumping it into the chamber he pointed up at the screen and changed it back to his visit. He couldn't take the added emotional stress of these other signals anymore.

While frantically pumping the new mixture into the magnifier, he viewed the scene when he entered Earth's solar system through the dome. He was aware that shortly, the screen would show him trying to crash his ship into Earth. After that, it would show the seven Earth men and women who had given him inspiration in the cave.

When finished, he adjusted the cell below, hoping for a blue glow, but there was nothing. On the screen, he expected to see his ship enter Earth's atmosphere—but it didn't. It somehow jumped over the scenes of his attempted suicide mission and his encounter with the seven philosophers. The screen now displayed the period of time during his visit when he found Deon's signal and realized Evion was OK.

He shook his head. He knew the events had occurred. What happened? He started to wonder if that part of his visit had been a dream.

Looking upward, he adjusted the angle of the magnifier to catch the sun's rays. Frustrated, he could see the massive dying sun sinking near the last part of the clear dome above. What was he going to do? They were running out of time.

Starion checked on Dustion, who was in a back v-room with his friends. Then he checked in on Bria. She was sitting on the floor with the other children listening to the teacher, Kelleria, in another v-room.

When Starion glided by the door, he heard Kelleria. "So what is Earth's atmosphere made of?"

He heard Bria answer. "It is seventy-eight percent nitrogen and twenty-two percent oxygen."

Starion stopped, putting his fifth and sixth fingers up to his chin; he smiled and hurried over into the main control room. He took the last remaining small tank of Earth's air, then brought it into the skyroid, repeating to himself, "Seventy-eight percent nitrogen and twenty-two percent oxygen—that's it! That's the mixture!"

Quarion, puzzled, shook his head from side to side at Deon, who had just joined them. They both watched while Starion held the small Earth air tank with a determined look.

Adjusting the magnifier again, he looked up. Just that fast, Starion's confidence diminished. He could only see half of the large plasmic sun's sphere. His planet had rotated too far. And its daily rotation continued.

"Oh, no…I just can't seem beat these evil forces," he shouted.

He glanced over at Ardia and Phileon standing in the doorway. They each gave him a mentor-reminder look while nodding.

Starion went into deep thought. He closed his eyes; they glowed a light blue. Soon he opened them. He had an idea.

He hurried down into the basement. He zigzagged around the large, dirty, silver hydraulic cylinders. Finally, he found a door to a room. He opened it and realized this was the room where, long ago, the I-mover director used a special IS unit to raise, lower, and move the building from side to side. Starion saw an old wooden bookshelf containing many of the old books he had been reading. He understood the director had used these books to follow along with the film in order to time moving the I-mover building to exact scenes in the film.

Next to the bookshelf was a control box with several levers linked to the IS unit. He moved each one, looking out the door to see if any of the hydraulic cylinders moved.

Finally, they moved from side to side. He pushed another lever and the cylinders moved upward. He pushed the same lever again then held it. He heard a loud creaking sound as the floor of the I-mover began to lift straight up.

He hustled out of the room to see how far up the ceiling or floor of the I-mover was. He was having a hard time breathing. He could see the dangerous outside environment in between the cylinders. He believed he had raised the floor about ten feet. At first he figured it would be far enough, but he decided he'd better raise it as far as he could so the magnifier was as close to the sun as possible.

He glide-ran back in, pushed and held the lever, and watched the cylinders rise until they finally stopped.

He hurried back out, gasping for air, now soaking with sweat. Surprised, he looked up and saw that the I-mover building was over an e-mile above him.

But now he had a problem. How was he going to get back inside the raised I-mover?

He searched for a way up, blinking sweat from his eyes. It was difficult to breathe.

There must be a way. What if there was an emergency and an Evion had to leave during a film?

Finally, he found a door in one of the cylinders. He stood in front of it and it automatically opened. Starion entered. Inside, he saw a thin ladder pointing up the side of the cylinder. But thankfully, it had the antigravity technology. He shot up to the floor of the I-mover.

Within seconds, he was standing in front of an open door inside the main control v-room, where Deon was working on a signal. Starion hurried inside, startling Deon.

"Oh! Starion, whatever you did, it worked. The skyroid glass dome is clear and we are closer to the sun."

CHAPTER 42

STARION HURRIED back to the skyroid, where he had left the small tank of Earth air. He started to pump the air into the magnifier chamber. Looking up, the full spewing sun's rays were now shining through. His efforts to raise the I-mover had worked.

At that moment, Dustion and his three other friends walked up to the room without their gliders. Dustion asked Starion, "Can we sing to all of you down on the I-mover stage?"

"Dustion, we don't have time…can't you see we are busy?"

The rebellious Dustion and his friends ignored him. They gathered their instruments and set up down on the stage in front. A few moments later, they started playing a song. The Evions watched and listened, some with curiosity, some in shock, while others were in sleep-mode.

Dustion played the instrument while singing.

"Words are flowing out like endless rain into a paper cup…They slither while they pass, they slip away across the universe…"

Starion, who had just finished pumping Earth's air into the magnifier top chamber, was adjusting the horizontal magnifier for the best optimum position to receive the sun's rays when he heard his son begin to sing this beautiful Earth song. *How does he know this song?*

Starion hurried down the aisle steps while the scene on the I-spacer showed him flying back to Earth to find London. As he approached the stage and the song was about three-quarters finished, Dustion broke down as he sang, *"Nothing's going to change my world…"*

Starion climbed up on stage. He hugged his son like never before. Dustion finally reciprocated, saying. "I'm sorry...I'm sorry, Dad."

"I'm sorry, too, my son. I should have been there for you...I should have been there for you, Bria, and your Mom."

"That's OK, Dad. That's OK. You were trying to save us all."

Bria had followed her father. She wrapped her arms around both of them.

"I'm so proud of you two," Starion told them.

Now, almost all the Evions had tears in their eyes—except for Judion.

Ardia took advantage of the moment and hurried down onto the stage. She changed the I-spacer to the one Judion had shown from Earth's past when they were ousted from the council. She displayed the young man who had lost his legs in a roadside bomb lying on the sidewalk, bleeding.

Then she fast-forwarded Starion's visit to a replay of Starion in the church, when the old man had talked about forgiveness. She played it for all to see and hear, but she prefaced it by yelling, "This is the same man in this I-mover image I just showed who almost died when he was a young man...and this is him again, seventy Earth years later."

They all watched this old man just as Starion had in the church. "One must forgive in order to be one with God," he said. "Whether it is as large as forgiving a whole group of people or as small as just one person, you must forgive in order to move forward with life."

Starion finally made the connection Ardia had found. He knew the old man in the church had looked familiar.

Ardia froze the image. "We all have to forgive, like this Earth man has done. And we have to forgive our previous generations' failure to find a solution—they did the best they could under the circumstances. We have no right to judge them. If we all can forgive them, we can move forward and take advantage of each of our own calls to adventure; otherwise, we can't. And you also have to forgive yourself."

"Forgive myself for what?" Judion yelled.

Suddenly, Quarion, who was still in the skyroid, yelled, "Starion…Starion…everyone—look!"

Starion and everyone else turned their attention backward. They could see a blue glow shining from the skyroid lab. They all hurried up the aisles, where they saw the star-power cell fully charged.

Starion hugged Deon, Ardia, and his children while his supporters cheered.

Judion's supporters had followed to see what all the commotion was. Two of them joined Starion's group, while the others went back to their seats.

One of those who stayed with Starion's group was Valkia. Starion was glad. He could tell she had started to come out of her shock at losing her husband. Then he saw Glenion, who appeared much better. "This Earth virus is not fatal," Glenion told Starion, painfully trying to smile.

Valkia found Ardia, and then broke down crying. "I'm so sorry, Ardia."

"It's OK, Valkia. It's OK."

Quarion also nodded to Starion in ashamed approval, wiggling his six toes.

"Earth's combination of oxygen and nitrogen did the trick," Starion proudly stated. "Now I know why Earth's atmosphere is so blue. I should have figured it out earlier—Vincion mentioned Evion's diminished nitrogen when we started losing our ability to create instant star-power cells. I didn't catch it. I didn't make the connection…maybe I was too complacent, like the previous two generations were."

Moments later, Deon joined them all. Ardia asked him, "Still think faith can't move planets?"

Starion pondered deeply, and then he said, "I think all we need are three more star-power cells, Quarion. Remove this one, and then charge up three more empty cells."

Starion looked down at the damaged v-breaker. "All we need to do now is fix this v-breaker."

Starion optimistically put his sixth finger up to his chin. He felt he couldn't be stopped now. "We need to somehow start a fire then melt the braydium so we can patch the v-breaker."

"How can we start a fire?" Deon asked.

Starion pulled out the book of matches. There was one match left. Phileon took it from him. "I can handle that, Starion."

Ardia sauntered up to Starion, looking at Judion's group. "We need to make sure all of us leave for Earth. You need to continue showing your visit to Earth, Starion...but this time, like Phileon said; you need to show what we have been missing."

Starion realized she was right. He pointed and chose the subcategory labeled "Earth Human Emotions."

Phileon reminded him, *Show the good and bad.*

Now, on the large protruding screen, there were scenes from when he interacted with the humans in England, San Francisco, and New York. He was witnessing the humans as they laughed, cried, yelled, sneezed, coughed, argued, and made different facial expressions. His fellow Evions saw and heard the young humans call Starion a creep.

Judion snickered. Starion wondered how he would know what that meant.

Then the Evion audience observed the two I-jet flyers land, with humans wearing masks while carrying guns and empty bags. They witnessed the two steal I-jet flyer tanks and fly up and away while someone followed, yelling and shooting at them.

Judion shouted, "Is this the kind of place you want to live, everyone?"

But after that scene, the large I-mover image displayed a large red surface vehicle driving by with its loud siren to help with a building on fire.

His fellow Evions saw two young men run inside. And, like Starion had experienced at the time, they couldn't believe it, either. Why were the humans risking their lives? Four other humans with strange uniforms ran out of the large surface vehicle dragging long hoses. Two of them hauled a ladder, dangerously placing it against the building, and then started climbing up.

Several Evions stood up in their seats, astonished, when the two young men ran out coughing and carrying a woman in their arms, then falling on the grass.

Then they witnessed the two in uniforms who had climbed the ladder. They returned from the fiery inside carrying a small child down while gasping for air.

Again, like Starion had when seeing this live on Earth, several on both sides of the I-mover had tears run down their face.

Then the scene changed to when the coughing uniformed man returned from the burning building with a woman limp in his arms.

The audience tensely watched as the two other humans tried to revive her. When they were unsuccessful and held a small vigil, more tears developed.

The image changed again to more human emotion scenes.

Everyone observed a human man run out of a building in anger and yell, "Keep those damn dogs out of here!" And then when a small white dog pranced by Starion, growled, and leaped toward him, there was slight laugh from someone in Judion's group.

Starion recalled the incident and contemplated if this was an appropriate scene to show.

Then they saw a young man chase his crying girlfriend and tell her, "I'm sorry, I'm sorry...I was jealous." When she took off her head IS unit with the face panel and threw it away, then kissed him and made up, Starion's side cheered. Starion was also worried about revealing this scene.

A couple in Judion's group stared at each other differently than they had before.

After that, they all saw two young Earth boys racing each other on the sidewalk. Bria and the young Evions paid special attention. "One, two, three—go," one boy shouted as they raced down the sidewalk with their shoes and caps.

Starion definitely remembered this, and he hoped his children could do the same.

Next, the large I-mover displayed a huge 4-D protruding image of when he had stopped for coffee with Mary.

A human man next to where he had been sitting asked a woman with him, "What do you call a crazy alien from outer space...an astronut!" The woman had laughed, sipping on her coffee. "Why did the alien leave the restaurant?" she asked him back and then answered herself: "Because there was no atmosphere." Shaking his head, the man asked, "Why did the alien cross the galaxy...to get to the other side."

Starion remembered he had not understood the first joke at that particular time and had turned his attention to something else—Mary. But now he understood along with the rest of the jokes. He cracked a huge smile, hurting just a little. Phileon, Ardia, and for some reason one of Judion's group were the only others to get the humor also.

Starion knew he shouldn't be watching this. He had other things to do. But as he was about to turn away, he heard a whoosh. Phileon had started a fire toward the back left of the I-mover.

Then, he heard the blower for the tank of Earth's air inside the v-breaker slow down even further. There were gasps from everyone; the air was becoming very thin. Several of them appeared lethargic and lay down on their I-mover chairs. Phileon's fire started to diminish.

"What else are you going to throw at me?" Starion said, looking up, struggling to breathe.

He had to start patching up the v-breaker, but air was more important at the moment. Glancing at the background of Earth's blue sky in the 4-D image, suddenly an image of his mentor Vincion popped into his mind.

He hurried into his v-room. There, he brought up the interview of his mentor Vincion again. He fast-forwarded to a place in the old I-spacer where Starion remembered Vincion had been interviewed one hundred years before.

The reporter was saying, "I understand you also are working on other inventions, such as developing a way for I-movergoers to join in with the 4-D image and interact with it?"

"Yes, that is correct; it would be called 5-D. But keep in mind my main reason to invent this is to help us easily divert future deadly hyper-asteroids. I was very close to succeeding, but ever since our atmosphere's gas composition changed due to the sun's sudden change, I have been having difficulty. It seems like the gas composition of twenty-two percent oxygen and seventy-eight percent nitrogen is what I need, but we are rapidly losing our nitrogen."

Starion shook his head from side to side. "Aha—why didn't I let him finish when I was listening before?"

His mentor Vincion continued on with the interview. "I believe I had the correct air mixture to succeed with creating a fifth dimension, but I just couldn't get it to work after our atmosphere started to lose its nitrogen—which, by the way, is why we are experiencing a change in our atmosphere's blue color."

"Yes!" Starion said to himself again. "Just like my star-power cell that needed the correct mixture of oxygen and nitrogen. Earth's air is what I need again."

Starion hurried back into the skyroid, where Quarion was charging the last cell. Starion grabbed the small tank of Earth's air. He shook it. There wasn't much left.

Starion hurried back to his v-room and closed the door. He pointed at the 4-D blank image on the desk e-screen and then pulled it toward him. He found the D-box and was planning to choose a live view of Earth, but strangely, a pulsating oscillating signal appeared.

He chose it.

CHAPTER 43

STARION SAW a silhouette of a man walking into a dark and dangerous area on Earth. Then he noticed a water canal parallel to the street and the sidewalk the man was stumbling along. The man was carrying his belongings, including a musical instrument. The word "life" was displayed inside on the back upper left of the screen.

Starion could tell it was his Earth son, Wayden. He watched him stumble, about to fall into the ice-cold canal. He could see this part of the canal had steep cement walls. It would have been impossible for Wayden to climb back out if he fell.

Starion's adrenalin skyrocketed. He put the mask and hose from the Earth air tank inside the floating image and turned the knob on the tank wide open. He chose the 5-D option.

He stood up gradually, moving his face and head into the image, and then he bent down even further with the upper part of his body. He was now within arm's reach of Wayden. Then, with all his energy, Starion lifted and pulled Wayden back toward the sidewalk by his coat collar and laid him down gently with his hand.

Starion sighed with relief. He was in euphoric shock. The fifth dimension technology worked! He felt half his body on Earth and half his body back on Evion. He could feel and smell the cool evening Earth air. He took a deep breath.

"Wayden—Wayden!" he shouted.

Wayden opened one eye but then shut it.

"Wake up, wake up," Starion kept saying, reveling in his ability to physically shake Wayden.

After a brief moment, Wayden appeared to be coming out of his drunken haze.

"Who are you?" he asked, looking up at what must have seemed a strange image.

"My name is Starion."

"Where am I?"

"You are safely on Earth's ground. You almost fell into the water canal," Starion reminded him.

"Oh, yes. I must have gotten lost," Wayden mumbled.

Starion knew he was lying, and he recollected his own mistake not long ago.

"Wow, I have to quit drinking," Wayden continued.

"Yes, you do," Starion counseled him.

Wayden looking around wiped the sleep and drunkenness out of his eyes. "What do you want?"

"I want to help you with your life," Starion pronounced.

Wayden struggled to sit up. "No one can help me. I have no family, no formal education. Hell, I can just barely read—the orphanage couldn't afford glasses for me. And people think I'm a creep because of my six fingers."

"Yes, I know what you mean," Starion sympathized, remembering his own visit there. "But I think you are in good company. There were many Earth people in your history who were misunderstood or different…use this difference to your advantage somehow."

Starion reached back into his shroud and pulled out the book, *Anciente Evion Adventura~Hero.*

Wayden squinted to see it. Then he reached into his bag and pulled out his own copy. Starion smiled more easily than before. *That's right,* he suddenly recalled. There was a copy of the book in the bag of clothes he had forgotten while in London. He realized his mother must have given it to him.

"Who are you? Are you my father?"

Starion pointed his focus finger into Wayden's eyes, and after a bright flash of light, Wayden had to close them. He put his hand up to wipe away several tears from the flash.

When Wayden could open them again, he looked at his copy of the book. "Wow, I can see it! How did you do that to my eyes? And what or where is Evion, anyway?"

Starion told him, "Never mind how I fixed your eyes for now. As far as the book, Evion is a planet whose sun is dying. The people need to migrate to another planet such as Earth to survive."

Wayden responded, "I have never heard that story."

Starion changed the subject. "Wayden, I need your help. Can I count on you?"

"I don't know. What do you need me to do?"

"First, I want you to get healthy...both physically and emotionally, OK?" Starion said in a fatherly tone.

Wayden looked around again, as if making sure this was real. "OK, I'll try."

"That's all I can ask: that you do your best. Along with your copy of *Anciente Evion Adventura~Hero*, I need you to study some information I am going to transfer into your brain. You have a special ability. You are able to scan data into your brain instantly, Wayden. I need you to learn everything I transfer to you. Also study all the philosophical and passed-down stories from Earth books you can find. And then you must take what you have learned and travel the planet to relate that knowledge to as many of your fellow Earth people as possible. OK?"

Wayden thought for a moment, still in shock. He shook his head again. "This is a heavy load...why me?"

"You have been chosen because of your deep understanding of the labyrinth. You have been down deep in despair. Now you must come back out of it and inspire others. That has always been the way the hero passes on a new or forgotten life force message to the rest of society or becomes the redeemer."

"Do I have to do this alone?"

"Sometimes...but usually no. Usually a magical aid or mentor will mysteriously appear. And always look for inspiration in your fellow people, nature, literature, religions, philosophies, music, paintings, sculptures, and I-spacers...I mean, motion pictures. And most importantly, act on instinct."

"Okay," Wayden replied again. "I will try."

"Remember, Wayden, I have faith in you."

Starion sent a blue data stream to Wayden, first transferring the Evion dictionary, then the rest of his memory. Starion finally pulled his head and body from the image, a tear in his eye.

Starion felt happy and sad at the same time. He had been able to help his son Wayden, but at the same time, he did the same thing his father had done to him: he left this lonely young man alone without a father.

Deon opened the door.

"Starion...we are almost out of air."

CHAPTER 44

THE EVIONS in the I-mover were breathing in the last of Earth's air. They were sweating and gasping.

"What are we going to do, Starion?"

"Watch this—and get ready to refill the v-breaker air tank."

Starion hurried out into the main seating area and down to the v-breaker and the large tank of Earth's air inside. He opened the valve as far as it would turn. Massive amounts of Earth's air filled up the I-mover. Moments later, the hyper-fan stopped.

"What are you doing? That emptied the tank," he heard someone yell.

Starion pointed at his Earth visit, which was playing the scene where he was flying above Earth with his head out the window.

He instantly changed it to a live view of Earth from its moon. He zoomed in on an ocean. In the background was a small land mass. The word "life" was up on the front upper left. Salty blue waves were splashing all over inside the image.

Starion pulled the I-mover image all the way to the back of the building with both his hands. Now, the whole building and all the Evions were engulfed inside it.

Everyone was startled. They put their arms up to block the Earth sun's rays. Starion brought up the D-box with the old links to "I-Mover Antigravity" and "Fifth Dimension (5-D)." He chose them both.

At that instant, everyone was floating right above the ocean, breathing in the fresh Earth air. They were now in both the fifth dimension and in zero gravity.

Starion slowly changed the image from 5-D to 4-D again, bringing the gravity level back to normal. Everyone began to land safely somewhere in the I-mover, still standing above the Earth Ocean and breathing the fresh salty air.

"Wow Starion...the fifth dimension...you did it...you did it!" Deon shouted, sucking in the new fresh air.

"Yes...Vincion was so close to inventing it, but, like the sudden diminished ability to create star-power cells when the sun started dying, he had to quit."

"Starion...why can't we show a live view of Earth's surface and then all of us jump into the 5-D image?" Deon asked curiously. "We could all be on Earth instantly."

At that moment, Judion landed next to them. He had heard them. "Ha," he exclaimed, scurrying back down where he was before with the others from his group.

"This has not been tested," Starion said, ignoring Judion. "It is possible not all of our molecules would pass through...it's too dangerous. Air is one thing, but the complicated Evion cells from our bodies are another and besides, we should properly introduce ourselves when we arrive on Earth. And furthermore, we now will have plenty of star-power cells to travel back in our spaceship."

"Spaceship? You mean our v-breaker?"

"No, Deon...the Earth people call them 'spaceships' in their stories. And by the way, Deon, once on Earth, you may want to find out what stories or mythologies you are living your life by. Or you may want to create your own and then live by it. But get ready for both intended and unintended adventures. Hopefully you will be able to live a life that was intended for you."

"What will that be?"

"That is for you to find out. Each individual must discover that him or herself."

"Starion, the fire is going strong again," Phileon shouted. "It started up again as soon as you filled the I-mover with Earth's air."

Everyone turned toward it. Most had never seen a small fire burning on purpose.

After seeing Phileon with his shroud holding his staff and then glancing at the vast ocean inside the image, Starion had a strange urge to ask Phileon to part the water with his staff, for some reason.

"Deon, fill up the v-breaker's tank. Then we need to melt this Earth's braydium and patch up the holes with it!"

Starion remembered seeing an old cauldron in the basement. He dropped down the long, tall hydraulic cylinder, found it, and then shot back up.

He set it on top of the fire and hurried to the back of the v-breaker, where he opened the hatch. He grabbed his shovel and hauled almost all of the braydium over to the cauldron.

Deon hob-glided into the v-breaker. He opened the tank in- put valve, filling it with the Earth's air that now permeated the I-mover. "The tank is full, Starion."

Starion poured two of the Earth bottles of water Deon had brought back into the cauldron. After stirring it, there was a milky, clear substance.

He found a small piece of wood from an I-mover table that had been destroyed. He filled it with the pasty-looking substance and then diligently started filling up the holes on the v-breaker.

"Deon, hurry—find a small piece of wood like this and help."

Starion glanced at the I-spacer. Now that they had their air, he felt renewed. He wanted to check on his other Earth son, so he pointed and chose the "Unknown Signal" link again, then "Signal #1."

Now on the large screen, Edison and his friend drove into an Earth parking lot with the large yellow digital arches Starion had seen while on Earth. After parking their old beat-up red surface craft, they hopped out and peeked underneath the hood. They adjusted the solar panels on the engine. Edison explained, "We have to figure this out somehow, Nikola."

Just then, behind the two Earth men, three I-jet flyers landed near them.

Watching from their room, Dustion and his friends moved out into the main seating area again so as to see clearer.

"Come on—I'm hungry," Edison said as they both strolled over to the front counter to order their food. Edison stared at the pretty young blonde cashier. "We'll take two Planet Macs, two Earth fries, and two Super-Cokes," he politely ordered. Then he aimed his wristwatch device at a scanner near the register. When he did, the young lady could see his six fingers and gave him an odd look.

"Hey, you sure are pretty," Edison told her anyway.

"Your food will be ready in a minute."

When she came back with the food, Edison asked, "Hey can I get your phone number?"

"No, you seem pretty strange."

"I'm only strange around other people," Edison replied.

The cashier pondered for a moment. "Hey, a person can't be strange when you're alone…you can only be strange around other people. That's dumb."

Nikola poked his head from behind Edison. "He may look dumb, but that's just a disguise."

The cashier laughed shyly.

Back on Evion, the I-mover erupted with laughter. A woman from Judion's group tried to laugh, but it hurt too much and she stopped.

The two young men on Earth took their food out to the car and started it up. The engine revved up and down intermittently.

Edison, in the passenger seat, grabbed a book sitting next to him. Starion zoomed in on it with his hand. It was an extra copy of his favorite book. He had given it to Amelia in San Francisco.

"Let's never give up on this solar engine, Nikola," Edison said to his friend, and they high-fived each other, but Starion could see that Edison had an extra finger.

"OK, buddy...your mom invented the hydrogen engine twenty years ago, and we will invent the solar engine. Hey, the presentations of energy inventions at Berkeley go on all day...let's go back."

Nikola and Edison high-fived (or -sixed) each other again. They drove to a college building and hopped out. When they opened the trunk, Starion could see another prototype of their engine. They took it, put on some type of backpacks, then they each strapped on a bulky waist IS unit.

All of Starion's side cheered. Dustion and his friends high-sixed each other; two of them awkwardly missed each other. They returned to their back room.

Starion then heard them creating a new song he had never heard before or could cross reference in his memory.

"*A new chance at life* . . ." he heard his son sing.

One more of Judion's group defected to Starion's side.

Still thinking about his son Edison's invention, Starion closed his eyes and replayed in his mind the scene of Amelia opening up the hood of her surface vehicle at Berkeley. He rewound it and played it several times. He now realized what had happened.

She *had* caught his thoughts when he had accidently sent the image of the hydrogen engine to her telepathically. He smiled. They wouldn't have to go back in time now when they traveled back to Earth. And he was proud of his Earth son for trying to invent an engine utilizing star power without his help

Judion, too, seemed to have finally made the connection. Now psychotic, he shouted, "Starion, you were not supposed to interfere with human history."

CHAPTER 45

"YES...WE know! I accidently changed Earth's history!" Starion proudly yelled as Ardia and Phileon nodded in approval.

Starion filled up one last round of braydium paste. "Only two more holes to fill Deon, we will have just enough."

Wondering how his poor new Earth daughter Dea was holding up, he pointed his two fingers, planning on changing the view to her live broadcast. But he looked away for just a second and accidently chose "Starion's Earth Adventure." Now, up on the screen was a close-up of his face, when he had awoken from drinking all the liquor. He was looking in the mirror with his red and yellow eyes.

"Oh, no ..." Starion uttered, embarrassed.

All the Evions laughed despite the pain in their facial muscles. Starion quickly changed the screen back.

Now, on the 4-D image, there were many Earth people who had gathered at Dea and her mother Mary's home. They were mourning while comforting each other throughout the house. Mary was searching for Dea and found her near a bookshelf in the living room. She was talking with guests showing them a book.

Starion noticed that Mary had aged, but she was as attractive as ever.

"Dea, I almost forgot, this letter came yesterday for you."

Starion focused in on the return address; it was from a place called Harvard. Dea opened it up and proudly proclaimed, "I've been accepted to medical school at Harvard! They liked my idea of the S-ray body scanner."

Mary and Dea hugged and cried, along with several guests who stood nearby.

"Your father would be so proud...both of them," Mary whispered to her.

"I am going to make curing cancer my lifelong task. I am going to cure all cancers. That is my passion," Dea confidently announced while she gently laid down the book she had been showing everyone. Starion zoomed in, recognizing it as his special tattered copy of his favorite book Bria had put back together. It was the one he had given Mary while on Earth.

Then, looking closer, he saw that there was another book next to this. It had a similar-looking cover. Zooming even further, he saw that it was in the Earth language. This must have been the book he and Mary had seen at the Museum in New York, the one from the famous Earth inventor Thomas Edison's private library.

Starion slapped on the last of the pasty braydium. He proudly shouted, "See? These Earth people *are* living our ancient stories of the quest."

Back on Evion, the whole I-mover of Evions erupted with cheers again. Two more of Judion's group defected, two from sleep-mode.

Judion, now beyond psychotic, shook his head while huddling with the last of his group. They were now down to only nine including Judion.

Starion didn't care about Judion anymore. After seeing and hearing his inspired daughter the inventor and Mary, he told Ardia, "I feel happy and sad at the same time."

They looked back into the large image again.

"Remember, if you do something you love to do, doors will open for you where they wouldn't for anyone else," Mother Mary told her daughter.

Phileon, Ardia, and now Starion all nodded to each other.

Inspired by what he was witnessing, Starion recalled when he and Mary toured the Museum of Natural History. Using his whole hand, he zoomed out above the city. He was surprised to see a large glass dome being built above where he believed the Hayden Planetarium was. He also noticed many more sky-roids above the Earth houses than he had seen when he visited. Then he saw hundreds of I-jet flyers cruising along air lanes designated for a certain direction.

Then Starion moved the I-mooncams view away from Earth to the next planet Mars. He zoomed in and saw an enormous large glass dome on the planet with humans performing different tasks. Ardia pointed at the few left in Judion's group while motioning for Starion to keep the positive news coming.

He brought up the D-box and highlighted the option "Earth Human Emotions" again.

He showed the man with one leg who had greeted him with the crutch and the smiling paraplegics near Berkeley again.

Just then, he saw Curion struggling with his broken leg while holding his broken arm.

"Bria, can you and the children find something like this man on Earth was using and then help Curion?"

"Yes—come on, everyone!" Bria yelled.

The children searched and found a long wooden splinter near the v-breaker. Apparently when Starion had landed it, it had broken a wooden table into pieces. They brought it over to Curion, along with some strips of fabric for tying it on. Curion sized it up and tried it. It worked.

Bria also remembered her studies of ancient Evion medicine she had told her dad about, and then created an arm sling for Curion also. Starion was so proud a tear ran down his face while he nodded in approval.

Starion turned back to the I-screen and showed the elderly Earth people who had landed near him with their strange-looking contraptions strapped to their backs. Once this scene was shown, the four elderly Evion citizens also hobbled over to Starion's side with a spring in their glide.

"This is good stuff, Starion...why would you have been

afraid to show us this?" Ardia asked.

"I don't know...I guess I thought our people would be afraid to enter such a world."

"No, Starion—this is what we have been missing."

Starion brought up the scene on Earth when he had scanned the books in the bookstore, the videos, and the music.

He told them, "Everyone, telepathically connect with me, and then download...I mean stream these Earth books, movies, and music into your memories. I will include the dictionary of their language first. The humans confirmed to me from their passed-down stories that our ancient Evion stories are still valid. And that is the story of the quest: to find your inner self so you can handle both the intended and unintended adventures in your life."

Starion was worried they wouldn't catch the metaphorical messages of many of the books and I-spacers. He and Ardia were the only ones who had been able to.

He closed his eyes and thought about the complex emotions of the humans, and the terrible circumstances his people had to endure. He remembered the tragic deaths of his wife, Lazarion, Zealeon, Kircia, and the billions of other Evions. He braced himself on one of back v-room walls.

All the Evions stared deeply into his eyes. Even the four remaining holdouts in Judion's group couldn't resist. Judion, however, turned his head.

Starion could see and feel them connect. He almost fell down from exhaustion within moments. Happily, however, he could see the data streams were blue instead of red. He knew they were able to get the inspirational metaphorical messages!

Once finished downloading, the Evions cheered again. And now the last four of the pessimistic Evions—except for Judion—moved over to Starion's side. One couple held hands and kissed.

"We are so sorry, Starion...you were right," several admitted. "We *were* missing something."

There was one more thing Starion wanted to show them.

He rewound his visit to when he was hovering above the large statue. They all could see the writing.

Give me your tired, your poor
Your huddled masses yearning to breathe free
The wretched refuse of your teeming shore
Send these, the homeless, tempest-tossed to me
I lift my lamp beside the golden door.

Starion remembered when, on his way back to Evion from Earth, he had contemplated if he was fulfilling the ancient story quest of bringing back a revelation of the life force—and, if so, what it was. He now understood: it was bringing his people back to experience life, no matter how terrible and tragic things were, and to look for inspiration in everything and everyone, whether in the past, present, or future. He felt redeemed.

"Let's go to Earth!" Starion yelled.

There was much excitement. There were a few new shining eyes along with several new painful smiles. Some lamented, looking around at what they were leaving.

They all gathered, waiting to board the v-breaker.

Starion, still standing in the back, noticed Judion still sitting in his chair with his arms crossed, facing forward. He couldn't see his eyes but didn't want to anyway.

Starion took off his gliders and walked down the aisle, feeling the cool metal steps with his reawakened muscles on his feet and six toes. "Judion, please come with us...please...we forgive you."

Judion didn't budge. His eyes were closed.

"We will need your medical knowledge...please come. You need to help Curion. And when we get to Earth, we will need to stay segregated from the population until you have tested everything and give us the thumbs-up, OK?"

But Judion didn't move at all.

Starion headed back up the stairs. He bumped into Quarion

and stopped. Quarion was tired from manually running back and forth between the v-breaker and skyroid. He had just carried the last of the charged star-power cells. He sat down.

"I suppose if we get to Earth, we will have to either provide the bionic technology to the Earth people or learn to walk and run like our ancestors did," Quarion concluded.

The old Phileon overheard Quarion and shuffled over. "Maybe you need to walk in these shoes for a while," he said wiggling his five toes in front of his sandals.

Phileon winked at Starion.

"OK, everyone...let's go!" Starion yelled.

All the Evions cheered.

"Deon, check the lobby. Make sure we have everyone."

Deon stumble-glided up the aisle.

Starion finally had enough of his awkward gliding. "Deon, take those damn gliders off!"

Deon sat on a chair and took them both off and tossed them down a few rows. He wiggled his six toes, stood up, and headed for the lobby. "This hurts, but it feels good," he shouted.

There he found the IS-man standing idle. But just as he turned to go back, the face pane mysteriously had a hint of light.

"Should we take that IS-man with?" he yelled to Starion.

"I don't know...it's just more technology, and like I have been saying all along, is all of our technology going to save us?" But then, changing his mind, Starion said, "Take him along, and also your equipment, including those O-scopes."

Deon turned it on and then guided the IS-man into the ship while the rest watched curiously.

Starion stood again in the back row, again pleading with Judion. "Judion, we are leaving. Please come with us. This is your last chance...you are forgiven...we have to leave."

Judion didn't move.

Starion realized they had to leave. And he knew he had to open up the dome, which would allow the air to seep out.

On his way to the main control room, he walked by the room

where Kircia and Zealeon were laid to rest. He stopped and covered them with a large white piece of fabric he had found earlier. "Dust to dust...ashes to ashes..." he said, bending his head down, remembering the small vigil he had seen along with Earth words from his memory.

He walked out, feeling the cool floor on his flesh again. He confidently shouted to Deon, "Make sure you connect all of Earth's signals, plus transfer any and all programs from these old I-mover IS units. Also lock in the fresh new Earth's air inside the tank."

Starion glanced up at the screen, which was now showing him quickly shoveling the braydium into the back of the v-breaker near Roswell. He felt the air was getting thinner, so he chose the 5-D link again. A fresh burst of air filled the I-mover again.

He could see the back of Judion's head in front of him.

He couldn't resist one last look at his Earth son Wayden. He pointed up at the screen and then changed the live 5-D image from the Roswell view to a live view of Wayden.

CHAPTER 46

UP ON the large screen was a live 5-D I-mover image that protruded out so far it almost touched Starion. It engulfed the v-breaker. He read the word "life" again and commented to himself, "Now it really is a life image...this is where dreams can come true if one doesn't refuse the *Adventura~Pathos!*"

Inside the image was Wayden. He was all clean-cut, shaven, and wearing clean clothes. He was walking along the streets of England with his friend Alan, who had also cleaned himself up. Both carried several books in their hands, including *The Hero with a Thousand Faces, Anciente Evion Adventura~Hero, The Adventures of Huckleberry Finn, Moby Dick, Greek Mythology, Arthurian Romances,* and several others.

Starion stuck his head into the image above the two. He had to squint from the bright sunshine.

"Why all the books, Wayden?" his friend Alan asked.

"I have been called to help our fellow Earth people...but before I can, I have to earn it."

"But why all the books on heroes and adventures?"

"Because that's what's worth writing and reading about. In all of history, it has always been the individual who has saved the day, not society. He or she must heed the *Adventura~Pathos,* not refuse it—otherwise, they cannot follow the life force clues and bring back the revelation," he proclaimed as the two walked along.

"The old story of the quest is still good...to find your inward self that you basically are," he gleaned as they strolled along in the sunshine. "Listen to this," Wayden proclaimed, reading from a book: "*And so Galahad decided it would be a disgrace to set off on a quest with the other knights. Alone he would enter the dark forest where there was no path...*"

The whole crowd inside the v-breaker erupted with cheers again.

Starion was as proud as he could be, but he was aware he'd better get going. He changed the image to a live view of Earth from its moon.

"Judion...Judion, we're leaving," he yelled one last time. Judion, all alone, was sitting like a statue staring up at the image. He didn't move.

"We're all set," Deon yelled through the v-breaker hatch.

Starion manually ran into the main control room, then hauled the old IS tower to the v-breaker. He loved feeling his leg muscles work. He ran back into the main control room and pushed the lever to open the domed roof. Then he hurried over to the skyroid. There he took the old star-power magnifier and cell mold-casts along with the new magnifier with him to the v-breaker. There was limited room inside, so he placed them underneath the floor next to the star-power cell compartment. He was aware that long ago, luggage was stored there.

He took one last look around him and shouted while the hatch slowly shut tight, "Judion, we're leaving." But Judion still didn't move.

Then, without warning, the whole building shook like never before.

Starion hoped the tall hydraulic cylinders would hold. They had to hurry.

Once inside the v-breaker, he saw there were twenty-three seats—just enough for their group. *How odd*, he wondered. *Maybe things are finally on my side.*

"Okay, let's go to Earth," he yelled as they all watched the dome slowly open.

Deon shouted, "IS unit, proceed to the galaxy coordinates I just gave you."

"All doors secured. Proceeding to Earth," the v-breaker IS unit replied.

Deon looked at the gauge. "Star-power energy gauge full, Starion."

"How long will it take, Dad?" Dustion asked.

Starion was happy to hear the word "Dad," but he turned to Deon for the answer.

"It will take about four E-hours—or, in Earth time, about eight hours," Deon explained with a new smile that didn't appear to hurt anymore while wiggling his six toes.

Starion was glad they didn't have to travel back in time again.

"Will we be welcome?" one of the newcomers yelled.

"I don't know," Starion acknowledged.

"Do we have a plan on how we should introduce ourselves and where we should land once we get there?" Deon asked.

Starion smiled, finally feeling no pain. "No. We were going to, but we didn't have time…I guess we will have to let fate take over."

When they lifted up, Starion saw the large 5-D image of Earth and Judion still sitting in the I-mover seat below. But something was odd. The view inside the image had changed from a view of Earth to a view of a large desert land mass, for some reason. Starion's eyebrows displayed a puzzled look as he felt the ship finally stop shaking while they lifted over the stilted I-mover building. He looked down again and noticed Judion was gone from his seat.

Just then, they felt an odd jolt underneath the v-breaker, as if something hit it from below. Then they heard and felt the same from the back of the ship. It sounded like something hit the clear shell.

"I wish we could have connected with Neilion and Shepion somewhere out there in the galaxy," Deon remarked. He seemed to believe the jolts were from the quake.

Starion still puzzled about the sudden Earth image of a

desert, asked, "When did you last try to communicate with them?"

"It was just after the devastating quake that destroyed the e-center."

"Once we get out of Evion's atmosphere—or what is left of it, anyway—try it again."

They veered up above the dying planet and directly away from the enormous sun. The sun was so close they could see its turbulent, fiery surface. Starion was aware they weren't completely safe yet. He could feel the gravity pulling hard at the ship. Suddenly, a flare shot out at them. Just before it reached the ship, it swirled. It almost looked like the flare had wanted to grab the v-breaker. They safely flew through it, feeling the heat.

As the v-breaker gradually sped out into the solar system, Starion and the Evion passengers turned and looked behind them. They saw their home planet, along with the dying sun, become smaller and smaller.

Then, as they passed by Galion, they witnessed their planet finally succumb to the large sun's gravity. When it collided with the massive sun, there was a heartbreaking explosion. It was a spectacle like none had ever seen before. It was sad, tragic, and sublime all at once.

Shortly, while still safely traveling away from the sun, they witnessed Galion follow suit with the same results.

Gaining speed, Starion and his fellow Evions watched in total silence as they saw their large, dying sun become smaller and smaller. When they couldn't see it anymore, they turned toward the front, where they could see only vast space ahead of them. It was as if someone had turned a switch that changed the past to the future, Starion thought.

"Deon…see if you can pull in Earth's video broadcasts," Starion requested, breaking the silence. "And put it on the navigator."

A 4-D floating I-spacer suddenly appeared. Gradually, an image of a human appeared. "It will be blue sunny skies with a temperature of seventy-five degrees in the big city," the man stated.

Starion, proud of Earth, explained, "This temperature is what the Earth people call 'heaven.'"

Almost all the Evions cheered.

After this, a good-looking Earth woman behind a desk spoke. "Our next story is not new: Earth's global water supply continues to diminish."

Suddenly, on the main e-screen in the front v-panel, a static signal came through. All of the Evion passengers stood, glaring at it. They saw a static and snowy silhouette of a man in another v-breaker. He was trying to say something, but they couldn't decipher it. Deon tried to adjust the signal to the right frequency, but it wasn't working.

Starion peered up into the universe for fate to help again. It had worked before. His confidence was so high; the signal suddenly came in clear.

"Evion…Evion…come in, please…come in, please. This is Neilion and Shepion."

Starion spoke into the unit. "Team leader Neilion, we have you…we have you…come in."

"We have you also," Neilion replied.

They could see the fifty-year-old Neilion with his short brown hair while the slightly younger blond-haired Shepion stood next to him.

"Where are you?" Deon asked.

"We are in the Milky Way's largest rotating arm called the Phoenix."

"Neilion, you will have to change course," Starion told him. "We have decided to migrate to a planet called Earth in the Optim section. Do you copy?"

There was a long pause.

"We copy Starion…we copy. But—"

Abruptly the signal was lost, and Deon struggled for a few moments to adjust the frequency again.

"But what, Neilion—what?" Starion yelled.

Quarion yelled from one of the seats, "Hey, everyone, look at Earth's broadcast…it says there is something called a 'special bulletin.'"

CHAPTER 47

THEY ALL huddled near the navigator where they could see the Earth man was in panic mode. He pronounced, "Our scientists have just found an asteroid hurtling toward us at an unbelievable speed...it will impact in a few hours."

Starion brought up two more broadcasts on two hanging e-screens. They were of humans in panic on the streets, running around in chaos.

Finally, the signal from the envoy came in clear again on the front e-screen. "We have found another planet that might work," Neilion reported.

Starion looked at Deon and the other Evion passengers. They were all stunned.

"Neilion, hold on a moment; Deon, in your presentation to us elders, you said you found a hyper-asteroid that was going to safely pass by Earth, right?"

"Yes, and I checked it out myself once I got back here from Earth. It was definitely going to pass Earth by thousands of e-miles."

"I wonder what happened," Starion said, pacing the ship's clear braydium bottom with his new legs. Moments later, he put his six-fingered hand up to his chin and blurted out, "Judion...Judion."

Neilion, still on the I-spacer, shouted, "Starion and Deon, come in...where are you? We don't have much energy left."

"Neilion, we have decided to migrate to this Earth...and like I just told you, it's in the Optim arm. Can you meet us there?" Starion asked.

"I think so sir...but we have some good news."

"What?" Starion replied as the others watched and listened.

"We have found a large blue planet similar to ancient Evion. It has a healthy yellow sun, lots of fresh air, and lots of fresh water, along with an abundant amount of green vegetation."

"What about life?" Starion asked.

"There is a variety of life."

"What about intelligent life?"

After a short pause, Neilion answered, "I don't think so, but we weren't able to confirm that. We didn't have time."

"Was there any sign of the mineral braydium?"

"Yes...it is plentiful."

"What about the climate and environment?" Valkia yelled with fresh new energy.

"Because of its large size and fast rotation, the winds and storms are much more violent than on Evion—but we could easily survive there," Neilion answered.

Starion looked at Deon, Ardia, Valkia, Quarion, and then all the rest of the Evions, including his children. It was now very quiet.

"Hello...hello...are you there? Please let us know what to do—we are running out of energy," Neilion urgently requested.

"We're here," Deon replied. "Stand by."

Starion turned to all the Evions and reasoned, "Evion's charter states that if at all possible, we are required not to interfere with an intelligent being's development and history unless absolutely necessary. But if I am correct, and it was Judion that diverted the asteroid...I think it is our responsibility to save Earth now."

Valkia and the teacher Kelleria sneezed in unison.

"Who is in favor of still migrating to Earth?" Starion pleaded while pointing to the chaos on Earth in the I-spacer.

Everyone except two of the newcomers raised their hands immediately.

"Neilion, we are heading for Earth...Deon will send you the

coordinates. Meet us near the fourth planet from their sun, the red one. Can we count on you?"

There was still much static. They could tell Neilion was saying something, but they couldn't make it out. Then the signal went dead.

"Deon, can you get the signal back?"

"I'll try," he replied, sending the coordinates.

"Meanwhile, head for Earth as fast as you can—the Earth newscaster said the asteroid will hit in a few hours," Starion ordered. He paced the floor with his bare feet. He was finding it harder to breathe.

Suddenly, his twinkling eyes opened wide with an idea. "Speaking of that…Deon, let's just travel back just a little in time and use the laser ray to divert the asteroid."

Deon observed the energy gauge needle was at half. "Starion how could we be at half-full so quickly?"

Starion opened up the compartment, where he saw there were only two star-power cells.

Quarion exclaimed, "That's impossible! I put four in there."

Starion also noticed that the two magnifier and cell mold-casts were gone, along with the new magnifier in the compartment next to this. He checked the bottom flap doors to make they were secure. "Hmm," he said, continuing to pace the floor, wondering how this could have happened and what else he could do. Then, he remembered the fifth dimension. He mumbled to himself, *did Judion do this before he perished?"*

Still pacing, he had an idea. *I could bring up the live image of the asteroid from Earth's I-mooncam, reach in, and divert the asteroid.*

Starion ran to an idle e-screen hanging down near the back. Again he felt short of breath.

"Deon…we need more air. And did you transfer the programs from the I-mover?"

Deon observed that the air pressure was low. "Starion, there must be a small leak in the v-breaker. And yes, the old programs are installed."

Just then, another Evion man in the back pointed at the clear rear hatch door. "Hey, there is a crack here. It is leaking."

Starion shook his head in bewilderment, wondering how that could have happened. Then he recalled the jolt when they had taken off. *Judion?*

Starion brought up a protruding 4-D image of Earth from its moon. Twirling his hand, he changed the view out into space. He searched and searched while zooming in and out. Finally, he located the asteroid. He zoomed in on it so it filled up most of the image. Then he zoomed in further until it looked like the camera was just a few feet off the surface. He chose the drop-down option "5-D." Then he slowly started putting his hand and arm into the image.

Everyone inside held their limited breath.

But this felt different from when he had saved Wayden. Starion wiggled his hand around and tried to feel the asteroid's surface, but his hand went right through the image and hit the e-screen instead. He tried again and again.

Then he realized what had happened. There wasn't enough of Earth's air. He pulled out of the image in despair.

"Deon, we are going to have to save Earth the old-fashioned way: Kick it down. Let's get trekking!"

Deon looked puzzled at the new words. Starion telepathically sent him an image of an I-spacer he had scanned in from Earth of a large spaceship zooming off into space. Deon got the message and sped up.

Starion manually paced the floor with his six-toed feet.

He felt helpless while gazing out into the vast universe of nebula clusters, galaxies, and space streaking by. He noticed his fellow Evions lose some of their renewed hope while the air became thinner. Several even went into sleep-mode.

He immediately pointed up at another e-screen and started up his recorded visit to Earth. At random, he chose a scene of when he was gliding down the sidewalk witnessing the vital humans in their variety of shops, professions, and clothes, each experiencing their own adventure.

"Everyone, once on Earth, follow your dreams of what you want to do there."

"Don't worry everyone, we will make it...have faith," Bria shouted.

"How do you know?" a man yelled out. Starion saw this was Lexion. Next to him was his wife Hildia. They were both in their late fifties. Even though Starion had apparently persuaded them to come along, he could see their eyes were still blank and cold.

Starion, proud of his daughter, remembered what Mary had told him while they hovered above the Earth. "Call it a sixth sense."

Just when he was afraid it was nearing the time the Earth broadcaster had estimated, he saw the most spectacular nebula he had ever seen. It had a vast array of colors that reminded him of the rainbow he had seen on Earth.

He closed his eyes for inspiration. His lips moved ever so slightly.

Moments later, Starion opened his eyes. He could see the same view of Earth's solar system ahead as when he had visited Earth before. "There it is, there it is—Earth's solar system!" he yelled, fully convinced of the power and magic of the old stories.

They all stared forward happily, squinting at the bright, healthy sun. Even though the planets were staggered in their own elliptical paths around the yellow star, they were all visible. As they passed by each planet, Starion proudly stated, "There's the brown-colored Pluto...there's the light blue Neptune...there's the blue Uranus...there's one of my favorites, the yellow one with the rings called Saturn...and there is the large orange planet Jupiter...and there is red Mars, where we will meet Neilion and Shepion, if they show up."

Starion turned back. "Deon, try Neilion again. Do you see him?"

Starion and Deon watched diligently out front toward Mars. Starion took out the handheld spacegazer and searched the planet's orbit and surface, but there was no sign of Neilion's ship. The passengers, fighting for air, tried to look out beyond Mars for Earth, but the large red planet was blocking the view.

He moved to the back of the ship, where he scraped up the little amount of braydium left on the floor. He spit into his hands, forming a paste. Then he slapped it on the cracked portion of the back hatch window.

Suddenly, without warning, the onboard IS unit's annoying monotone voice stated, "Low on energy...Low on energy."

To everyone's surprise, Starion shouted, "Shut up!"

He rushed over to the compartment, opened it, and then shook the two cells. Nothing happened. He noticed that some of the braydium paste had since dried on his hands. He placed his hands on the cells and then rubbed them. The warning stopped.

"Travel to the other side, Deon."

When Deon headed around Mars, Earth started to appear. Almost everyone cheered. They stood up, crowding toward the front of the ship for a better look.

But then Deon, who was looking in a different direction suddenly yelled, "There it is—the asteroid—there it is!"

Everyone turned to the side of the clear v-breaker, where they saw the asteroid hurling toward Earth.

Lexion, who hadn't cheered, stood up and yelled, "What are you going to do, Starion...what's your plan now?"

"When Neilion arrives, we are going to each point our laser blaster rays in a V shape at the asteroid and then split it in two. The force should push the two pieces on safely past Earth, one on each side."

"Ha—that's the same thing you failed at eight years ago when you tried to save our sun. It didn't work, Starion. It didn't work then and it won't work now."

Starion searched for Neilion's v-breaker, but again he was unsuccessful.

"We have to try without him," he finally stated. "Deon, match the asteroid's speed."

Suddenly they heard a crackle, and then: "We're here...what do you want us to do?"

The passengers cheered.

Starion put up his hand to quiet them. "Neilion, you will fly to a forty-five-degree angle at the same speed of the asteroid, above it. I will do the same, and then we will each point our laser blaster rays at the same point on the asteroid. OK?"

"OK, Starion...but I don't know if we have enough energy."

They both maneuvered their v-breakers to their positions as they and the asteroid hurtled toward Earth.

"Hurry, Dad," Bria yelled.

"OK, Neilion, on three: one...two...three!"

Starion's ship blasted a ray at the designated point on the asteroid. Nothing came from Neilion's ship. The single ray hardly affected the asteroid.

"Neilion, what's wrong?"

"We don't have enough energy, Starion."

"Reach inside your cell compartment and shake the starpower cells."

A moment later, Neilion confirmed. "OK—ready to try again."

Now they were so close to Earth they could see the blue oceans and swirling clouds.

"One...two...three!"

Both rays hit the asteroid in a V shape. Starion peered up into the sky at the constellation Prometheus, like he had when leaving Earth.

Just then, the asteroid split in two. The two giant pieces streaked by each side of Earth's atmosphere and safely by the planet.

The whole v-breaker erupted in joy. There were high-sixes.

The two negative souls, Lexion and Hildia shook their heads in defeat.

"Hold up, Neilion," Starion said, walking back to witness the happy humans in the live newscasts dancing in the streets. "Deon, send the Earth people an I-spacer recording of what we just did. I think we will be welcome now!" he told everyone.

Starion squinted while happily staring at the healthy and young shining sun.

Phileon shuffled up to Starion with his staff. He pulled out another old, tattered book he had taken from his bag of books. He handed it to Starion and then went back to his seat.

Starion took his eyes away from the healthy sun and read the title of the book to himself: *Ancient Earth Adventures of Heroes*.

Starion's eyes opened wide.

"Recording sent," Deon yelled.

Starion stared at the two mythological figures on the book and noticed they were the same as his Evion favorite book. He looked over at Phileon, who had a strange smile on his face. Starion decided to put the book in his pouch for now. When he did, he felt the scroll he'd found on Zealeon—he'd forgotten about it. He pulled it out and opened it.

It was in a language he couldn't decipher.

He remembered Ardia's comment about it at the Elder meeting. "Yes, it is possible the scroll contains the oldest story ever told of the master. The master in these ancient times was not only successful in following the hero's journey and lived to tell about it, but had gained enough wisdom to master the two worlds; the real world and the spiritual one."

Starion saw that Ardia and Phileon had wise grins on their face. He put the scroll back in his pouch.

"Starion…where to now?" Deon asked.

Starion looked at the swirling blue planet. He realized they were directly over where he had found the braydium.

"To the mystical blue planet Earth."

"When are we going to meet our Earth brothers and sisters?" Bria suddenly asked.

"Soon my daughter…soon."

"What shall we call them?" Dustion followed up with.

There was a long pause. Then, Bria spoke up: "How about Earthions?"

Starion nodded in approval while the rest used their new-found facial muscles to smile the best they could.

Deon brought the ship down into Earth's atmosphere, while Neilion followed behind. When they hit the five e-mile mark, a squadron of Earth aircraft suddenly appeared behind and to the side of them.

The Evions worriedly looked back. Starion began to wonder if they should have waited a little longer to make sure the humans had received the recording of them destroying the asteroid.

Starion took control of the ship and flew further downward.

"*Low on energy . . . low on energy . . .*" the IS unit blurted.

Deon jumped up and down on the compartment. The warning stopped.

When they neared the one e-mile mark, Starion opened the windows to let the fresh air permeate the ship. Everyone's hair and shroud hoods blew around. They all took deep breaths.

Finally they landed near where Starion had loaded up the braydium. Neilion landed next to him.

Starion opened the hatch and walked out first. Deon, Ardia, and Phileon were next, followed by the rest—some with gliders, some without. Curion was behind them, wearing his arm in a sling and using the wooden crutch. Many pulled their hoods over their heads by habit, but then realized they didn't have to. Everyone except Starion put their hands up to their eyes, trying to block the powerful sun's rays.

"Be careful, everyone. Even though you feel lighter, remember that Earth rotates opposite Evion," Starion warned.

Neilion and his copilot Shepion met them outside, but they didn't hear Starion's instructions. They both stumble-glided for a few moments before figuring it out.

All the Evions worriedly watched as the squadron of twenty-five aircraft also landed near them.

Starion and his people stood, hoping they would be welcome. They watched as fifty Earth men and women hopped out of their crafts wearing sunglasses.

Approaching closer and closer, Starion started toward them, his people following.

When the two groups met, the leader of the squadron stood face to face with Starion. Then, a man wearing a slightly different uniform joined the squadron leader from behind him. He was carrying a familiar hat. Starion immediately knew that this was the man who had been after him while he was visiting Earth. He was now twenty Earth years older.

Starion noticed their serious facial expressions behind their sunglasses. His heart was racing with fear. *Have they not been informed of our efforts?*

Suddenly, the man holding the hat took off his sunglasses, smiled, and put out his hand.

Starion, feeling a rush of relief, took it and engulfed it with his hand and six fingers.

Both sides cheered. Two Evions sneezed.

"Welcome!" the man said, handing him his pair of sunglasses.

"Thank you. We are glad to be here," Starion answered, motioning no to the sunglasses, "I want to experience your starshine and its life-creating rays the best I can."

Starion turned and squinted at the sun. He dug his six toes into the ground. Several tears ran down his face.

JIM EVRY was born in the small town of Ashby, Minnesota, near Alexandria. When very young his family moved to the Twin Cities. He grew up in the small town of Maple Plain, about 20 miles west of Minneapolis and graduated from Orono High School. He also has lived in Golden, Colorado, twice in his life. He presently resides with his wife Julie in St. Louis Park Minnesota and works in the small business brokerage industry.

Jim originally wrote a screenplay for his debut story but his mentor and friend Phil Cousineau suggested he "cotton" a book. Three years later, each has enriched the other. He hopes this book inspires the reader to follow their inner call to adventure and look for inspiration where ever he or she can find it. And never quit!

Jim loves the outdoors and is an avid fan of many sports including basketball. He enjoys all kinds of music and movies along with his favorite which is science fiction. He likes lively discussions about any type of new ideas, inventions, concepts, philosophy, religions, politics, sports, movies, and music.